THE RESERVATION

An Iroquois Book

THE RESERVATION

TED C. WILLIAMS

Illustrated by the Author

SYRACUSE UNIVERSITY PRESS   1976

Library of Congress Cataloging in Publication Data

Williams, Ted C   1930-
    The reservation.

    (Iroquois books)
    1. Tuscarora Indians—Fiction. I. Title.
PZ4.W7273Re   [PS3573.I4557]   813'.5'4   75-46585
ISBN 0-8156-0119-0

Manufactured in the United States of America

To Rain

Theodore C. Williams was born on the Tuscarora Indian Reservation in western New York in 1930. His father, Eleazar Williams, was sachem chief of the Turtle Clan, whose skill as a medicine man was sought by many non-Indians as well as Indians. Ted's mother, Amelia, is clan mother of the Wolf Clan.

After graduating from LaSalle High School in Niagara Falls, New York, Ted spent four years in the United States armed services as a paratrooper. Under the GI Bill he studied trumpet and modern jazz arranging at the Knapp School of Music. He later toured the country as a professional archer. Ted's hobbies include stone carving and ceramics. He is employed as a crane operator for the Eastman Kodak Company in Rochester, New York.

A grant from the America the Beautiful Fund, through the New York State Council on the Arts, facilitated the completion of this manuscript.

Dear Readers:

At first I was sad to have to call this book a work of fiction. But now I don't feel that way anymore. It may, in many ways, be much more accurate this way. This way, many more Indians of the Tuscarora Indian Reservation are in the book. Even the dead are alive again, because names, events, faces, physical descriptions, philosophies, voices, etc., have been resurrected, borrowed, and exchanged among and between those people of the reservation that I have known.

Next, I began to have a fear that my people, my friends, and relatives would think that I had inserted someone else's cruel happening into their lives in a spiteful manner. Truth, though, has much power, and the knowledge that my heart is not that way stopped that.

Many more stories could have been told but I am only one existence with just so much memory. In the four or five years that it took to write this book, many Indians slipped away and even more were already in the cemetery on Upper Mountain Road. It is a nice feeling, though, to have said something for them that may otherwise have been lost to written history.

I want to thank all those speakers and tellers who spoke to me, either with their lives or with their lips, for the material which formed this book. I want to thank You-thaw-huh-TU(T)-oit (The-paintbrush-is-big), Wayne Trimm, art director of the New York State *Conservationist* magazine, for directing a couple of my first writings to the Syracuse University Press. Most of all, though, I guess nothing at all would have been written had not Professor Peter Marchant of State University of New York at Brockport encouraged me by saying, "That's it. You've got it. You have more story material in you than all of us here."

Rochester, New York   Ted
Spring 1976

Contents

THE RESERVATION

When I Was Little

MOTHER was about twenty years younger than Father. She liked the wooden leg that Father made for her out of willow. It was hollow and light of weight but the knee joint wore the wood and got rattley just about the time she became skillful and began buzzing up and down stairs. Of course she fell quite often but she got used to that. That and whatever bruises or cracked elbows or some other bones that go with falling. Well, you'd probably fall quite often, too, especially if one of your eyes were half-cataracted up like hers.

However much she liked her first leg, she liked the second one better. The first one looked good, even better than her real leg, but the second one was stronger and more comfortable because it made use of any mistakes made in the first one. Both legs stayed on by use of a harness. The harness was like the ones horses use, although she didn't have to wear a collar. Arthritis was what drew her joints in tighter and left her not able to straighten them all the way out. That's why she decided to have one leg cut off. It just wasn't any good to her at all.

One thing Mother was good at was housework. Plus sewing and beadwork and cooking and canning. Once she made Manylips a man's suit because he said he never owned one and craved to have one. He paid her two whole dollars and an eggplant, which is something we never took time to grow.

We knew Mother could do things, even play piano with her bent fingers, but once she got skillful with her wooden leg, she was all over like a hand grenade. I never had a hand grenade, but I hear they get around. Soon she was chairman or president of whatever ladies organizations there were on the reservation or between the other Iroquois reservations.

Between Mother and Father, I don't know which one could say funnier things. They spoke Tuscarora between themselves but I knew perfectly well what they said. One Sunday after church Mother was bouncing about getting Sunday dinner which was about the middle of the afternoon. Whatever the preacher had said was still running around in Father's head so he was letting it coast to a stop by talking. Every once in a while he would get in Mother's way and she would say something like, "Thot-neck-gu." That means, "Escape out of my way."

We were taking places at the table when Mother said, "Oh hush up. You don't know anything about the Bible anyways."

Father said, "Sure, sure, I know about the Bible. The Bible says we must multiply!" And then he began saying grace so Mother couldn't answer back. She bowed her head more than usual so we kids couldn't see her smiling so easy.

Whoever first thought of the Tuscarora language and maybe any of the Indian languages made lots of room for laughter. Groups of Indians are always laughing. Mother could be funny too. One day the women were at a quilting-bee. I should say comforter-bee because they made comforters with patchwork designs on one side, cotton batting in the middle, and flannel on the other side. Anyway, the women were talking about their hair. Someone asked Mother if she used anything on her hair. She said, "Raid! Makes the bugs nice and shiny." Another time she told the women that she used D-con for upset stomach. "D-con" is mouse poison.

Others, too, would get a laugh. One day I was playing with water. Pouring it from one tumbler into another, back and forth. Father said, "Look, he's going to be a doctor."

See More said, "You mean a bartender."

Another time, Jeeks, who was a Medicine Man too, was trying to pry some herbs out of my father.

"Don't you know anything else for a cold besides wild cherry bark?" Jeeks teased.

"Sure," Father said, "Pinus Strobus."

2

"What's the Indian name of that?"

"Most Indians call it, 'Christmas Tree,' " Father said, smiling.

Hardly anything escaped joking. Even death. When Bad-News went to the hospital with a ruptured appendix, the surgeon said, "I doubt I can save you now."

Bad-News said, "All I want to know is, if you cut me in half, will I have to pay double." He died during the operation.

Lots of Indians knew the signs that someone would die and some of them could forecast things in a dream. Mother was one of them. She told me that once she dreamed twelve years into the future. It was a simple dream and at the time, she could not walk because of the arthritis. She dreamed she was walking under two large trees when she heard a noise behind her. She looked back and a leghorn rooster was following her. Twelve years later, after she had married Father and was cruising about on the willow leg, she suddenly recognized the big sugarpear tree and the black walnut tree as those in her dream. She said, "I knew when I looked back, the rooster would be there." And it was. It was making those noises that chickens do when they try to talk to you. You know, "gaaaaa-ga-ga-ga." Soft-like.

Geese-a-geese, my grandmother, had been taught some way to read some English. She had been up late sneaking a look at a newspaper that Father had brought in. She had been reading about some earthquake in Japan and picturing in her mind how awful it would be if the earth cracked open and swallowed her up. Mother was dozing off beside me. I was asleep already. That's when the Skeleton hollered the first time.

"I had never heard that sound before," Mother said, "but I knew, right away, what it was. Some people say it sounds like a cow bawling, but to me it sounded like a man frightened. I was nearly asleep but I remember thinking, 'Oh, I know what that is. It's a Skeleton.' It didn't frighten me because I know death signs. The sound was to the south. I was just dozing off again, maybe five minutes later, and I heard it again. This time to the southwest."

Grandmother said, "Well, I heard it the first time but I didn't want to believe it. I let myself think I was hearing things. But when it hollered again I threw the paper down and came upstairs. It was dark in my room and I was so frightened I couldn't

3

go in there. I slept on the davenport."

In a couple of days we heard that Blind Pearl had been babysitting five children for two mothers who had gone picking fruit. The children were playing with matches and trapped themselves in the barn when the hay caught fire. They all died. The barn was three miles south of us. The children's homes were to the southwest. Blind Pearl suffered a stroke from the shock. She didn't live long afterward. The children burnt on the day after the Skeleton hollered.

I started out to tell you about what Mother could do but I almost forgot the most important thing. She had some magic words. If Weedy, my sister, or I got to feeling blue about anything, Mother could stop it right away. I don't know how it worked but all she would do was grab us in her arms and pull us toward herself. Then she would chant a little tune, although the notes did not change. She would chant "Sa-ga la-ga-la la-la-la" and on each note she pulled in just a teeny bit tighter. It always worked, too.

Father called me Luck-Ins. The Tuscaroras took Christian names before most of the other tribes. Missionaries probably got more scared of the Indian ways than the Indians got scared of theirs, so they probably threatened the Indians to hell if they didn't change their ways, or at least their names. Nobody on the reservation paid much attention to anybody else's Christian name.

It took quite a while for my mother and father to realize that I fully understood the Tuscarora language. Weedy, my younger sister, never learned it all but that was probably because she knew how to mind her own business. Also, Geese-a-geese, who was my father's mother, couldn't handle the English language too swiftly and she spoke half and half to me before she died. Father was fifty when I was born and Weedy was born three years later. What I'm getting at, I had a three-year jump on Weedy on listening to Geese-a-geese.

Why I learned to understand Tuscarora more than Weedy doesn't matter, though, because hardly anybody can speak it anymore. Teachers like Geese-a-geese can't just keep on living. Take her, for instance. She was ninety-two or ninety-four when she fell out of a cherry tree. Didn't last more than a year after that.

What happened was, she went out one day and saw a flock

of starlings gobbling up her wild black cherries. "Niih! Set-gee-heh-waah," was all she could say, being as there are no swear words in Indian. It means, "Oh isn't that too bad." The tree was fatter than I could get my arms around and I don't know, to this day, how she climbed up it, but the next thing, BAM, there she was, flat on her back with a broken hip.

Father was working on WPA so all Weedy and Mother and I could do was look at her while we thought of the next step. Finally we decided that Soo-heh might be home so I ran across the valley of grass and climbed a tree to take a gander to see if I could see anything moving around his house. It was another half to three quarters of a mile to go yet. What do you think I saw? On a warm day, smoke coming out of the chimney.

When I got to the house I went right inside. Now here was another obstacle. Sitting in front of the kitchen cook stove was Geeeks, Soo-heh's wife. I don't know but what she had been born cripple, but for sure she was cripple now. She used a rocking chair for a wheel chair and some way she could rock-and-skid, rock-and-skid, and get around that way. But worse yet, she was deaf. And this time, when I say deaf, I mean real bad deaf. So now, what do you think she was doing? Playing with fire. Just like a kid does. She had a little piece of kindling and as she jabbed it good and glowing she swirled it around in the air, sort of writing in air.

Why we called her Geeeks was because that was the noise her rocking chair made. I was sure she would never hear me but I hollered "GEEEKS!" anyway. I was right, she didn't hear me. Well, I thought, might as well see how loud I can holler. "GEEE-EEKS!" Believe it or not, she turned around. After she saw me, her body gave a little jump. I had scared her because she hid her writing stick, just like a bad little girl. Well really, she wasn't very big but I don't think that had much to do with it. She was nothing but skin and bones except her cheeks stuck out like a chipmunk's full of seeds. Her tongue went in and out all the time, wetting her lips. On top of all this, I think she needed glasses because it took her a while to see that I wasn't a big bad man coming to kill her. She smiled. Her tongue stayed in while she smiled. "Geese-a-geese fell out of the cherry tree," I said. She smiled and nodded her head. She thought I had come to visit with her.

She threw her writing stick into the fire and then she started

6

her rocking and skidding. And pointing. She pointed to the parlor and then to her ear. What she wanted was her trumpet. I went to get it for her but PHEW! did it stink in there. Half the wall was covered with pots of geraniums and some were so big they were starting to crawl on the floor. And you know how geraniums smell. The trumpet was a silver one, a real one, the kind a band plays with.

My father told me about it once. His father, Dehh'WEESE, owned it. At one time Dehh'WEESE owned a stable of show horses. He traveled around putting on wild west shows. With the show was an orchestra, which Dehh'WEESE led. But he got to drinking and gambling and pretty soon somebody he owed money to burned the stable down, horses and all. All them stones at the edge of the valley of grass were part of the foundation of the stable. Dehh'WEESE finally drank himself to death and in the process, he hocked the silver trumpet to Soo-heh for five dollars. Soo-heh wouldn't sell the trumpet back to my father because Geeeks needed it to hear with.

So here I was getting the trumpet for Geeeks. It was in an open case with red velvety stuff inside. The silver was blackish or sort of purplish. Into the kitchen came John Bunker. He was a white man that Soo-heh hired for nothing. Except, he could eat and sleep there. John could talk and understand some Tuscarora. "Chweant (hello)," he said, to let me know he had come in.

Now here's about how John Bunker used the language. "Wehh-dooge" means "It's raining." John would say, "It's wehh-dooging."

I told John about Geese-a-geese and we took off. But first I gave Geeeks her trumpet. We didn't talk going across the fields. That was partly because John was saving his breath for walking purposes and I kept getting ahead of him. Also, I couldn't help laughing about something that I was thinking about. And I couldn't help thinking about what I was laughing about. It was about John Bunker so I couldn't let him catch up to me until I was through laughing. My buddy Eel told me about it. He said that one night his folks took him to Wednesday night prayer meeting at the Mission. Who should show up for the only time of his life but John Bunker. He sat down right in the seat behind Eel. To honor his presence the preacher asked John to stand up and pray. Eel said everybody closed their eyes and John was so scared his hands were jiggling when he took a hold of the back of Eel's seat to stand up. Eel said he strained his ears and when John did speak, you could hardly hear him. "I can't," he said, "my heart won't let me." When John sat back down, people began peeking out to see if he was finished and gradually they all straightened up and smiled, like, "Atta boy, John, you pray with the best of them, don't you."

When we got near the house John was puffing. I don't know how old he was, maybe fifty and he looked, well, to me looked like all white men do, if they let their whiskers grow a few days. Mother was outside with Geese-a-geese. Probably giving her a pep talk. John picked Geese-a-geese up and she hollered, "Thaw-hree-yot-nus-heh? Wah-gyah-neah-hreht-het-gat (Are you out of your head? I've been injured as a matter of fact)."

John said, "Chweant," and took her on into the house. He wasn't sure what she said.

As I said, she didn't last more than a year after that but before that I had some good times with her.

Wild strawberries lived beyond the sumacs and this was a time when they were ripe. I saw Geese-a-geese go out across the garden and into the sumac. I wanted to follow her but I didn't dare. I never knew when she was going to toilet. She would not use the one everyone else used. She was gone, maybe a half hour, when suddenly she came tearing back through the sumacs. Her long white hair was flailing and at first I thought her mouth was bleeding. She had been eating wild strawberries.

"Hroosquatneh (snake)!" she cried.

She had been startled by a huge blacksnake sunning itself on a stump. She hurried on into the house.

I had to go and investigate that. Sure enough, I found the low, barkless stump. On top, in a neat coil was the huge snake. It never blinked an eye when I got near it so I got a long stick and poked it to see if it was dead.

Move? Man, that snake leaped off the stump like a whip and sashayed through the small trees at tremendous speed. It was all of six foot long and I needed a better look at it so I dashed after it. It

8

must have heard me coming so it climbed a big thornapple tree.

I went back to the house to tell Grandmother that it was alright to go and eat the berries now. She was up in her room with the door closed. I could hear her singing, "Nearer My God to Thee."

I don't remember much about Aunt Lizzie except she was awful frail. She had TB and when she found that out she turned fiercely to religion because three of her sisters and one brother had already died from it. But she did too, though, anyways. She got it into her head that germs were everywhere and were after her.

Our drinking water came from a spring at the base of a limestone hillside. Father had the water tested and the inspector said it was the purest water he had tested in a long time. The spring was about a quarter of a mile away through the woods. Aunt Lizzie was always going after water. She was so weak and awkward that she would start out with a half a bucket and by the time she got back, half of that would be splashed out. Then she would have to wash her hands and that would use up most of what was left. She would never dry her hands on a towel for fear of the germs that lived there. In fact she hated to touch the wash basin to empty the water out afterwards. It seemed she was forever flipping her skinny fingers about in the air to get the water off. I think she was the one that got Grandmother to shitting in the woods, away from the germs. No wonder nobody married her, I know I wouldn't have. Besides, she was a school teacher and hounded me no end, even when I skipped a grade in school.

Now Uncle Go-beddy was different. He wasn't a bit afraid of germs. I don't know how smart he was but he was always traveling about giving lectures. He could also pitch a baseball. That's what he wanted me to be, a baseball pitcher and that's what he lectured about to me. Why I say he wasn't afraid of germs, he would sometimes spit on the ball even though Aunt Lizzie told him never to do that. Scared or not, he was the brother that died of TB before Lizzie did. Later on, when I spit on the ball, I was told not to do that too. I was told it was illegal.

It was usually very quiet where we lived. We were quite a

ways from any main road. One year though we tried to raise
turkeys. They could be pretty noisy if we went near them. One
day they broke loose.

The day the turkeys broke out of the pen was a sunny one.
They came out one by one. Mother called me. "The turkeys are
out!" she said.

"We'll never catch them," I said. "Let's see what they do."

Well they didn't do anything. They had never been on grass
before so they just stayed under the russet tree picking the grass.

In the evening when Father came home we formed a ring of
three people and tried to herd them back into the coop door. We
were quite a ways yet from surrounding them when they all
pricked up their heads and gave each other the alarm signal. Then
they ran through the cucumbers and the pumpkins. I ran to head
them off but they took to the air. Half of them landed in the
walnut tree and the other half landed in the big sugarpear tree.
That was that. They teetered and bobbed up there all night long
and once in a while during the night one of them would get scared
of some noise like a katydid or something and start the whole
gang off clucking again.

We never did catch them. Mother didn't seem to care because
now it cost less to feed them. They did often come back to the
coop and some would go inside and eat. Quite a few would always
remain outside acting nonchalant but daring anyone to take a step
towards them. They had taken to roaming the woods too and they
never had a set pattern.

About sneaking back to the coop. The only time they would
fly was at sunset when they would fly into the sugarpear tree to
sleep. Maybe they didn't know it was possible to fly to anywhere
else, that having been their maiden flight. Some of them must have
had some mighty restless nights because they just about blackened
the whole tree as big as it was and some of them must have had
poor footing. Some would even be on limbs barely strong enough
to carry their weight.

One day Mother said, "I wonder what people are going to
say when they come for their Thanksgiving turkeys and I'll just
point to the pear tree and say 'There they are.' " I guess she
mentioned this to Father because one evening shortly afterwards

10

he come home with a box of .22 bullets and gave them to me! All he said was, "These are for the turkeys."

I thought it would be a hectic thing, getting the turkeys for Thanksgiving, but all that happened was, when they came to bed, I went under the pear tree with the rifle and plunked them all in the head. I simply lined the shiny reflection of the setting sun along the barrel with their heads and binged them out of the tree. I asked Father why they didn't all fly when I shot the first one. "They knew it was time for Thanksgiving," was all he said.

Once I got to wondering how my father courted my mother so I asked her. She said that with her one leg curled up and crippled she never thought anyone would marry her. She said that The Whisperer used to bring her wild flowers once in a while but that her mother told her that it was a trick; that, Gawreesnet, his mother, had spilled the beans on him at the quilting-bee. Why Gawreesnet told about her son was because she thought he had a very good head on him and she told how he had cleverly made up a list of the girls he might marry, with first choices first. Wolf Ma, who was my mother's mother, then told her that this happened quite some time before, that my mother's name wasn't on the list then. Also that The Whisperer was becoming meaner and meaner because his idea didn't do its job.

Wolf Ma got her name because she was the clan mother of the Wolf Clan. The Tuscaroras followed the mother's side, like if your mother was a Cayuga of the Eel Clan, then that's what you are, a Cayuga of the Eel Clan. So Wolf Ma probably didn't want her daughter raising any mean kids, which, one of them would have been me. So she told my mother that a lot of flowers had been wasted already. Wolf Ma died before I was born, so this is secondhand news.

The Whisperer wasn't dead, though, and I remember him. He was tall and dark, had a high forehead with lots of lines in it. Something had gone wrong with his vocal cords and all he could do was whisper, even when he laughed. Of course when I remembered him, he had gotten older so maybe that's where all the lines in his forehead came from. Or else he got them from wondering who he was going to marry. He wasn't fat or skinny, just big and tall. And slow.

Well, what happened was that Mother didn't listen to Wolf

Ma when The Whisperer came around with his flowers. Probably she was only too glad to get a boyfriend by then. She was probably twenty-five or thirty and I don't think she had gotten her curled-up foot cut off yet. But then she said he never whispered about marrying her but he was getting sexier and sexier with her.

Once in a while Indians who had been away to school or someplace came drifting back to the reservation. One Tuscarora came back from Carlisle Indian School and went to work quarrying limestone near the reservation. He carved handles for sledge-hammers and mauls and hammers and axes. They called him Steelplant because he knew strong medicine plants and he was later to become my father. So, according to Mother, Steelplant came around one day and put a handle at one end of her father's crosscut saw. Her father's name was Chew. Chew offered Steelplant some wood in return but Steelplant told him to forget it, that he had all kinds of wood. The men got to talking and visiting and telling stories as Indians like to do, and come to find out, they both knew Indian medicine and could trade knowledge. Mother made Steelplant some met-met (moccasins) and they struck up a friendship. Steelplant called Mother Mischew at that time.

Mischew dreamed one night that a stranger came to the door and in the dream, she wouldn't let him in. The next day, she was home alone because her sister had, quite a while before that, married a man named HAA-hree, and her parents had hitched up the horses and gone to Niagara Falls. Towards evening, a car drove up and the man in her dream came to the door. This time she let him in. He told her that her parents were dead. The horses had panicked at a hissing locomotive and bolted right in front of it. In those days, there was no bridge at Hyde Park where all those railroad tracks are.

People came to stay overnight with Mischew. Among them were Steelplant and The Whisperer. The Whisperer had black-eyed susans and Steelplant had catnip. The Whisperer got there before Steelplant. He heard that Steelplant was friendly to Mischew. The Whisperer stood about six foot two or three and Steelplant was about five foot eight or so.

When The Whisperer saw Steelplant coming he went and waited on the porch for him. As Steelplant came up the steps, The

Whisperer kicked the catnip out of his hands. Steelplant picked the catnip back up again and broke four of The Whisperer's ribs with his elbow. Then he went on into the house and made catnip tea for Mischew. Later they got married.

Father

FATHER was tricky. He could do lots of things. He could carve
most anything he wanted to out of wood. Whistles, bows, arrows,
flutes; you name it, he could carve it; but mostly he carved more
needy things. Handles for axes, saws, hammers, spouts for tapping
maple trees; or like when he carved a wooden leg for Mother. It
was willow. The leg, I mean; the wooden one. Or like, he made
everything into a game. If we were cutting wood we'd see who
could make a wood chip fly the farthest. Or if we were felling
trees, see who could drive a peg into the ground by hitting it with
the falling trunk. Or if we were plowing, see who could plow the
straightest line.

Wait now. I just thought of a question. Why is it, when you
plow, there might not be a single seagull in the sky but then all of
a sudden, there they are, fighting over the worms with the
chickens? Where do they come from? Worse than fruit flies. Well,
anyhow, back to Father. He was good at laying around too, telling
stories or maybe carving a pipe out of that stone that, when you
first dig it up, it's still soft. Mostly, though, he was busy because
he was a chief. Also a medicine man.

Probably with medicines is where he was the trickiest. Or
with the Ouija board.

Now I'm going to tell you something. It's best to believe
your father even if you can't hardly do that sometimes. Like,
when he told me he used to play with elves (eh-GEWSS-hi'yihh)
I didn't believe him. So this one night we went down the Lower

15

River (Niagara) for sturgeon. Towards morning, just as the dark starts to lighten up, I thought I heard a noise. Father was standing on a rock dock like a shepherd with a staff, except Father had a spear. I thought maybe he had kicked a pebble but he said, "Did you hear that?"

I said, "Yeah, what was it?"

He didn't answer me the way I wanted him to because he said, "Kee'uh." That means "listen," so I did. In a minute the noise came again. This time it sounded like a pebble struck my father's spear pole, which I think it did.

"Somebody's monkeying around," I said.

"No," he said, "there's a sturgeon coming up. That was eh-GEWSS-hi'yihh telling us to get ready."

"Poo too," I thought to myself, so I said, "If there's a sturgeon coming up I'll — I'll carry it home for you." (This was the second night now and we hadn't seen sturgeon one yet. I was hoping we'd run out of kerosene for the lantern.)

Father didn't say anything and after a half hour or so we could start to see around us fairly good. Father left the lantern on the rock but he came off it and started downstream, towards Lake Ontario. He only went about twenty or twenty-five steps or so, to where there was like a small pool. The next thing I knew, JA'WOKS! he thrust his spear into the water and pulled out a huge splashy fish. It was a sturgeon alright, because later when we sold the eggs for caviar, we weighed it. I could never ever even lift it up, much less carry it home because it weighed over a hundred pounds.

Next, the Ouija board. Now here was something that wasn't like hearing a story and then getting a chance to wonder if I believed it or not.

One evening in the middle of the wintertime I tried to get out of chopping wood because the axe was dull. Father says, "I know, and the file is lost so we can't sharpen it. I better ask Weegee (Ouija) where the file is." He got out the Ouija board and we sat down on two chairs facing each other with the board on our laps. I had to have a couple pillows to get the board level. "Weegee," he said, "where's the file?"

16

The pointer went to S-T-E-P. Father put the Ouija board away, went out, and pulled the step away from the house and picked up the file and sharpened the axe. I had to go to work anyway.

Father very seldom used the Ouija board. Once Mother lost her scissors for almost six months before Father got out the Ouija board. The scissors was in the box of Christmas things, put away in the attic from the year before.

Another time was when I got accused of stealing twenty dollars. It was during one of the times when the women of the Ladies Aid were at our house sewing, on patchwork quilts. I never did really get along with one of the women. Her name was Edith Johnathan. I didn't like her because if I said "gosh" or "gee" she would scold me and tell me that I was using bad words. Just the same I was in and out of the house and in around the quilt makers all day long. After all, Edith Johnathan was at the house only to sew quilts; I was there to live there. Anyway, about the middle of the afternoon Edith said that her eyes were getting to bother her. She said she probably better go home but first she was going to buy a pie from my mother. She went to the kitchen to get her purse but then she hollered, "Hey! (a bad word) somebody stole twenty dollars out of my purse!" Then of course, she almost killed me with her bothered eyes. I don't know how many people, including my parents, thought that I took the money. All I knew is that everybody got riled up. All the women got up and went home. Father was riled up too. How I know is because he got the Ouija board and worked it all by himself.

"Weegee," he asked, "where's the money?"

"P-A-R-L-O-R," Ouija said back.

Around suppertime, little Eddy Corn, Edith's son, came puffing into the house. "My mother said to tell you," he gasped, "that she found her money. It was in the parlor in her other purse." He spun around and started back out of the house.

"Wait!" my parents both said, "Stay and have a bit to eat!" I think they were both very glad to hear the news.

Little Eddy Corn came back in. "I ate already," he said. I looked at his belly. He was skinny except for that spot. As he went on out the door I pictured a little bag of something in his guts. Corn probably.

18

Another time that Father used the Ouija board was during the war. Being as he was a half a hundred or more when I was born, the government thought he was too old to fight when he was only sixty or sixty-two so instead he went to work at the Bell Aircraft where they made airplanes. After a while some of the airplanes began to crash. Maybe two every three weeks or so. When one crashed on the reservation (near Homer's which was only a couple miles from our house) Father figured that that was too close. Enough was enough, and he brought out the Ouija board.

This time we had trouble figuring out what Ouija was saying. Something like "P-A-U-L-H-A-N-S-R-E-I-C-H-H-E-I-N-Z-..." Finally it came out that these were names. However Father was able to tell the guard at Bell that such people might be causing the planes to crash, he did it. Not too long afterwards it was in the Niagara Falls Gazette that three men were caught goofing up the planes at Bell. I remember one man's name was Paul Hans. He was a foreman. He got caught putting steel wool into the fuel tank of one of the planes. All three went to jail.

In the line of medicines, Father might have been even harder to believe. Or scarier. I mean, there, he was sort of regulating life and death. Sometimes it seemed like he could be in two places at once. Like I'd think he was in the house, then I'd see him coming out of the bushes. He gathered lots of medicines but he seemed to want to do that all by himself. Kind of secretively like.

I think he had lots of guts. I don't mean his belly stuck out, I mean he was brave. I mean I think he did things that the Baptist teachings might not approve of, and here he was a deacon too. What I mean is, lots of Indian ways were called pagan ways but probably Father felt as though as long as he was saving lives, what did it matter if he prayed to medicines or used the Ouija board or listened to eh-GEWSS-hi'yihh or crushed snails for a healing salve. What mattered is that things happened for the best.

Others, even others in the church too, must have felt that way because one day I realized something. Before we moved to Dog Street I realized that some people visited our house by com-

ing up past the spring. To come from the east like that was a
harder way. I realized after a while that they came that way if
they had unusual problems, like if a witch or ghost was bothering
them and they wanted that kind of medicine; or if they had VD.

Now there ain't no use you and me knowing those kinds of
medicines because we ain't my father or someone like him that
knows how to handle such things. Lots of medicines are deadly
poison and the power medicines, the kind you pray to, even
though they are not poison, are not to be fooled with or they
could backfire on you and destroy you.

Oh I know the simple medicines. They seem to be able to do
enough miracles for me but most of them I just know by their
Indian names. Sqa-HREE(t)-nu(t); You-h'DYEH-hra-wee; thoo-
HRO(t)-na' gi(t); things like that. Plantain; that's even more
common. In fact you can't build a house without it crowding in
next to the foundation. One day a little dog bit me. Hung right on
to my ankle too. I didn't think nothing about it until about six
hours later when my ankle was hurting so much I had to look at it.
Here it was all red and swollen. I just chewed a plantain leaf to
mash it up and put a little ball of it on the three holes from the
dog's teeth. I put my sock on to hold them in place and went to
bed because it was dark out. In the morning I would have forgotten all about it except for one sock on because I could barely
see the teeth holes anymore. Another time I burnt my foot trying
to make a deer slug. I was pouring melted lead into a hole in a
potato. The lead made the water in the potato boil and it popped
the lead out. Wouldn't I have to be barefooted and step right on a
gob of it? Yes. I hopped around and hopped right on outside the
house. It was late fall and all I could find was one scroungy little
plantain leaf. It was half yellow at that. It was yellow around a
place where a bug had bit a bite out of it. I put that on the burn
as is, without chewing it any smaller. This time the leaf stuck right
to the runny blister. I was also thinking of going down to the
spring and putting a big ball of cold white clay over my whole
foot (the kind we used for bee stings) but before I could get
around to doing that, the hurt went away and I went into the
house and played dominoes with Mother instead. (To this day
you can't see a mark of where that burn was.)

There seem to be about three kinds of medicines. First

20

there's the common simple ones like plantain. Also there's wild
cherry bark for sore throat and sweet flag for cough, slippery elm
and Oo-HOOS-stu(t) bark for drawing out poisons or the cores of
boils or slivers, old puffball dust for stopping nose bleeds, things
like that. Father says if you live right and don't pick your nose
too hard, these are all you ever need. These are some of the
common ones I know.

The second batch are not so simple. These are the ones that
need knowing how to prepare, when to gather, how much to use.
I sort of stop here because like with may apple, I know that three
are a physic and more than that is a steady stream; and that the
plant and root can be poison to some people, if you use too much.
This second category is a big category because lots of common
sicknesses are taken care of here like dropsy, snakebite, sore eyes,
gallstones, pleurisy, arthritis, palsy; things like that. Some of these
medicines I know, but where I'm not sure, is where do these
medicines cross over into the third group. Or is there a third and
fourth group.

For me, there is just a third group. These are the medicines
that hide and the medicines that are spiritual and the witch medicines. This is the group that brought people to our house from the
east entrance.

Father said that Indians very seldom got sick years ago but
now quite a few come for medicine. I take it he's talking about the
second group sicknesses. His mother and sisters were so religious
that they wouldn't use any of his medicines and three sisters and
one brother (only brother) died of TB which Father could cure. So
most of the people that came for medicine were white people. For
many of them the cure was a miracle. These are the ones that
would say, "My doctor says I have six months left to live" or
"You're my last hope." And then after they were cured, they'd
come back and say something like, "How much do I owe you?
You've saved my life!"

One day after we had moved to Dog Street, I came home
from school and Bluedog was dead. A car had hit him. He was
laying in the ditch all bloated up, stinking and covered with flies.
I shooed the flies off and tried to wiggle him to life but it was no

use. In a little while my father came home from work and I was still just sitting there crying. He felt Bluedog around a bit then he said we might as well get the shovel and bury him. I wouldn't move, though, and after a minute or so Father said, "Wait a minute. I got some medicine that might work."

I stayed by my dog while Father went into the house to make the medicine. When he came out the medicine was soaked into a washcloth and Father stretched it out, hanging in front of him. It must have been hot because he ran to cool it. He jammed the wet rag in Bluedog's mouth and picked the dog's head straight up and squeezed its jaws together. Then he rubbed and shook Bluedog's throat to get the medicine down it. The second time he came out he took a stick and poked most of the rag down Bluedog's throat, then he squeezed the lump it made. Father kept saying, "Ahh — you'll be alright." I felt that he was doing all of this just to make me feel better.

About the fourth time father did this though, Bluedog's whole body started jerking and all of a sudden he stood up. Father jerked the rag out and big globs of black blood came puking out. I felt so good I cried again. Blue had to rest up for quite a few days but he lived for four or five more years.

With Bluedog and all these people getting their lives saved all the time, somebody was bound to wonder about that and get nosey and ask questions. One day a white man came driving in and asked my father to see "the famous Chief and Medicine Man." He said he wanted to talk business so Father took him under the sugarpear tree where there was a bench to sit on. I crawled under the house so they wouldn't know I was watching. Well I could see that they were talking but you can't see words with your eyes so I shut mine and pulled my ears out from my head and aimed them at Father and the white man. I began to hear the white man; but then too, I think he was raising his voice. I gave up though because I didn't know what he meant. ". . . but you have an obligation to society! . . ." ". . . unethical to deprive the world of pharmaceuticals. . . ."

When I opened my eyes the man was walking towards his car. He was quite a tall man. He was carrying the coat-part to his grey suit. He was also carrying his glasses and hat and necktie. At first it seemed like he had rosy cheeks but now it seemed like he had rosy ears, rosy head (no hair), and rosy neck. In fact, a very rosy neck.

The car door slammed and as soon as the dust rose up in the driveway I came out from under the house. Father was still sitting under the sugarpear tree. I walked over as big as you please; as though Father wanted a good listener. What it was probably more like was that I was wanting to hear something and now might be my best chance. Well I got an earful alright but I don't know if Father was really talking to me. Maybe just talking.

"I been half waiting for this," he said. "I had a feeling somebody would be here one of these days — trying to buy some big secret. The earth is no secret, we walk all over it. If our hearts are glad for the earth, the earth will be glad. God will be glad and all will be well; we will not be sick. I guess lots of people don't know that. But the earth doesn't get mad because of that. The earth is in balance because the Creator made it that way. I guess lots of people don't know that. Lots of people get mad. Then they don't want to have anything to do with anybody. By and by they get sick. The earth doesn't do that. It doesn't get mad and jump away from us. If it did, we would have nothing to walk on; nothing to live on. I guess lots of people don't know that. They think the earth has always been here or that the earth has been provided for them. No. The earth was created. And the water was created. And the air was created. And the plants and the animals and the people. But lots of people think they are different from creation. They think everything has been provided for people. I guess lots of people don't know that we are all part of the balance of the earth. People could be thankful and glad that we have been given the power of choice. Of all of creation, people can help keep the things of earth the most in balance. If we take and never give, we work against the balance of creation. If we take from creation we take from ourselves. If we harness the earth we harness ourselves and we blank out of our minds what we don't want to know. We want to believe that only WE, the people are important. We want to believe that there is no God; that people alone have power over everything. We don't even want to believe that some day we will die. And even then we give ourselves back to the earth grudgingly.

We have to hide in a casket because we are not just fertilizer, we are PEOPLE, he(t)-ga(t) (it is so). It's people that think this way the most that I've been expecting. These are the people that speak of discovery. As though I have discovered a secret medicine. These are the ones that say that man alone has the power of choice. These are the ones that order choice beef and then call their children animals if they misbehave; as though animals are shameful. With the beef they order wild rice; but they call those with sick minds vegetables. And now one of them comes to buy a secret medicine; to 'discover' it for the world. To be rich and famous. What a pity. Here is a person who has studied hard; but he blanks out what he doesn't want to hear; that plants have the power of choice too. Just can't believe that oo-D'HRUSSschh won't work for him; probably won't even grow for him. He chose to blank that right out. I doubt if he blanked out the 'rich and famous' though. I expect he will come again."

Sure enough, just as we were getting ready for State Fair, the same man came back. This time though, he didn't come by himself. There were two others with him. He didn't drive in as fast as he had driven out and he wasn't mad anymore. He had a big smile on his face as he waved hello to my father. Father told me to pick out a melon that would be sure and win first prize at the fair, then he went to talk to the men who were walking towards the sugar-pear tree.

Doggone but if all them melons didn't look all the same to me. The next thing I knew I was looking at cucumbers and I realized then that I was wandering closer to where the men were talking. Why was it now, both times when strangers went under the sugarpear, that I got extra interested in what was going on? Well I just knew something was different. I got that feeling, the first time, when that one man came alone. Strangers just didn't come to our house unless they were sick or bringing news. But here's why MY ears pricked up. I had heard, here and there, that my father was a good fist fighter but never had I seen him fight. Another thing; he always kept track of any big boxing matches and he'd always find out who had a radio that was working when these dates came and he'd go hustling through the fields to that person's house to hear that fight. So I watched pretty close so as to be sure and be around to cheer in case he started swinging. So here I was now, close enough to watch the fight if there was going to be one. Close enough too to hear the talking. I mean, you know how talk gets louder if somebody is getting mad. The same man that got mad before wasn't the man that was mad this time. I can't tell you who it was that got mad because, well you know how white people seem to all look the same. The difference was, this man had on short pants, no suit, not gray either; tan. He was saying " . . . the great numbers of people you could help back to health simply by showing me this herb. I'll even write the check out right now before we go into the woods. Five thousand dollars."

"No," I heard my father say, "I can't do that. The medicine doesn't grow around here but it knows what I'm saying to you. It has that kind of power. I can't betray that medicine for money. There must be a pure need first. I must feel right in my insides first, then I must talk with the medicine. Otherwise its power might be lost to me forever."

"I don't understand what you're trying to tell me. We don't seem to be understanding one another here for some reason. Maybe you can understand this. You have no license to practice medicine in the State of New York. Maybe we can come to some understanding that will keep you from being arrested for that."

If you were me, you'd probably do what I did. I took a couple steps closer. Get a GOOD view of the fight.

Father didn't do anything though. He didn't even talk for a minute or so. I could tell he was getting mad though because when he did talk I heard him loud and clear; the same voice I heard just before I got spanked.

"Last fall four men came in here in a big foreign automobile. They come from that rich section around Lewiston Heights. The older man in the back seat was in great pain. I charged him one dollar and ten cents for bladder stone medicine. The dime was because silver is alright if you don't have Indian tobacco. Not long after that them four fellas came back again. That old man came out into the garden where I was. He said his name was Steve and he shook my hand. He pressed two one-hundred dollar bills into my hand. And he told me to get ahold of him if I ever needed anything. He said just to call the Maggadino Funeral Home in Niagara Falls and leave word for Steve that his doctor wants something.

Well I don't approve of them fellas. They're gangsters. Sometimes they make people disappear. I don't approve of that. But I approve of some things. I approve, if you three fellas here get into your car and go back to where you come from."

Heck! Just when I thought I'd get to see my father fight, guess what them three men did? Nothing! They just got in the car and went home. I wouldn't even wave to them. Heck! That's not the way us kids would do; not when we got mad like that. One of us would of pushed the other then we would of settled it by punching. That's how some of my best friends were made.

Father was coming towards me. "Hey," I yelled. "The melons look all the same to me. What'd them guys want? Buy medicine again?"

"Yaaas," Father said, "I guess they think I only want more money."

"How much did they want to give you?"

"Oh, enough to buy a big chicken house. Maybe two chicken houses."

"We already got a big chicken house," I said, trying to get more on Father's side.

"That's what I thought too," Father laughed. I laughed too, not really sure what was so funny.

Father started walking towards the garden. I wanted us to stand around and talk some more but all of a sudden I couldn't think of much to say. Finally I said, "Who is stronger, God or the Creator?"

"Neither," he said, keeping on walking. "God IS the Creator."

There still seemed to be lots of questions in my head. I wasn't sure why Father didn't take two chicken houses worth of money for a medicine. "I wouldn't of known whether to take money for that medicine or not," I said. "How would I know?"

"Oh sure you know," he said. "Just do whatever you know is right. Look at the melons again. You'll know which one is the best one."

I went over and grabbed whichever seemed like a good one. On the way back to the house Father told me that if he had shown the medicine to these men and sold it to them so that they could use it for what they wanted it for, they would have come back. He said they would have come back to take him to court.

26

They would have said the medicine was worthless because it wouldn't have worked for them. "I don't think I could have found the medicine if they came with me anyways. It only grows on a certain kind of tree and even then, not often," Father said. It's one of the medicines that ju-gwa T'HHHHD used to call spiritual or ceremonial or the-medicines-that-hide."

"Boy!" I said, "I was ready to watch you punch them guys out. What happened? Were they scairt of you? I don't understand what you could of said to them. Maybe they'll be back again. Maybe ten will come next time."

"No. I don't think they're coming back," he said. "Not the same ones anyway. I think I was able to tell them, in their own way of thinking, that somehow, the earth is balanced."

I felt like I was getting no place. I was still half not satisfied that there was no fight. Father took the melon from me. In a little while it would be on its way, with my mother and her friends, to the State Fair. I seemed to want more answers. "What medicine was that?" I called quickly to Father. He was going up the steps into the house. "What was it good for?"

"Cancer," he said, going on into the house.

Five days later a postcard came from Syracuse, New York. It was from Mother. All it said was, "Melon won first prize."

As I got older I came to a night in late summer when Father said, "Look at the moon. It's full now and it's starting to get smaller again. Tomorrow is the best time to gather some medicine. I gotta work so I want you to go after powerful medicine for me. It's called oo-de'HEHH'ryeh-OO-skuh-hreh. Take the path west of Miles until you get to Doo(t)-hrut's field. In the middle of the field a small creek comes out of the ground and flows north. Follow it and you'll see some blue flowers. Be careful now, these are not the ones. Go right in the water and you'll notice the flowers there look just a little different. That one will be the medicine. This is one of the ways this medicine hides; it grows next to another plant that looks the same. If you don't see two kinds of plants, if there's nothing growing in the mud, it's hiding on you. In that case, don't pick anything."

I looked up at the moon. All of a sudden it moved sideways.

I kind of jumped until I realized it was clouds passing by that were moving, not the moon. Father said, "Pay attention now, this is important. There's some Indian tobacco in my medicine bag. You must talk to the medicine."

"What shall I say?"

"Whatever you feel — how healthy and strong the medicine looks — how beautiful the flowers look — greet the medicine like an old friend — but most of all, thank the medicine for being there — and don't forget to say you have come for it. Then before you pick any, you do the Exchange. You sprinkle the Indian tobacco all around the medicine. Indian tobacco is a powerful medicine too. It is valuable in the Exchange. That's why we can't hog Indian tobacco, or hoard it. As you sprinkle the tobacco, say, 'Neow-wehh! ooneh it'wa joss hoo(t)'. Don't pull the medicine up by the roots, at this time of the moon the power will be in the leaves and stems and flowers. You can leave a little Indian tobacco in the bag to ride home with the medicine."

The next day I slung the old white medicine bag over my neck and took off for Doo(t)-hrut's field. The bag never seemed so big when Father was wearing it but now it seemed to have grown to be quite a baggy bag. I had to double up on the carrying strap. It was made out of clothesline tied around little stones in the top and bottom corners of the bag. And you know me — I couldn't be bothered with going around the lane that Father had prescribed; I went crosslots straight through the woods.

I came through some wicked places. Thorn bushes and wild grapevines and blackberry prickers. Next thing I knew, here some of the Indian tobacco had fell out of the bag which was twisted half upside down around my neck. I got worried and now as I think about it, I'll say it again, "It's probably best to listen to your father. If he says to go on the road, then GO on the road." So now here I was backtracking and not even knowing where it was that I had walked. And talk about trying to find leaves among leaves! Finally I realized I was wasting time and also, the bag was turning on my neck again. I bunched the top of the bag shut and took a death-grip on it. I ripped through one more wicked place then BANG, I was standing at the edge of the field I was looking for. It was mostly timothy.

I came to the creek and turned north. It wasn't all that big

28

of a field and pretty soon I was coming to the end of it. There wasn't any blue flowers anywhere; just a reed here and there. Sickening. I looked in the medicine bag. There wasn't too much tobacco in there either. I got kind of mad because I figgured I'd be back home by now. "HEY!" I yelled into the bag, "Where's them blue flowers?" Of course I never got no answer. I took off my sneaks and rolled up my pants and went right in the water. Well, there was hardly any water, mostly mud, but what little there was, I went in it. Guess what! I found the flowers. I was almost out of creek though. I don't know how I missed them the first time. I could tell that there were two kinds of plants. I was fairly glad and I almost started picking before I remembered I was suppose to do something. Now here was the wild part. I couldn't think of what to say. I felt foolish. I even looked around; see if anybody was looking. Nope. They weren't. I reached into the bag to get out the Indian tobacco. Dang if the bag hadn't dragged in the water and the tobacco was soggy. I broke the leaves up into smaller pieces to make more of it. I threw it all around as best I could. "HERE!" was all I could think of to say.

I picked the medicine and went home using the lane. None of the medicine spilt out. When Father got home he thanked me and hung the medicine up on a nail. It stayed there and I don't know if it ever got used. When Father died, Mother gave all of his medicines to Mirror Jack's son because father and son were both medicine men. I don't know if he used the medicine I had gathered or not. Maybe he didn't know what to use it for. Lots of medicine men guarded their medicines from each other. Sometimes they traded knowledge. But no matter what, wherever that medicine is, I know it's still good yet. I know because that's the way I feel.

One time Father told me that he had married two other people before my mother but they both died. I'm sure he started doing medicine then so that there could be an end to his burying wives. One of them was from Canada. Maybe that was the one named Myrtle. She thought she was pregnant but it turned out to be a giant tumor. The Indians in Canada were scarier and witchier and mediciner than on our reservation. Father said that there were all kinds of scary stories among the Indians in Canada and some were not true. He said that a few medicine people pretended to have great medicines but all they wanted to do was make money. He said they'd put worms or spiders or anything in their mouths and pretend to suck this thing out of a witched person. He said that there was a certain kind of witchcraft people that could shoot things into people and others that could someway put small living things into people. He said that one of his wives, maybe Myrtle, had this happen to her. Also, Father said that there were medicine people who WERE close enough to the earth and the Creator to get these things back out of whoever had 'em in 'em. These people were hard to find because they never spoke much to people because people generally made fun of them.

Here's what happened to whichever of the wives that it happened to. First they had a son named Huron. Huron got into some kind of a squabble with some other kid. On that reservation, quite a few different tribes lived, mostly Iroquois but some Delawares and Crees and Wyandottes and so on. Some families of some tribes never got along because maybe somewheres way back one family had fought each other; one family with the British or French or Americans or whatever. Or maybe Huron fought over marbles, who knows, but he picked out a family of strong medicine people. Poof! In a year, Huron was dead. No doctors, Indian or white, could find out what was wrong with him. Next, Huron's mother got sick. Same thing, even the hospital didn't know what was wrong.

One evening Father saw an old Indian stuck in the edge of the Grande River. That is, the old man's wagon was stuck. The wagon had a horse in front of it too. He had been gathering drift logs for fire. Father helped get him out and they got to talking, which, up alleys, is right up Father's. Father happen to tell about his sick wife and how nobody knew what was wrong. The old man says, "Come on, I'll show you what to do," and he showed Father a medicine. I think it was some kind of fungus. It turned out, the old man was strong medicine people because the medicine worked.

Father did what the old man told him and in the middle of the night his wife let out some screams. Father lit the lamp. His wife looked dead but all she had done was faint away. No wonder though; she had passed a six-inch shiny black lizard. It was dead. I don't know if she peed it out or pooed it out but from then on, Father knew that not all stories were lies. It didn't matter, though, because later she got sick again and this time nothing saved her.

One day Father says, "One of these days I might die."

I said, "Why don't you show me the medicines then," as though he would never die if he did.

That's when I learned that it takes years to learn the medicines because right from the step of the house Father started saying, "There's one, there's one, there's one, there's one. . . ." Of course he explained each one but, what the heck, after about three, I got ALL scrallered up.

There was plantain, sorrel, yellow dock, burdock, smartweed, knotweed, nightshade, chicory, and all like that before we even got to the garden. Then we crossed part of the garden and walked along the edge. There was carpet, purslane, chickweed, cockle, buttercup, St.-John's-wort, mustard, cinquefoil, black medic, oxalis (sorrel), mullein, mallow (I called them little breads), primrose, wild carrot, dogbane, pimpernel, butterfly weed, bindweed (wild morning-glory), heal-all (Dug-de-Han'a Hres), Jimson weed, ragweed, yarrow.

Man, we weren't even to the woods yet. I felt like saying, "Sorry I asked," or at least, "Hoe! Let's start over, only slower this time." At this point Father stopped. He seemed to know that my brain was spinning. All I could remember was which smartweed was good for heart in case I got too excited.

Father said, "We'll just go in the woods a little ways; then tomorrow I'll show you the medicines in the fields. Then we'll do the creek and the swamp. Then I'll show you the places where the scarce medicines are. Then we gotta go all over it again and I'll show you which part of the medicine to use so you won't forget. There's lots of medicine looks the same; all the ones that look like small sunflowers, they're hard to tell apart. When you learn all this, I'll show you some of the stronger medicines." Then we went into the woods.

We just took a small swing around the wooded hillside to the north. That was too much, plus what was already too much. First there was mandrake, then coltsfoot, then bloodroot. On the side hill there was squirrel corn, Solomon's-seal, vervain, digitalis, poke, crowfoot. Mind you, these are only the names of those medicines that Father and I knew the English names of. Towards the bottom of the hill where it was more moist there was touch-me-not, gentian, borage, poison hemlock, Lobelia, yellow violets. As we started back Father pointed out trees. Elder, red maple, basswood bark, prickly ash, wild cherry, sumac, slippery elm. Once in a while we'd see something different like puffball or brake or toadflax. By the time we got back, I'd HAD it. I probably haven't mentioned quite a few medicines but maybe you get the idea of what it's like to learn medicines. It's ROUGH! In fact, I never did do it. I know enough though. I'm alive ain't I? But what I mean by rough, I mean tough; tough to remember everything. Now you just take the one single medicine that's most common to me: plantain. It's not just good for cuts and burns and bites or stings. It's also good for bed-wetting people. And runny ears. And sore guts (inflammation). And ulcers; or when people spit blood. And eczema. And worms. And the shits. And regular earache.

Now Father is very often in a joking-thinking place. So after he had told me this number of things that plantain was good for, I had to try and be funny and say, "Is THAT all?"

He said, "No, there's more," very seriously. "It's also good for neuralgia, diabetes, impotence, to stop tobacco habit, spleen, hemorrhoids, and too much menstrual flow in women. And them little green seeds are good for yellow jaundice, dropsy and epilepsy."

He might as well have said, ". . . and Constantinople," because I didn't know there were such sicknesses with such names. So go ahead and tell me — that I SHOULD have remembered all the things my father told me; then go ahead and recite what I just told you. That's what I mean by ROUGH.

Father loved to sit and talk and laugh, especially with his old buddies. Maybe all Indians do. They'd tell hunting and fishing and sports stories half the night long. Most of all though, even when he went blind and couldn't gather medicines or show them to me, he loved to have some medicine person come and swap medicine stories. This was especially true if he had a visitor who was a medicine person that he had never met before. That may be because in his retirement, nobody kept secrets from him.

Some of the most powerful medicine people would come from long ways to see him. They would smoke Indian tobacco and giggle like kids. Some of the greatest medicine people were women. I say they were great but none of them believed that; not those that were. They say the Creator is part of all things and all things are part of the Creator, but it is only the Creator that has the power. I often tried to stay up and listen to the old stories and I always thought I missed the best ones by falling asleep. Why I say that is because medicine people get sleepy too. In order to stay awake as long as possible, they had to tell trickier stories. Or scarier.

Here's about the type of story that would be told while I was still awake. It's about two sisters that lived about a half mile apart. Sa-nit was fat but her sister was fatter. The sister of Sa-nit was named Ga-ruh-geh. Father was telling some medicine man from Canada about them. He said, "Sa-nit got pneumonia and when Ga-ruh-geh found her she was too sick to cook or make fire so she brought her home to her house in a wheelbarrow. That cold ride made Sa-nit worse. Ga-ruh-geh came and got some medicine. She stayed up doctoring her sister. Two days later Ga-ruh-geh was all bushed out trying to save her sister's life so she went to the bedside and said, 'I have to lay down for a while.'

"Sa-nit opened her eyes and looked around. I guess she could feel that she was cured. She took one look at Ga-ruh-geh and told her, 'MY GOSH! YOU'RE the one that's sick,' then she jumped up and pushed her bigger sister down on the same bed.

"Ga-ruh-geh struggled back and the two sisters got to wrestling. Ga-ruh-geh said, 'Tha-hree-yot-nus oo-neh,' meaning that Sa-nit was so ill she was delirious.

"But of course even though Ga-ruh-geh was bigger she was no match for her sister, who after all, had used my medicine. Naturally, then, the little one got the best of the big one and she grabbed her coat and headed for the door. 'I GOTTA GO! RIGHT NOW!' she said.

"Ga-ruh-geh said, 'WHY?'

" 'Because I don't live here,' she said, and she went back home."

Father and the medicine man laughed quite a bit but while
they were still laughing, Father said, "Wait, that's not the end of
it. A little later on there was a knock on my door. Ga-ruh-geh was
back again. I think she was ashamed to talk very loud. She said,
'Have you got any more medicine? My sister and I got into a little
scuffle and I'm not feeling so good.'

"I said, 'Wait now. Let me understand you. YOU want
medicine because you're sick of your sister.' "

And the two men went tee-hee-heeing on into the night.

After I got into higher learning and all kinds of sports and
feeling that girls seem to be getting friendlier, I didn't seem to
notice the passing of time. There was no end to it and Father
could always teach me about medicine. One day, though, Father
died. The bell rang eighty-eight times.

The next thing I knew I was looking at him in a coffin at
Pike's Funeral Home in Sanborn. I realized then that quite a bit of
knowledge was going to have a lid put on it and covered up. Years
ago his pipe and bow and arrows and some cornbread would be in
there too. Instead there was nothing. I didn't like that and I went
outside.

There was snow on top of most of everything but I didn't
want to look at much anyways. All I could see was a bunch of
dried stalks in an old flower bed. I've always had a habit, when I'm
walking through a field, of breaking some old stalk of something
off and poking it into my mouth to diddle on so I went over to
the flowerbed and did it again. When the snow fell off the top of
the stalks, what do you think I saw? I was holding red LOBELIA!
— and all of its properties had gone back into the ground too. I
took the bouquet of dead red Lobelia and put it in my father's
hands. It would be a more peaceful hibernation. Red was his
favorite color, too.

The funeral was regular until the Baptist minister finished
speaking at the graveyard. For a minute I wondered why nobody
walked away. Then the chiefs came forward. The chairman of the
chiefs' council spoke in Tuscarora. Before he spoke, though, he

had made sure that the wampum signifying the title, Saw-gwaw-hree(t)-thre(t), was in safekeeping somewheres. The message was long but I'm not allowed to use ceremony words just to tell them. The ending was something like this: "With great reluctance we receive and pass on your title. You have left giant footsteps and together those of us who remain will try to fill them."

Mrs. Shoe's Gang

ABOUT A MILE from where we lived there was a narrow and dusty road that we called Shoe Road. The woman that lived on it had lots of children and she was called Mrs. Shoe because it made everybody think of the old woman that lived in a shoe. Even the house had sort of a shoe look to it. It was a small log house with an upstairs to it and a ladder to get there with. Two rungs of the ladder were missing and that made it so that only the best climbers could sleep upstairs. There was a shed made of poles that leaned against the back of the house. That's the part that made up the toe of the shoe-look of the house.

There was no way that anyone could ever keep track of how many children or grownups ate and slept in the shoe. Or died, because my father said that that shoe was older than Fort Niagara. Another reason you could tell that the shoe was old was because there was a little backhouse that had to be moved every time the hole under it got filled up and now it was almost a quarter of a mile away from the shoe.

Only the people that lived in the shoe were of the Beaver Clan and nobody monkeyed with them, like as though they were a separate tribe. Most other people on the reservation did things at a certain time, like eat and sleep, but not Mrs. Shoe's gang. Well, really, the shoe wasn't big enough to let them all do that so they formed two crews, the day crew and the night crew. And talk about eat! Why, that gang went through tons of food. Once Boneset said they could have some white corn and that night the night crew went through his cornfield like a flock of locusts. Picked Boneset dry.

And what do you think they kept in the toe of the shoe? Dogs or cats or pigs or chickens. Strays. Any stray thing that wandered too close or into their path. Sometimes I think their paths wandered into the animal and made it stray. We had an old cat named Kitty Girl. One day Mrs. Shoe came to do housework. Nobody ever asked her to do any work but it always meant she was going to do something no matter what you said. Then she would ask for canned goods or squash or apples or anything in the straw bin in the cellar for pay. I mean, that's what she asked for at our house. Mother had only one real leg and didn't get around to the neighbors so she never heard about the eating of cat soup by Mrs. Shoe's gang. So now here comes Mrs. Shoe. Sometimes people called ker Kangaroo because her legs were very big and hung over her ankles. But even more so, they called her Kangaroo because her lower arms stuck out like she was forever playing a piano. Never before had Mrs. Shoe ever gotten any of our animals except those put up in fruit jars and given to her by Mother so I didn't think anything when I saw her plunking up the path. As far as work went, the only thing safe to let her do was empty the slop pail and even that was risky but in my mother's mind, she let Mrs. Shoe pretend to work so as not to have her feel as though she was begging. This time though Mrs. Shoe saw Kitty Girl by the fire and right away she said, "We need a cat."

Never did I expect my own mother to say what she did. No more had she said, "Go ahead," when Mrs. Shoe made a beeline for Kitty Girl and threw her in a grain sack. Mother told her that the cat's name was Kitty Girl and not to worry about feeding her; that she would eat every mouse in the house plus outside mice too. Kitty Girl put up such a struggle in the bag that Mrs. Shoe left right away. She never even had time to light her pipe. She must of found it in some trash pile because it had only half of its stem. As soon as Mrs. Shoe was out of ear range I said to Mother, "How come you gave Kitty Girl away?" Mother just went on doing whatever she was doing and told me never to mind, that it was a good way to get rid of her. I said, "I didn't know you wanted to get rid of our cat; I could of done that." She said no, that she didn't mean the cat, she meant Mrs. Shoe. That Kitty Girl would be back before morning; that that was why she told Mrs. Shoe what a mouse-getter Kitty Girl was. And sure enough, about two or three or four in the morning I heard Kitty Girl crying at the door. I ran downstairs and grabbed her and took her to bed. I made a long tunnel out of my quilt by lifting it up and pulling against my foot and Kitty Girl went all the way down to my feet and purred herself to sleep. I think Mrs. Shoe knew she had been tricked because she never came back for a long time and when she did, she never mentioned any animals. Only vegetables.

I was one of the few people that ever went to the shoe to visit. In a way I didn't like to go there and in a way I did. Why I liked to go there was because you never knew what tricky toys the day crew children had invented from the junk that the night crew brought in. The thing that I didn't like was, so few people came to see them that, like in my case, all the kids would pour out and crowd around me like I was famous. Once I yelled, "Hey, stand back, you're breathing up my air," but they only came in closer anyways. So this day when I got there I brought a penny and dropped it four or five hundred yards from the shoe and as the kids spotted me and came yelling, I felt my pockets and started looking around saying, "Hey, I lost my money." That did it. In a minute there was nobody to talk to except Snotnose and Toy Man.

Toy Man must have been almost thirty years old. When he was little he showed a knack for inventing toys so Mrs. Shoe gave him the job of seeing that the kids always had toys. I asked him what new toys he had invented. He showed me a bundle of rags wired into a ball. It was all black. "We can't touch that," he exclaimed. "That's for the night crew kids. They pour kerosene on it and light it so they can see it, then they kick it around. They call it nighttime lacrosse. Whoever gets burnt is out of the game."

There was a very tall elm there too. It had four long strands of wire hanging from a very high limb. There was an old car tire at the bottom. I asked Toy Man where did he get such long wires. "Mr. Nichols loaned it to us," he said. Mr. Nichols was a fruit farmer farming on Ridge Road off the reservation. "From his grape vineyard," Toy Man added. It didn't look like many had used the swing and I asked about that. "The reason we can't hardly use it," said Toy Man, "is because Snotnose won't let us. It's his swing. Kangaroo gave it to him because he put it up, but while he was climbing back down, he fell and wedged one of his arms between two trunks. It broke his arm and I think it stretched it too because, look, show him Snot, how your arm does." Snot, with snot running down his nose, gave me a demonstration. He could fling his right arm in any direction, like as though it had a ball joint above his elbow. "We're thinking of making him a baseball pitcher when he gets bigger," Toy Man said, "but right now we never know which way the ball will go when he throws it."

Snotnose was limping so I asked what about that. "Oh that," said Toy Man, "I was giving him a ride on the lawnmower and he stuck his foot down in the blades. He said he thought that was the way to put on the brakes." I asked why didn't Snotnose talk. "He don't want to," Toy Man explained, "Kangaroo told him he could do anything he wanted to, since falling out of the elm was in the line of duty. Once in a great while he lets us use the swing."

Just then we heard a swarm of kids and it was the money-lookers coming back. "We went all the way to your house," one of them yelled. "Your mother said you were visiting us so we remembered and came back to visit you."

"Let's play El Booto," Toy Man yelled. I asked what that was. "Oh, you better not play," Toy Man said, "too complicated for you. I won't play this time," Toy Man went on, except now he switched to the Indian language, "so I can explain the game to you." All the kids darted around the giant trash pile behind the shoe. "This is individual effort. Each player is trying to find the biggest tin can that he can hold in one hand, because they have to try to catch the boot in it." By now the players were picking up white wooden paddles that were stacked by the shoe. I could see that they had once been somebody's picket fence. "The paddles are to hit the boot with." Just as I began wondering if Toy Man was really saying "boot," out of the shoe came Mrs. Shoe. "Kangaroo is the chief scorekeeper," Toy Man went on. Mrs. Shoe was carrying a small red thing. What it turned out to be, it was a rubber plaything for a dog. Probably a thing that rich people would buy for their dog for Christmas because it was in the shape of a Santa Claus boot. "Let the game begin!" shouted Toy Man, just as though this was a terrific event. There were four kids of different sizes and sexes on each side of the sagging clothes line. Somebody's brassiere was hanging on the line but nobody moved it or nothing.

Mrs. Shoe was dragging a wooden kitchen chair but it only had the front legs on it. She said, "Hi, Beh-Beh," to me and I just waved to her because I didn't like that name. She was at our house watching me get born and she put that name on me for her own self to call me that with. There was a big spike on the shoe house and she hung the back of the chair on it and sat down and lit her short pipe. "Now how this game goes," Toy Man said, talking Indian, "is somebody bats the boot over the net." He meant the clothesline. "Then those on the other side, whichever of them think they can catch it, yell either, 'Booto' or 'El Booto.' If you yell 'Booto,' that means you're afraid you might miss it, which, if you do, you only lose two points. Or if you want to you can just bat it back because whoever misses it, while they lose points, the one that batted it, gains points. If you're pretty sure you can catch it, it's best to holler, 'El Booto,' because then you can get four points. But then you could lose four too, if you miss it." The game was already on.

I was just thinking about how gamey the rules were when two kids crashed their heads into each other. Tweeeeet! Mrs. Shoe had blown a police whistle. She got up and plunked over to the two kids who were wailing very loud. They were still laying on their backs and she stood between them looking at them. "Three points for bloody nose!" she called out. "Two for lump on cheek." I had just been thinking of asking to play but now I didn't know if I wanted to score with my face. I had heard that Mrs. Shoe could read minds and wouldn't you know, she said to me, "Don't worry, you can't play. All the players have numbers and that's as far as I can count, to eight. And another thing. You don't have no hitter stick of your own. We don't want one giving the other any germs." She blew the whistle and the boot started flying over the net again. It seemed like only a couple minutes went by and Benna, who was the largest, hollered "El Booto," and was just about to catch the boot when the whistle blew again. "Time out!" Mrs. Shoe said, "No score on that last play! Dinky needs more power." Benna was ahead in points but the smallest player, Dinky, had no score. "January!" called out Mrs. Shoe. Out of the shoe came January carrying a small baby. She layed down in the grass and opened up her blouse. Dinky went over there and sucked some milk. "Too much milk for Hitler alone," Mrs. Shoe said. The baby was named Hitler because they had heard that there was a bad person named

41

Hitler and when the baby was born it came out hitting and hollering, so Mrs. Shoe figured that there was no better name for it than Hitler. "Okay, that's enough!" Mrs. Shoe said to Dinky. Dinky got up and went back into the game but he never scored anything. Pretty soon, tweeeet! went the whistle again. "Rest period," Mrs. Shoe said.

All the players layed down right where they were. "Wait a minute!" Mrs. Shoe said, and she blew the whistle. "Game called on account of time to eat," she announced. All the players sprang from their positions and began scrambling to the other side of the shoe. But as fast as I thought they were, some of the people living in the shoe were even faster and they came out of the door like a school of fish. Mrs. Shoe motioned to me, "You're our guest," she said, "so get in line." With all them bodies moving so fast I automatically went right with them. But even if I was a guest, I must have been thought of as a slow guest because when I got there, the line was already formed. I couldn't believe how fast some people were. Even January and Hitler were near the front of the line.

There was a great big black pot on stones and a little dinky fire under it. It was the kind of pot that maple syrup makers use. There was a long wooden spoon or dipper in the pot and each one ate a dipperful then passed the dipper on to the next one. Then the first one came round and got back in line again. "You just keep going around until you get full," Mrs. Shoe said to me, "I don't get in line. I can eat anytime because I'm the boss." I asked her what was in the pot. She said, "Oh, everything. We just keep adding to it. Sometime it rains and makes more or we add water from the well. We don't dip down too far because the latest things are down there and might not be all cooked yet." She went over to the pot and started poking around into it with a stick. Her pipe was out so she spit it out and kicked it towards the shoe. It was getting fairly close to my turn and I was watching Mrs. Shoe fishing out bones and tossing them towards the toe of the shoe.

If there was anything that I liked to do where Mrs. Shoe was concerned, it was to watch her face. Something on it was always moving, like her bottom lip was always playing around. Her bottom jaw stuck out and so did the bottom of her forehead. Her face was dark and small. Well, her whole head was small and with her big tall body it was almost like somebody carrying

42

MRS. SHOE

around a head on a pole. I was just thinking about that when, Lord have mercy, she fished out a skull that looked like her own but smaller. "What's that?" I said out loud. She laughed, and she looked like Popeye laughing in the comics. "Oh that ain't nobody but Pete," she said. "I got him at New-dow-wit-eh" (which in Indian means 'water pouring downward,' and that's the name of Niagara Falls), "when I worked there. It was Mrs. Bostwick's pet monkey and she donated it to me because it bit her two times. I told her I had a good place for it. That was three days ago and it's too bad you didn't get here sooner. I don't think there's much monkey meat left." She played with her face again, then she said, "But we put two rabbits in there and half a dog and there's lots of corn. "Yessir," she said, "there's lots of corn."

In two more turns it was going to be my turn to dip into the pot that cooked a monkey head. And a half a dog. "Mrs. Shoe," I said, "I gotta go home."

"No," she said, "your mother will be mad at me if I don't feed you."

"No," I said, "she'll be mad if I eat because it'll spoil my supper. It's my father's birthday and Grabber will be there with his fiddle and we might have pig guts." Pig guts is blood sausage we make with pig guts and blood.

"Oh," she said, "No wonder you want to save your belly."

I got right out of line without looking into the pot. Next, I was embarrassed because I stepped the wrong way. I was in the middle of a circle formed by the day crew. As I squeezed out, Ferret grabbed my hand. She said, "If you stay, you can play nighttime lacrosse with the night crew. They don't have no referee."

I said, "Maybe I can come back," and she let go my hand. I dogtrotted along the dusty road, looking back often to see my- self making dust puffs behind me. I was quite sure that I wasn't coming back. Maybe even for six months. I liked to be around the shoe for looking purposes but not to live there. I crossed the little footbridge in the valley of grass and from there I could see Grab- ber's bicycle leaning against the house. Bluedog came trotting half sideways to meet me. I thought of half a dog in the syrup pot. "Get back," I said to Bluedog before I could stop myself. But he just started wagging his tail.

44

Bedbug

ONE DAY Bedbug came over and I could see that he had been crying. We called him Bedbug because his face, his whole head, looked like it had someway been flattened. "Our house," he said as he began crying again, "It burned down last night!"

"Live with me," I said right away. "We'll have more fun than a barrel of monkeys." I was thinking as fast as I could to cheer him up. "You can always make another house but you can't always live with me."

"Yeah, but you don't know the half of it," he sobbed, "I was gonna be twelve today but now our house is burnt and I got no place to have my birthdaaaaa." He cried the word *birthday.* He was going to be tough to cheer up.

Twelve years old is an old age to be crying as loud as Bedbug was crying. I almost put my arms around him but his face was such a mess I couldn't. Mother opened the door and hollered out, "What's the matter?"

"Bedbug needs a house," I yelled back. "His burnt."

We went inside and Mother gave Bedbug a big cup of sassafras tea with milk and honey in it. Just the smell of it would stop anybody's crying.

Bedbug didn't have a father. Never did, that I knew of, but his mother, Naw-Root'na-Root never gave up looking for one for him. "Where's your mother?" my mother asked.

"I don't know," Bedbug said. "She went to Sanborn last night but she might of got drunk because she didn't come back."

45

I was feeling so bad for Bedbug that I said to Mother, "I KNOW! Let's give Bedbug a birthday party!"

You can always count on Mother in such emergencies. She said, "O.K. but it's going to take time to get things ready. You boys go out and play. I'll make a cake and some eats."

Now I began to feel good. I got to thinking, "We might even have Kool-aid." I got so excited I even took Bedbug along the big maple hillside and let him shoot away half a box of .22's. Well some of 'em wasn't wasted. We found a big long wild grape vine going up to a squirrel's nest and being as we didn't have any knife of any kind I let Bedbug shoot off the bottom of the vine so we could swing out over the hill.

Just as Bedbug was out at the end of our first swing on the swing, a squirrel came out of the nest. Bedbug wanted to shoot it but I said, "No. It ain't the time of the year yet." This made Bedbug cry again. By the time he swung back in again the squirrel was gone anyway so I let him take another shot at just anything. This he did. He shot just anywheres into the trees.

We played on the swing but after a while our arms got tired because the swing swung so far out we had to hang on for a long long time. From there we went back home and got a sharp knife (paring knife) and went towards the springwater spring. Along the way I showed Bedbug how to make a sliding basswood whistle and gave it to him for his birthday. This he tweeted all the way to the spring.

At the spring we dug out some of the white clay that lives nearby and made some clay animals and some marbles for Bedbug to cook in a fire after they dried.

Bedbug kept asking if I thought the birthday cake was ready yet, because when we got the paring knife we could smell it baking. I told him that lots of other good things had to be cooked yet and this made him almost smile.

Next we lifted up rocks and found crabs and pushed them together and made them fight. This made Bedbug laugh. We had to quit this though because Bedbug got to jabbing the winner crab with the paring knife and killing it.

In order to keep Bedbug from crying again, I told him it was time to go and get some blankets to make a tent in the woods so we could camp out tonight. This took his mind off the crab jabbing so we took the clay things back to the house and set them in the sun to dry.

By this time the birthday cake was out of the oven and cool, and Mother said we could decorate it. And BOY did we ever decorate it! In fact, we had to make a second batch of icing because Bedbug ate quite a bit up of the first batch.

Father came home just in time to join the party and eat. Bedbug had a whole dumpling in his mouth and was starting to chew before he realized that nobody else was eating yet and that Father was saying grace. He did wait though, to hear "amen" before he chewed more. Bedbug forgot about the cake as he stuffed himself with chicken and dumplings and homemade bread and strawberry jam — never touched his vegetables. How I know he forgot the cake was, as soon as we lit the candles, he left all of what was in his plate of his third helping. Also, after he made a wish and blew out the candles and we sang "Happy Birthday dear Bedbug . . . ," he could hardly eat two pieces of cake.

After the eating part of the birthday we took blankets and axes and matches and went into the woods and made a little low tent. Then we made a fire and told stories until quite late. One of the stories that Bedbug told was of his house burning down. Finally we got sleepy and went to bed.

During the night it rained some; about enough to put our fire out and wet everything. Towards morning, Bedbug woke me up. "I gotta pee," he said, "But there's a ghost outside."

I peeked out. Sure enough, there was a white thing out there. Maybe if I didn't feel that I was taking care of poor Bedbug I wouldn't of been so brave. I had heard that ghosts were afraid of light so I tried to strike a light but the matches were all wet. To act brave, I crawled out and touched the white thing. It turned out to be a wet old rotten stump. Something in the rotten part, maybe fungus, made it glow in the dark. Everything in the tent was wet but it was a warm night and I went back to sleep. I don't think Bedbug did though because in the morning, he was gone. Of course, lots of birds were singing by the time I woke up.

I ran back to the house to tell Mother. She was just putting her wooden leg on — that's how early it was yet. I told her too about the stump that glowed in the dark. She said that probably Bedbug was scared out of his wits. I offered to take Mother back

47

in the woods and show the stump to her. She said no, that I didn't need to worry about her seeing any stumps and that if Bedbug could make out as well as he did at our house that I didn't need to worry about Bedbug either, no matter where he was. She also told me that I had done my duty to poor Bedbug but that I hadn't done my duty to the chickens; that I had forgotten to gather the eggs because of the birthday party. I went out and looked. Sure enough, I hadn't.

You know, it's no good to let chickens see their eggs for too long. They'll get to thinking that they can have them to hatch. It's a mean thing to do — to let chickens have their eggs for too long before you take 'em away from 'em. While I was carrying the eggs I realized that I had also probably forgot to draw water and knock the potato bugs off the potato leaves and burn 'em in the knocker-inner bucket with kerosene.

After lunch I told Mother that I was going to track Bedbug. It was easy. You know how rain does to dust in the driveway. It makes lots of little prickly looking things. Bedbug's tracks went towards Wah-hraa-hreh-d'yehhs (where the sun goes down, or west). From then on I didn't even try to track him. I just figured on stopping at houses and asking, "You got Bedbug?"

Well I didn't have to go very far. The first house I came to was BilMeehhrruh's and THERE he was. And guess what? Mother was right when she said not to worry about Bedbug if he could make out so well as he did at our house. Know why? Here he was, playing with little Prince Albert and having himself another birthday party!

I ran home and told Mother that I was going to be invited to another Bedbug birthday party. She smiled and told me to watch out for belly aches. When I got there, to the middle of the party, sure enough, I WAS invited. We played hard for quite a while — in fact, until little Prince Albert quit showing off when he fell off a barn beam and broke his arm. We stood around and watched him cry while his mother made a sling for him out of one of her old aprons. What made little Prince Albert mad was, we had been playing tag when he fell. I had been chasing him because I was "IT" and while he was laying on the floor with a broken arm, I tagged him and made HIM "IT."

This didn't stop us from eating though. Bedbug, "as long as

it was HIS party" he said, claimed that he had a right to make the eating rules, so we ate the birthday cake first.

After the party, I started to offer to walk Bedbug home but then I remembered his was burnt. Instead we just all went for a walk; down Upper Mountain Road; towards my place. Who do you think we met? Bedbug's mother. She smelt a little drunk and wasn't really paying much attention to us until Bedbug saw her and yelled, "MA!"

When she saw Bedbug she started crying a loud scarey cry and kept yelling, "MY BABY! MY BABY! OH MY BABY! YOU'RE ALIVE!"

After a while she said something that made me giggle inside. She said, "Oh my baby! I almost forgot your birthday. COME ON! We're going to REALLY celebrate!"

We watched them walk down the road with their arms around each other. Maybe, and probably, Bedbug's mother had been on her way to Red Book's to get drunker. Now, though, they were going to have Bedbug's third birthday party — at least it was the third as far as I knew. I don't know where they were going to have it but they didn't seem to care. They were just walking to it. I watched them get smaller and smaller. They were walking to Wah-hraa-hreh-d'yehhs; to "where the sun goes down."

The Picnic Snake

ON THE EVENING of the day before the Tuscarora Nation Picnic, my slingshot crotch broke. Now at this time of my life, for me to be without a slingshot was like me without arms. So I went out looking for a slingshot crotch. As everybody knows, when you don't need 'em, good slingshot crotches can be found in almost every tree. When you need 'em, they hide because it probably hurts to be cut off by a knife. Also, I was very very choosy about my crotches and I knew it might take quite a while to find one. Even though it was light yet when I started looking, I took the lantern and matches.

Good thing too, because it was fairly late and night when I found one. Only thing was, I didn't have no knife so I hung the lantern in a tree to mark the spot and went home to get a knife. When I got back to the lantern, a snake was there. I never knew that snakes stayed up late. I thought they went to bed with the sun. You ever hear that if you cut the head off a snake that its tail will wiggle 'til the sun goes down? Well, probably that don't have nothing to do with it but anyways, THIS snake was up yet. It was a greensnake, about a foot long. It was up on this big yellowdock plant, catching tiny flies that got attracted to the lantern light. As soon as it saw me it sat still and never moved a hair all during the time I whittled the crotch off the tree. I think it thought I wouldn't notice it and would soon go and leave the lantern there for it to hunt little flies with all night. I fooled it though. I took the lantern and IT too!

51

In the morning I slept late. Then I took my good old time making a very good slingshot. While I was making it I had the greensnake in an old horseradish bottle. Nailholes were in the bottlecap. The bottle was hanging by a string around fourteen inches or so off the low butternut tree limb. After a while I got to thinking that it might be getting kind of stuffy in the bottle so I took the tin cap off.

I kind of forgot about the snake because I was trying to be so careful with the slingshot. In fact, I was doing such a good job that I even caught myself biting my tongue as it hung out the corner of my mouth. When I looked up at the snake, here the little son of a gun was crawling up the string. This was interesting. I didn't know that greensnakes could walk right up strings! It was a neat trick and the trickiest part was when the whole snake's body was touching only string. I was so interested that the snake almost got away from me. When I left for the picnic, I had my slingshot in one pocket and the snake in the bottle in the other.

At the picnic, people were just starting to get there, same as me. The picnic grove was a bunch of trees with the bushes cut out from under 'em. One of the people or whoever had cleared out the grove had trimmed the bottom of a thornapple tree so somebody else could stand under it. That must of been hard to do because those long jabby things can really jab you. Here was a perfect place for me because lots of tiny apples were on the ground and limbs for my slingshot. I hung the snake bottle up and began slingshotting the little wee apples around. Quite a few older people said, "Better put that away. You'll put somebody's eye out." They probably didn't think I was a very good shot.

Picnics are fun; especially if your mother works at the food stand. This way, you can eat free anytime. You can look around at stuff; run around here and there seeing what's going on, then get free corn soup if things get dull. There's no hurry then, at any time.

It wasn't long before a bunch of kids my age were asking for turns at my slingshot. Pretty soon there was about eight of them or so, so I said, "I bet a nickle that that snake can walk up that string instead of jumping to the ground." Some of the kids argued about that for a while and finally four of them bet me. I took the cap off but for a long time, nothing happened. The four that bet

began trying to make me pay because they said I lost. I argued back that the snake never done nothing yet; that probably we were scaring it. By arguing, I got everybody to move away and watch.

Just about the time I started getting yelled at again to "pay up," the snake's head came up out of the bottle. Everybody got quiet. Once the snake got the feel of the string, it inched itself right on up. The kids that didn't bet cheered it and I told them to catch it quick before it got away. I was busy collecting my nickles before THEY got away.

I could tell that Cardriver-uh (means little cardriver) was mad. Probably he had lost his only nickle. As for me, I had been fairly worried; I hadn't even had a nickle to start with.

To kind of smooth things over I showed whatever kids didn't know about biting greensnakes. I showed 'em how Geese-a-geese showed me how to do it. You stretch 'em out like a cob of sweetcorn or a mouth organ then you bite lightly along the snake's body. This causes you to have good white teeth. Quite a few kids will have good teeth. Some, though, buggered off on biting the snake. That's O.K. with me. They'll pay later with rotten teeth.

After we all had a turn or a chance, we put the snake back in the bottle and capped it up. As the kids wandered off I began thinking of letting the snake go so I wouldn't have to carry it around. Just about then, some kids that were just getting to the picnic came towards us. "Let me borrow your snake," Cardriver-uh says to me. "I wanna try get my nickle back."

"You can HAVE it," I said.

I stuck around to watch Cardriver-uh do the same thing that I had done. He was even more clever and got into a hot argument first. When betting was mentioned, then, one guy bet a dime. I was kind of thinking that I had been a dummy when the snake came right on out of the jar and fell on the ground. Worse yet for Cardriver-uh, the kids beat him up for not having any money.

It wasn't long before Cardriver-uh's mother was getting after the other kids' mothers and soon the minister went over to see what it was all about. I was still under the thornapple watching the greensnake. It had "frozen" again, hoping that nobody could see it if it kept still. I was just trying to think of what kind of a noise a snake makes to call another snake. I was going to try to learn to call snakes. I never got a chance to call this one though because before I knew what was happening, the minister walked right up and stomped the greensnake's head into the ground with his heel.

"HEY!" I yelled, "That's bad luck. Don't you know it's bad luck to kill a snake?"

He just said, "You kids were gambling," and walked away, leaving the snake to wiggle until sunset.

I never did fully enjoy myself the rest of that day. Lots of things were going on and I wandered around watching the Indian dancing for a while and going away during the speeches and eating and watching the lacrosse game and the archery and the penny pitching and watching the dancing and singing again and eating again. All the while though, every little while, I would look for the minister to see what bad luck had happened to him. It was O.K. for him to meddle into our business because most grownups can't help that. But it was bad luck to kill a snake. Grandmother Geese-a-geese told me so. And besides, how come he didn't stop people from pitching pennies? I went to look at the snake again; see if its tail was still wiggling. I couldn't find it. Somebody had put up a booth right over the spot where I last seen it. They were selling Indian things; mostly to white people.

Late in the afternoon, after the girls' softball game, a men's softball game started. Who do you think was the pitcher? The minister. Even though I was mad because he had stomped the greensnake's head, I had to admit — he had a real whizzy pitch. Softball games take a long time to end and besides, Geese-a-geese had told me to watch out for sun strokes so I only came back once in a while to watch it — see who was winning. Also — see if the preacher had bad luck yet.

As I say, I never did get to really enjoy myself because that crushed greensnake's head had ruined my day. Also, one deerfly stayed with me for a long time; even biting me once and circling me when I slapped at it. It could fly as fast as I could run. Also I hate loud noises and some old guy's voice kept yelling, "PEA-NUTS — POPCORN — WATERMELO-O-ON!"

Turkey buzzards, you know, very seldom flap their wings. I like to watch them sail. One had been circling the ball diamond but it kept going up until it was sky high. Between the sun and that deerfly I was about done watching the buzzard when suddenly it began to flap its wings. Down it came in a long low glide towards the northeast corner of the reservation and disappeared. I had to go all the way to the outside of the other end of the picnic grove to see what made that buzzard do that. Thunderheads were coming from the southwest.

I went back to see if the ball game would finish before the rain came. The players and the watermelon man were making so much noise they'd never hear the thunder until it came over the tall trees. I ran over and told Mother to pack up her corn soup. "I'm sold out anyways," she said.

You'd be surprised how fast a thunderhead can run. I sort of forgot about it because I was watching the preacher steam 'em in. He turned loose a sizzler when POW! the ball came right back off the batter's bat — right smack dab into the preacher's thumb. As the ump called time, the big black thunderhead came over the sun. I ran out to see the preacher's thumb. It was a mess. "SEE! SEE!" I said, "You had to go and stomp that snake DIDN'T you? I TOLD you it was bad luck!"

Just then the dark air shook from a terrific thunderbolt. I took off in a straight line — like a fox runs — for home. I could hardly wait to tell Geese-a-geese what had happened. And just like a fox when you shoot at it, everytime I looked back at the thunderhead, I could gather some more speed from somewhere. I knew, too, what Geese-a-geese was going to say. Once more, "NEVER KILL A SNAKE!"

Cassandra

AT FIRST there were two people on the Indian reservation named Less Laughing; one was the father of the other. They were almost the same size because they had twelve cows and little Less drank lots of milk and got very big for his age. Then one day a train smashed into little Less's father when the horse panicked and bolted in front of the hissing engine. That left only one Less Laughing on the reservation. He was thirteen years old.

YuLAY'le was the mother of Less and they lived on this old, old farm with YuLAY'le's mother, Cassandra. No matter how old Cassandra got, she seemed to oversee the lives of YuLAY'le and Less. I think they were afraid of her. She wore long dark dresses that fluttered and flowed behind her when she walked. She had quite a collection of huge old-fashioned hats and she loved to wear them. I never saw her without one of them on, even when she was reading the Bible in her rocking chair. She had a raspy voice and very thin lips and there was something about her that give me a little fear of her too. She had a habit of looking at you but not saying anything. All I can ever remember her saying to me was that I'd be going to hell if I wasn't good even though I was trying to be. I felt she wouldn't hesitate to kick me with her high-top shoes if it would save me from the devil.

When her husband died, YuLAY'le took a job doing house-work. Little Less pitched into the farmwork like a madman, hoping to persuade his mother that he was a man; that she wouldn't have to work. Cassandra simply patted each one on the back approvingly; maybe there would be enough money and she could buy a new hat. So little Less carried the big milk cans up the hill for the milk truck and wrestled bags of grain and bales of hay and straw and by the time he was fifteen his arms and shoulders were large and muscular. I was in the same grade at school as Less was even though I was only twelve because I skipped a grade but Less had to do fourth and fifth grade over again.

One day Less came home and announced that he couldn't wait for his birthday so he could quit school. Cassandra went into a fit and began to pray that Less would become a lawyer or a doctor. I remember Less bringing a note to Miss Felsy telling her not to let Less fail any more grades. Even Less himself began to picture himself becoming a doctor, being as Cassandra had willed it and was praying for him constantly. The next thing that I noticed was that Less began staying after school once or twice a week so that his marks would improve. There was no more talk now about quitting school to run the farm. In fact, the farm began to run down and Less didn't seem to care. He was going to be a doctor now anyways.

There came a day, then, that the cows escaped into the woods because Less had given up mending the fences. Cassandra had seen them running away because she saw just about everything that ever happened on the farm and she had fired the shotgun into the woods to head them off. This only frightened them and made them run all the more. It had been years since she had hitched a horse to a wagon but all that milk running away might mean that she couldn't buy another new hat. Less was staying after school that night, which was to Cassandra a very important thing, but not as important as the milk.

School was out and I was passing by the school on my way home from the store when I saw Cassandra driving the horse up the hill and hanging on to her big hat with one hand. At the top of the hill the horse began to walk and it looked as though Cassandra was thinking about something. She must have wanted to see her dear grandson cramming his poor head full of learning because as I say, she wanted to see everything. She drove the democrat right up to the school window and stood up on the seat and looked in.

Suddenly she let out a little cry and fell back into the seat. With one hand on her head and the other slapping the reins against the horse's rump, she came charging across the road and straight through the field in a cloud of dust. There was no reason for her to be racing across the field that I could see and only Old Shrinkable, the witch, lived among the pines. Surely Cassandra would not allow herself to go near Old Shrinkable's log cabin. The church would frown on that.

I ran to the edge of the field to see where Cassandra was going. I was sure something had snapped in her head. I had never seen such a wild look on Cassandra's face and I felt that something dreadful was happening to Less. Perhaps Miss Felsy was beating him for being so dumb. I ran to the door of the schoolhouse but it was locked, so I shinnied up the flagpole and looked inside the window. All I saw was Miss Felsy buttoning up her dress. I looked across the field and saw Cassandra bouncing through the small pines on a straight line towards Old Shrinkable's house. I slid down the pole and began looking for my bag of groceries. I wanted to get out of there. Just then Less came out of the schoolhouse.

"The horse is running away with your grandmother, Less," I shouted, pointing across the field. "You'd better go help her!"

Less said nothing. He just dashed after Cassandra. I was glad he didn't talk because with that flush on his face, I was getting scared of HIM too. I just took my groceries and hurried on home. I was even afraid to tell my mother what I had seen.

Less did not come to school the next day. In fact, I never ever saw him in school after that. Then one day not long afterwards, Miss Felsy said she wasn't feeling well and sent us home for the day. In the morning a man named Mr. Singer came to teach us. We kept waiting for Miss Felsy to get better and come back and finish teaching us but she never did.

I say I was scared of Cassandra and yet I couldn't help wanting to look at her. Now somebody else was scaring me. It was Mr. Singer. Maybe I was imagining things but I thought Mr. Singer put his hands on me too much. Miss Felsy never did that and also it seemed that he touched the boys in class but not the girls. He even combed and patted little Web's long black hair every morning.

What it seemed like to me was, something should be done

because I wasn't used to two people scaring me. Father had filled Mother's cupboards full of jars and bags with Indian medicine and I wondered if he could give me something to braven me up. So I told Father all about Cassandra and Less and Miss Felsy and Mr. Singer. I told him I didn't mind being scared of Cassandra but not Mr. Singer too and did he have any medicine to stop me from being afraid of anybody. Father laughed and said well maybe if Less wasn't going to be a doctor then maybe I could be, and that fear was nothing; that I had too much curiosity for fear to last very long; that fear was only not knowing about things. So then I asked him if he had any medicine that would hurry up my curiosity, and when he laughed again, I said also that I couldn't see what could be so funny. "O.K.," he said, "I'll give you catnip tea and you'll sleep good tonight. Tomorrow you won't be afraid to tell Mr. Singer how you feel and also you can ask him what happened to Miss Felsy!"

Sure enough, in the morning I woke up early and ran to school. In fact nobody was there yet and I had to wait for Mr. Singer to get there to unlock the door. As soon as he opened his car door I started telling him and asking him everything I could think of. What was tricky was that it was so easy to do. In fact, sure enough, even though I didn't realize how brave I had become, HE did, and all during the time I helped him carry in the wood and make a fire in the stove, he never touched me once. (Even to this day he hasn't touched me again. And I always thought catnip was only for cats.) So I almost forgot to ask him about Miss Felsy. "Oh," he said, "I'm not supposed to tell you this because Miss Felsy doesn't want me to. Can you keep a secret?" I said well not as good as my father could; that I could tell my father and he could keep it for me.

Mr. Singer was a person that never laughed. In fact he could barely smile. Now all of a sudden he laughed and I felt as though he might be a real person after all; like a crab coming out of a shell with no big pincers on. That's when I realized that I wasn't one bit afraid of him anymore.

He said, "To make sure that your father keeps the secret, tell only him about this. Miss Felsy is afraid that nobody will believe her anyways but I have seen her. First she had pains in her chest and she thought she was having a heart attack. Doctors at the hospital could find nothing wrong and the pain went away. She was told that the stress of teaching may have caused it and that she should remain in the hospital for a few days. Then something else happened that the doctors have not been able to figure out. Her face broke out with three skin growths that appeared to be warts. However, they grew to about a half-inch long and as one doctor described it, they appeared to look exactly like budding potato eyes. The dreadful thing about it," he went on, "was that as soon as they were removed, three more came out but at different places on her face." Being as I wasn't afraid of Mr. Singer anymore, I started asking all kinds of questions but just as he was starting to say something we heard Charley Redwater's horse clomping and snorting outside so all Singer said was, "The children are starting to arrive now and they are not to know your father's secret." I told him O.K. and went out to help Charley tie up his horse.

When I got home I told my father how the catnip had braved me up like magic and that I wanted another cup tonight. He said no, that if I got too brave I would start telling him what to do and that the only medicine for that was a willow switch. Then I told him his secret. I told him too that it was his job to keep it for me. "See!" he said. "You drank too much catnip tea."

We both laughed. He said that it would be nice if we kept the secret together; that it was easy to keep a secret but that probably I needed some help to get started with. He went to the cupboard and took out a bag of dried plants. There were some short little pods or something in the bag too and right away I thought of the potato eyes on Miss Felsy's face. He crumpled up the plants and together with pods, put them on a clean cloth and picked the corners of the cloth up and held the small ball of medicine hanging out between his thumb and pointer finger. Then he got Mother's flat iron and a hammer. He sat on a chair and put the flat iron upside down between his knees and pounded the cloth ball of medicine. "This is squirrel corn," he said. "It will help you keep a secret and maybe tame down some of your bossiness."

I wanted to know how could it help me keep a secret so I asked him. I didn't think he heard me at first because he began talking about Cassandra and Miss Felsy and Old Shrinkable. "It's too bad we didn't know about those potato eyes on Miss Felsy sooner," he began. "We might have stopped any more from growing. That's one of Shrink's tricks, those potato eyes." When he said "Shrink," he meant Old Shrinkable, the witch. "Cassandry got scared that Miss Felsy would keep Less-uh from becoming a doctor. She was afraid that Less-uh would run off with his teacher and the farm would go to grass." (Father always kept the two Lesses apart by calling them Less-oit and Less-uh; *oit* means big and *uh* means little.) "So Cassandry told Shrink to fix the teacher and stop her from running off with her grandson. And that's one thing that Shrink can do, is put potato eyes on you." I kept trying to ask questions but every time I talked, Father paid no attention and kept right on. "Now Cassandry needs the farm to go on more than ever," he said, "because Shrink don't do anything for free and she knows Cassandry will always be paying her with vegetables because Cassandry won't want Shrink to tell the church about her. Shrink is afraid of me," Father said. "She thinks I might be a witch, too," and before I could ask, he added, "but I'm not."

Father got up and got a tea cup of hot water and jiggled the ball of pounded squirrel corn into the water. "When this cools," he said, "we'll drink it down. What the squirrel corn will do, it will make you wonder if potato eyes will grow on your face if you tell anybody what we know." We drank the cup of squirrel corn. Boy! I was sure going to keep this secret.

On Saturday morning early I was upstairs laying in bed when I heard Pony make a friendly horse noise with her mouth. I jumped up and looked out the window and saw Father leapfrog onto her back. He always said he was too heavy for Pony but yet he would have her pull a wagon of wood plus him riding. I pulled the cardboard off the hole where I had broken a pane trying to kill a mouse on my windowsill with my slingshot. "Hey," I yelled, "where you going?"

"Shrink's place," he said in Indian. "Mind the house."

Pony stepped out quickly. Her head was making quick jerks up and down just like she was saying, "Yeah, you stay home."

When Father got back I ran out to meet them. "I forgot to tell you something," he said. "I forgot to tell you that we can't talk about our secret because we can't tell anybody about it. Not even each other."

62

"That don't make sense," I began.

"It might to the squirrel corn," he said.

I just stood there for a few minutes. Father woke me up. "Get the .22 rifle, Bluedog has a coon up the buttonwood tree on the second ledge. Listen. Hear him? That's a coon he's got, you can tell by his bark. We can have corn soup and coon."

I ran to the house to get the gun but I was pretty sure I would rather hear how Father had made out with Old Shrinkable than to go and get the coon. But then, Bluedog would be mad at me if he had to track a coon for nothing.

I kept wondering what was going to happen but I let almost a week go by. Friday after school I grabbed the .22 rifle and muttered something about there might be another coon in the same tree to my mother and headed for Less Laughing's place. I wanted to see if I could notice anything different going on since Father had spoken to Old Shrinkable. If I didn't notice anything there I wondered if I dared to talk to Old Shrinkable herself. No, I thought, even with another cup of catnip I couldn't do that. She might be a mind reader and find out that I know the secret. Now then, it seemed very important to keep my eyes and ears open when I got to Less's place. I even caught myself digging out any extra wax in my ears with my little finger. I was unbelievable how much courage a person could get from curiosity, which, even my father could see.

When I got near the farm I began wondering how I could get to talk to Less without Cassandra seeing me first. I had to laugh when I thought of something. It was unbelievable how Cassandra could change the size of my curiosity. Here I was, standing still. Then I heard the sound of wood getting chopped. That would be Less. I was glad I had picked at my ears. Wouldn't Cassandra think what a good boy I was if she saw me carrying in an armful of wood?

Just the same, it wasn't so easy when I got there, mostly because Less had picked up some shyness towards me. I didn't know if it was because of that happening he had with Miss Felsy or because I was going to school yet and he wasn't or if it was my imagination. One thing was clear — if I was supposed to be looking for a coon in the buttonwood, it wouldn't take very long would it? So I went right up to Less and asked him what he was doing;

even though any fool could see he was cutting wood. Less was used to such questions and he said that he was building up the farm and that it would someday pay off. "In fact," he said, "we're getting Big Egg's bull over tomorrow to make more calves. Red Cow hollered all night long."

"Oh," I said. "Hey, you know something? I gotta be getting home, it'll be time to eat supper pretty soon."

He said, "We're getting rich again. We got corn soup with meat in it. Why don't you stay and eat here."

I said, "No, I think we're gonna have coon in our corn soup. I'll see you," and I hurried off on home. I had almost said, "I gotta hurry because I have to shoot the coon first."

That night was a long night but finally it got to be morning. It was only two miles to Less Laughing's house so I ran all the way. Mother had given me permission to go because I said, "Less might need some help to do some farm work and maybe he'll pay me."

When I got there the steam was puffing out of my mouth because the sun wasn't up very high yet. And who do you think was already out on the porch in her rocking chair? — Cassandra. No matter if she was the churchiest-going person I knew, she still scared me with that big hat and long dress and that wild stare. She didn't say anything. Many people were beneath her talking to, and so far, I was turning out to be one of them.

As I got closer to the house I could hear Big Egg's voice yelling at the bull. What I did, I made a big circle around Cassandra, pretending not to see her, but I could feel her stare right on me, like, what business have you got coming here?

As I started down the hill, I could see the huge black bull with Less on one side of it and Big Egg on the other. O-Gee was behind it jabbing it along with a stick. Big Egg was doing all the yelling because O-Gee couldn't. O-Gee was Big Egg's sister and though she looked bigger and stronger, she was deaf and dumb. They were not far from the barn door, maybe twenty yards, and the barn was quiet. I had expected to hear that cow bawling inside but I guess all the commotion outside had got its attention for the time being.

Just as I started catching up to the bull helpers, the bull stopped and looked at the strange barn. Then he layed down. No amount of prodding or yelling or spanking could make him stand up again. I looked back up at the house. Cassandra had been watching all of this; had even turned her rocking chair towards the action, but now she wasn't rocking.

The horns of the big bull had been sawed off so nobody was afraid of getting hooked. It just looked like a heck of a lot of animal to be messing around with. I mean, I didn't get too close to it. Big Egg, though, I guess it was because it was his bull, was working up a sweat hollering and kicking at the animal. O-Gee kept prodding it and once she pulled its tail. Still the animal would not move. Less went to find himself a stick and he looked up and saw Cassandra coming down the hill with a white cane. The white cane made it flash through my mind that maybe all this time she was blind and I didn't know it. "Watch out, Grandma!" Less called. "You might fall. We'll get the bull up somehow."

Cassandra said nothing. She just kept on picking her way down the path. She had on that big flowery hat and that long black dress with the tiny polka dots and I wondered how many of that same outfit did she own or did she wash that dress every night or what.

Then I noticed that Cassandra was carrying a dinner bell with her. What with that flowing black dress and the white cane for a staff and the bell in her hand, she looked like a figure that might at any moment pronounce Judgment Day. Maybe Big Egg felt the same thing; I mean about his lazy bull; like she might pronounce it unfit and tell him to take it away without giving it a chance. He was now really whaling away at it, but even with Less helping and O-Gee starting to kick, nothing was doing any good.

I just couldn't help but feel that when Cassandra got there that something would happen. Well it did, but it all seemed so simple. All she did was hit the bull with the bell, BONG! on one of his stubby horns and instantly it jumped up and went on into the barn like it was supposed to. Less shut the gate and latched it.

Cassandra said, "Alright — everybody just go on home now and let that poor animal alone." To Big Egg she said, "Come back Tuesday or Wednesday and we'll see about paying you."

It all seemed so final, the way she said it; and we all just reacted like it was just the perfect thing to do. I was already quite a ways down the road when I started to get that cheated feeling.

Pretty soon I was good and mad. Here I had gotten up early on a Saturday and now it was going to be all for nothing.

I had planned heavily on watching Less and Cassandra to see if I could learn anything about the secret by how they acted. Not only that, I had somehow expected that we would all go into the barn and see how much the bull liked the cow that hollered all night. Even my legs didn't like it because I could see that they were going slower and slower and pretty soon they stopped altogether. I began throwing stones at a tree while I thought about it. I thought of talking to my father about it but then he would know why I had gone to Less's in the first place. I thought about what he had said once before. "Everything that happened yesterday and all the days before that is nothing now. But while it was happening it was like making a road that you couldn't walk back on because as you made it, it became only a vision. You have to keep making New Road or stand still. All the vision was good for now was to look at and if it looked like it was going to the wrong place you could make New Road to the right place." He said, "It's a sin people don't see such simple things." I told him then that I may be mixed up about what sin was and he said, "Nahh, you know only too well what sin is. I'm only saying that lots of times we don't pay attention to what we know. Like you, you keep asking me how long do you have to wait before you'll be grown up. And yet you know full well that you can't STOP growing up. And you know what patience is too. I think sometimes you have fun trying to use mine up." I thought about that next. Probably my father was all done growing. That's why his patience might get used up. But I, I could grow more patience, and what if I got too much by saving it. I'll bet that's what's wrong, I got too much patience. It was affecting my throwing arm. I was missing the tree sometimes.

I left the road and cut out across the fields and began to circle into the woods. I was headed back towards Less Laughing's barn. To keep sort of hidden from view, especially from Cassandra's, I came through the grape vineyard and up towards the lower side of the barn behind the manure pile.

Half of the cellar part of the barn, where the cows were kept, was dug into the side of the hill. The other part was a wall of field stones to level up the ceiling and make the bottom walls. There was a small window on the side wall but it was very spider webby. I had to crawl through the hollyhocks and burdocks to get to it. At first I couldn't see anything, even after I wiped the dirt away and cupped my hands along my eyes.

Then I could see something moving. It was the big black bull on top of the cow. There was something else moving on top of the bull. Pretty soon I could see what it was. It was Cassandra's big flowery, wide-brimmed hat. She was standing there fanning the bull. She had a big grin on her face. It scared me to see her grin for the first time and I wanted to run. But then I saw that she wasn't looking at me at all, and do you know? That was the first time I had ever seen her without that huge hat on. And do you know what else? Cassandra doesn't have a bit of hair on the top of her head.

Manylips and Lala la

BLACKLEAF was good at booklearning but slow with
common sense. He was dark and good looking and as it seems
to always happen, good looking people get lots of attention.
Probably, the feeling is, ugliness might be catching. They might
cough in your face. So what happened to Blackleaf when he was
about fifteen, was, his grandmother chose him to be chief of the
Snipe Clan. Father told me that the other chiefs asked that Blackleaf's father, Isaac Tree, come to council with him until he was
twenty-one.

As you know, kids tell one another things before their
parents do. During the winter, after Blackleaf had been raised as
Snipe Sachem Chief (Sachem is like senior), we ran a trapline
together. I don't know how we came to run the trapline the way
we did but it worked out very well. Blackleaf lived quite a ways
from me, and, before school, we checked the traps, working
towards each other until we met. This way, if one of us got sick,
the other finished the line. We sold the furs to Walibur and split
the money. Sometimes snow or sleet would ruin our sets, freeze
the iron traps, or cover the snares or crack the little tip-up trees
and so sometimes we caught nothing. On those days we walked on
to school from wherever we met. We had quite a few chances, then,
to talk.

On one of these days I happened to tell Blackleaf that it was
kind of odd that I hardly ever saw Manylips because he kept to
himself so. Manylips was our closest neighbor but he sent his wife,

Lala la to the limestone spring where we drew our drinking water. I don't know where she came from. She couldn't speak Tuscarora. All she said was "Hi" to me. ("Hi" is a word used in the past by Indians greeting other Indian-looking strangers. And for all I know, it was North America-wide. It is pronounced as a quick, chopped off sound, almost as though it was a tap on the head. If the sound came back, it meant, "Yes, I am Indian.") I don't even know what her name, Lala la, means, if anything at all. Blackleaf, being older and school crazy, liked to talk to me as though I was a dumb little brother even though I had taught him a lot about trapping. Well, also he was Chief Blackleaf now, and since Manylips was a chief too, he told me about Manylips.

Manylips and Lala la had three beautiful daughters. In fact, they were so beautiful that they even knew it themselves. Manylips told them that they might not even find a man handsome enough on the reservation to marry. As they got older they began wondering if they might never ever find such a man, so one night they snuck out of the loghouse and took off for New York City, where they believed not only handsome men might live, but with pockets full of money too. They never came back.

Manylips was a chief of the White Bear Clan. When his daughters left, he became very bitter. He had become used to having three beautiful girls at his beck and call. Also, any visitors might praise him for fathering such beauty. Now he had only Lala la left to wait on him. His bitterness began to be felt at the chiefs' council.

It got to a point where, at one council, when the other chiefs refused to go along with his demands, he threw himself on the council house floor and began kicking like a baby. Three times, Turquois, who was what you might call the chairman, ordered Manylips to get up, but he stayed thrashing on the floor. Turquois went out of the council house. When he came back he had Babymind with him. Babymind was the wisest man on the reservation and had a great knowledge of Indian medicines. For some reason he always wore what looked like a woman's dress made of leather. The right side of it was stained purple and other side was cream-colored. Babymind claimed that it meant that he was just as capable of stupidity and cruelty as he was of wisdom and kindness.

Babymind came into the council house walking slowly with his slender ironwood cane. Manylips was still flat on the floor. Babymind stood and looked at Manylips for quite a while. Finally he put his hand on Manylips' head. Manylips slapped it away. Babymind closed his eyes to think. In a few minutes he spoke softly in Tuscarora to Manylips. "I know your problem, White Bear Chief. In a little while you will be alright." Suddenly Babymind hit Manylips a sizzling blow across his backsides. "There's nothing wrong with you!" Down came the ironwood cane again. "Get up! Get up if you are a chief."

Manylips jumped up and behaved himself for three months.

Three months later Manylips was on the rampage in council again. Turquois lectured him sternly, as he had after the kicking-on-the-floor-time. This time Manylips shouted back. Turquois turned to the other chiefs and asked for a vote to de-horn Manylips. This meant that Manylips would have his title of chief taken away. The vote had to be a hundred percent and it was not. Turquois could not vote unless other chiefs could not agree. They couldn't. Turquois gave Manylips another chance.

Manylips lasted about half a year before he flared up again. This time he got a total vote to be de-horned. I liked to have Blackleaf tell me all this because I could see better why Manylips kept to himself. He was like, in hibernation.

If you had a neighbor like Manylips, wouldn't you want to see for yourself what he was like? Yes. Me too. I did. So I went.

Not knowing what to expect, I figured by bringing him something I would at least have something to talk about. It was near Thanksgiving and many Novembers were snowy, but this Friday night was warm and starry. I set two snares and sure enough in the morning I had two rabbits. Near noon I put one on my belt and took the slippery elm bow that Father had made for me, plus one arrow, and took the path to the spring. From the spring there was a steep and twisting path up the other side of the wooded valley to Manylips' loghouse. Halfway up this path I sat on one of the big limestones. No wonder Manylips sent Lala la after drinking water, he himself might not make it back up the hill.

One of the things about the limestones was you couldn't help looking at their shapes; like the water might have beat them and scrubbed them and worn them into animals and faces — whatever your imagination let you see. Why I think it was water was because you could pull off the moss and see shells and little skeletons of things that were supposed to be in water, like crabs or fish. I'm just taking a wild guess but the rock I was resting on was twelve, maybe thirteen miles from Lake Ontario. Maybe the world is running out of water. Maybe pretty soon Lake Ontario will be fourteen miles away. Maybe when I'm an old man I can walk right to Canada. Maybe I'm stalling for time because I don't know what Manylips will be like.

The loghouse of Manylips and Lala la is old. I hear that it once was a storehouse for bullets and guns for war. It had those same big square logs with the house corners locked in. The roof was a little saggy and patched up but the lawn was short and there was a rock garden full of strawflowers on the sunny side. There was a big elm near the house. It was kind of white because it was dead and barkless. My feet made just a little noise when I walked but nothing else did. Not even the wind.

Right by the doorway, which stuck out about three feet, a sort of entranceway, grew some tall sunflowers. Their big heads hung down as though they had done something wrong. I was quite near the entrance then before I saw Manylips. He was sitting on a bench near the loghouse wall, almost hidden by the sunflower stalks. His legs were out straight and the bench was beginning to tip forward a little. If Manylips slouched more than he already was, he would end up on his fanny. I could see the middle of his big belly moving so I knew he wasn't dead. He had a big neck and big jaws and he was breathing through his mouth which was wide open. There was a clear gallon jug on its side by his foot. A little something was still in it, maybe grapejuice. Before I knew it, I had stepped right up close and was just about looking into his mouth. Some fruit flies were flying small circles around his mouth and I could smell a smell of rotten fruit. He was drunk on wine, that's what it was, and what if a thunderstorm came up. He might drown, what with breathing through that big mouth. Father had told me that Saw'wot, who was dead and gone and who had taught Father a lot about Indian medicine, had saved Manylips from smallpox when he was a boy. I could see the little wells on Manylips' nose and skin and I thought that this too, might be why we didn't see

him very often. Maybe it was that people thought they might still get the smallpox from him. "Hello," I said, but not too loud. Remember, the bench was tippy-looking. Manylips did not wake up.

Lala la, though, heard me. She came out and recognized me and smiled as she always did when we met at the spring.

"Hi," she said.

She wasn't tall and she wasn't fat. Probably she was fifty years old, but however old she was she seemed about ten years younger than Manylips. Her hair was black and flat against her head because she kept it braided in back and wound in a big flat bun which was pinned to the back of her head. She seemed to have no colorful dresses and they were quite long. She wore men's wool socks and either bedroom slippers or sandals. I don't mean she had two pairs, I mean, I don't know what to call them. Under her heels it was just a flat sole, flapping. Maybe she just didn't like to waste time untying shoes when it was time to sleep and she wore these things on the rugged path to the spring water spring. She had lots of forehead, probably on account of the pulled-back hair and her face was smooth; kind of manly. You might say she was handsome.

After I had seen Lala la at the spring a few times, I began to like her. Her eyes were dark and, well, you could say they were always laughing. So after she came out of the house and smiled and said "Hi," I saw for the first time, a different look to her eyes. Tiredness, maybe. Some sadness. Now she fooled me even more. She put her hand on Manylips' shoulder and said in perfect English, "Papa, you have company. Papa, open your eyes and see who's here to visit you."

Manylips closed his mouth and said, "Huh?" He managed to stay on the bench but he looked like he didn't know where he was for a minute. He had that sour why-did-you-wake-me-up look. He rubbed his tongue on his lips and said, "Get me some water."

Lala la said, "I'll bring some tea out for both of you."

"I said, I want water!" Manylips hollered. Then he noticed me standing there and he began squinting at me in the sun. "Oh, hello there," he said, blinking and squaring himself on the bench. He had a loud voice. "What have you got there?" he asked.

"I brought you a rabbit," I began.

"No, no, the bow," he said. "Let me see the bow. That don't

look like hickory. I make bows, you know, but I use hickory. Nothing like it and they last a lifetime. Had a fellow from Pennsylvania come up 'bout a month ago. Said he heard I was making bows again. Don't know how he knew, maybe just talking. Anyhow I sold him a sixty pounder. Charged him twenty-five dollars. Gave me twenty and said he'd be back with the five. Never expected to see him again but here he came again day before yesterday. Know what he said? Got a big eight point the first day out. Paid me the five and you know what else? A gallon of wine. Called it a bonus. Drank it up already. Lala la! Bring me some water! Bring us some tea! My mouth's so dry I can't talk!"

Lala la had already been out and a bowl of water was on the bench next to him. I pointed to it and he gulped it down, spilling quite a bit on each side of his mouth. Lala la came out with another bowl of water, thinking that he needed more already. Well, he did because he drank that too. "I'm heating water for tea," she said, taking in the empty bowls.

Manylips went on like he hadn't even seen Lala la. "You must be a good shot to be plunking rabbits with a bow." I handed the rabbit to him and told him that I had snared it. "Lala la, get my change purse!" he yelled. I told him he could have the cottontail and this time he heard me. "Nosiree!" he said. "Anybody can hit a rabbit with an arrow needs to be paid for it. Now when I was a young man I used to be able to shoot the whiskers off a mosquito. Here have some tea."

Lala la had come out with a teapot and two heavy white cups. She put them on the bench next to Manylips. He stayed in the middle of the bench, taking up most of the room so I sat on the grass near the tea. He talked right at me and his breath stunk. I noticed how small his ankles were. They didn't match, at all, to his belly.

"Come on," Manylips said, getting to his feet. The wind caused him to have to take some extra steps in order to balance to walk. "Rheumatism. Come on, I'll show you some real bows. Let that tea set. I don't like it weak." He pushed off the loghouse wall and walked on those small ankles faster than I thought he would. "How do you like my garden?" he asked, waving a hand towards some vegetables in a small plot. It looked like any other garden to me but before I could say anything, Manylips disappeared into a shed. "Come on in, come on in," he said, "A big boy like you is all done playing with playthings like that bow you got, now take a look at these."

A horse-vise took up most of the shed. A horse-vise is a wooden horse. A piece hangs down through the middle with a head on top and a foot bar at the bottom. When you sit at one end and swing the bottom with your foot, the head swings down toward you and squeezes whatever piece of wood you put in there so you can carve it with a draw knife. My father had one. "I never let anybody in here," Manylips went on. "I don't tell anybody what kind of wood I use or how I dry it." There was about six pieces of hickory tied into a bundle leaning in a corner. The bundle was about as tall as Manylips. Each piece looked as though it had come from a small tree, split into fours. There were some smaller bundles of elm and ash. Probably for arrows. What caught my attention, though, was a small kettle of stones hanging from the ceiling. Manylips saw me looking at this. "Don't touch that!" he said. "She might spring loose and unwind. That's another reason I don't let nobody in here. Don't like people seeing how I make bowstrings. Pure linen. You gotta twist it the right way too or you'll untwist every thread. Lotta bowmakers don't know that. Got my own secret wax too. Beeswax and candlewax." He winked at me and tapped the side of his brain with his pointer finger.

The shed was so small that with the wide door swung inward, it covered quite a bit of wall. Manylips swung the door away from the wall. Five new bows hung from nails near the ceiling. Once, at the end of a school year, the principal surprised us. He had a magician show us some magic. I thought of the magician when Manylips showed me the bows. That's the way the magician looked after he did his magic. "Well what do you think? Let's take 'em in the light where we can see them." He unhooked two bows and took them to the teapot. His face got red but he managed to string one of them up. He handed it to me. "Notice the finish on it," he said. "That's another secret. Hand-rubbed linseed oil. They're worth thirty dollars but I'll let you have one for half price. Drink some tea first then we'll let you shoot it."

We drank tea and I looked at one of the bows. The string on it was so big it would never fit the arrows that I had sent to Sears Roebucks for. The face of a bow is the part that faces you when

76

you shoot it. The other side is the back. The face of Manylips' bow was rounded. The back was flat. Both ends of the bow were not much smaller than the handle. It weighed a ton.

"Let's shoot," Manylips said. He went into the loghouse and came out with three arrows. "I make three arrows. This is what you call a blunt," he said, holding up one of them. It was blunt alright. It had a big square knob on the tip, which probably was the shape and size of the wood bolt before he shaved the shaft down. "That's for small game. Punches 'em to death. Knocks the dickens right out of 'em."

He handed it to me. It was as heavy as my own bow and as long as a baseball bat; the ones grownup ballplayers use. "Now here's one I bet you never seen." He was holding up another monster arrow. "This is a dog arrow." It had that same oblong squarish knob on it too but the tip had been whittled and a short point stuck out of the knob. "It's good to have some of these around if you got a female in heat. Had a little lady beagle once. She got in heat. Used to pick her boyfriends right off her back. I tell you, I was a good shot them days. Don't hurt 'em none; just lets 'em know you mean business." I was glad I wasn't a boy dog. If I was, I'd stay away from Manylips.

"See that pile of ashes? Let's see you hit that rusty can. Get over some so's the can will be more in the middle of the pile." Not many Indians on the reservation had tin cans in the ashes. Most everybody made corn soup and they soaked the dried corn in hardwood ashes to get the black eyes out of the white corn. Plus ashes is good fertilizer. "That brother of mine's been promising me some bales of hay to make a target. That stingy bastard, I'll never see 'em." He handed me the heavy blunt arrow. "This other arrow," he said, "it's a deer arrow. It ain't got no point though. That's up to the hunter to put on whatever he likes."

In order to shoot such a long bow I had to tip the bow quite a bit or the bottom limb would touch the ground. The string hit my chest but that was about as far as I could pull it back anyways. I was just going to let go when Manylips says, "Recognize these feathers? Came off them turkeys you had last year. Your old man says I could have all the feathers I want but he quit raising 'em. Says the death rate is too high on the young ones. Go ahead and shoot!"

I had let down and was looking at the feathers. They had a nice long oval shape. "Bet you don't know how I cut them feathers," Manylips said. I drew up and let fly at the can. The heavy bow limbs banged forward and jarred the bow right out of my hand. "See what I mean," Manylips said proudly. "That bow's got a lot of wallop. You got to hang on to her. That's no toy, that's a man's bow."

The heavy arrow never got to the tin can. It was a close, easy shot but I was about a foot short.

"Get the arrow," Manylips said. "You come close enough, you would have hit a deer. Come on, let's put the bows up. Not good to keep 'em strung too long, they take a set. One thing, you can let my bows lay right on the ground. Dampness won't hurt my bows. It's that linseed oil. Keeps 'em shiny too." His face got red again as he unstrung the bow. The sun made the bow glisten. On a sunny day, you might not get near a deer with it.

I felt like taking off my sweater. It seemed more like September than November. Even one of the windows in the loghouse had been taken out. Not a whisper of a breeze had stirred yet today. Smoke from the chimney went straight up and the lace curtain in the open window never moved. Just as we started into the shed I saw a faint pattern to the lace in the curtain. As we went on in, I realized it WAS a face. Lala la. She had been looking and listening all the while.

"I use this," Manylips said, handing me a thin curved piece of metal. I didn't know what he was talking about. "Watch out! It's sharp. Cut them feathers neat and clean. Here, I'll show you." He put a turkey feather on a hardwood block and when he put the curved metal on it, I could see that it was curved to the shape of the feathers on his arrows. "Old hacksaw blade," he said, "All I did was sharpen the bottom edge. Clever, eh? Now if I was to rap this with a hammer —— well, you get the idea now. That's the way I cut my feathers so's they's all the same shape."

I liked being in Manylips' shed and seeing how he did things. I liked just about everything except the roughness of Manylips himself and, at that I felt he was forcing himself to be the gentlest that he could ever be. I felt he liked my visit to him; even kind of needed it. He needed to be praised but if I was a little slow doing

78

it, well he could pitch in and rush it a little. "You're a very smart man," I said.

"Well," he said, "I'm the mother of invention."

"I'm going home now," I said, "but I'll be back."

"You do that and don't be too long," he said. "I'll have those bales and we'll have a contest. And mind, you talk to your dad and maybe he'll buy you one of these bows for Christmas or else maybe your birthday comes first."

Funny how I liked being there and yet suddenly had to leave.

Snow came two days after Thanksgiving. I went to bed with big plans for fooling around all weekend. In the morning I had to change my plans. There was four inches of snowfall on everything. More inches were still coming out of the clouds. It was the beginning of winter.

Two times during the winter I stopped in to see Manylips. Both times I brought him some small game. Both times he invited me into the loghouse. Once I ran into Lala la on our water-drawing trips.

On the first visit Manylips was in a good mood. By accident, a strong wind had given him a windfall. A big old Y-shaped greening apple tree had split down the middle. One side fell to the ground. Here was extra firewood already cut down. But trickier yet, he found a big comb of honey inside. When I knocked on the door, I heard Manylips holler, "Come in if you're fat!" I couldn't see at first because my eyes were used to looking at the bright snow. Manylips saw me though and he said, "Come in anyway, I'll fatten you up." I don't know where that come-in-if-you're-fat saying comes from but quite often Indians say that if you knock on their door. Probably the Wolf Clan started it, to tease other clans, as though they would eat them up if they were fat enough to make it worthwhile. Even though my eyes were slow, my nose was not. I could smell the ghost bread frying on the stove. Later Manylips and Lala la tried to fatten me up on ghost bread and honey. Ghost bread is fry bread. It is really nothing but one big flat biscuit fried to whatever size frying pan you can find.

Why it is called ghost bread is because long time ago, the Iroquois set the table for a person that died, for ten days. For their spirit or their ghost. I think ghosts like fry bread.

Anyways, I had two squirrels on the first visit. When I got to the living room I threw them on the floor. Out of the woodpile behind the stove came Cooney, Manylips' pet raccoon. Cooney grabbed a squirrel and ran into the dark kitchen. "COONEY!" shouted Manylips, "Gawdammit! Lala la! Get a broom! Cooney's eating up the squirrels!" But before Lala la could get on to what was happening, Manylips was hot after Cooney. I heard a scuffle in the kitchen. "Gimme that squirrel," Manylips hollered.

"Grrrrrr," said Cooney. Raccoons are wicked fighters.

I looked around the room. The ceiling was rough boards and big beams. Lots of things hung from nails on the beams or else layed on the nails. There was white corn, eagle feathers, bunches of bittersweet, some pennyroyal, corn of many colors, a couple samples of those heavy arrows. Manylips was still in the kitchen.

"Lala la! Get some water!" I jumped because the voice was close by. It was not Manylips'. What it was, was a big green parrot. Someone had nailed short grey tree limbs to the wall as though they grew from the wall. Probably to hang things on. The parrot was sitting on one of these in a corner near the ceiling. It was picking at its own chest. It had picked a patch of bare skin.

"Hello," I said to the bird. It just kept on picking. I went closer to it. "Hello there, Mr. Green Parrot," I said.

Very loud, the parrot screeched, "Tha-breh, tha-breh, tha-breh, tha-breh, tha-breh!" five or six times. That means, "Be quiet, be quiet, be quiet, be quiet, be quiet!" If that bird was anything it was nervous.

Manylips was still scuffling with Cooney. Lala la was frying fry bread. I liked their living room. There was a lot to look at. The windowsills, shelves, china cabinet; anything flat, even the top of a foot-pedal sewing machine was full of little things. Figures made of glass or wood. If not that, small green plants in small pots. Some were cactuses. The china cabinet was jam-packed full. After a while I noticed something. None of the figures were of people. The closest thing that was people-looking was a group of apple face dolls. They all had on red velvet dresses specked with white beads. But the faces were not people's faces. When you jab a stick into an apple and carve a head out of the apple, when it dries, it looks like a wrinkled old person's face. These, though, looked like animals. Like a dog or wolf or a bear or something in between. With a dress on. I liked them.

Lala la came in with a tray. On it was a big chunk of honeycomb full of honey and the ghost bread. Manylips came in too. "Jesus Christ that Cooney's stubborn. Never did that before. Feed him, good too. Blast his hide, he got under the stove and wouldn't give up that squirrel for nothing." Manylips picked up the chunk of honey and bit a piece out of it. He squeezed off some fry bread and started chewing and talking. "Go ahead, eat some. It won't sting you. All the bees are scraped off. Wax won't hurt you either."

I picked up the honey and ate it like Manylips did with the bread. I saw some faint lettering on the try. It had been a ouija board at one time.

Lala la started upstairs. She was barefooted. "Where you going?" Manylips asked her.

"Put something on my feet," she said, but she never came back down.

The day I went after water and saw Lala la she was sprinkling ashes on her way down the steep path from the doghouse. "Hi," she said.

I said "Hi" too but after a minute, I said, "How come you only just say 'hi' to me here at the spring?"

All she did was come down and look into the spring. You could always see yourself in there. I often wondered why it never froze over because you could never see the water move. After a while she talked.

"I'm sick of talk," she said. "That's all people do. Talk. My girls are gone now. They used to talk too. They used to tell me they would never go away. But they did."

I said, "Here, I'll get your water out for you." All she did was quit looking at herself. She wouldn't get out of the way. She stared out to where the valley opened up. Out past the poison hemlock.

"I like it here," she said. "I like it down here by the trees

and water. They don't tell me lies." A few snowflakes were floating down. Some hit her face and melted. "But I want to go home.
My husband keeps promising to take me. But it's only talk." She
kept looking far away. I needed to get my water too but she just
sat there. After a while she looked at me. "You never said anything either down here." Then she got up and got out of the way.

I filled up all the water buckets. "Where is the place you
mean when you say 'I want to go home'?" I asked her. I picked up
my buckets of water.

"Georgian Bay Reservation," she said.

I was almost out of sight of the spring when I looked back.
Lala la was still sitting there. One summer three Indian boys came
to Tuscarora looking for work. They were from Georgian Bay.
They were thin and had smooth skin, kind of Chinesey looking.
In summer they ran us ragged at lacrosse and in winter they skated
rings around us. They didn't talk much either. When they left, we
became experts again.

Late in January or the first part of February we gave up on
the trapline. That is, Blackleaf and I quit doing business together.
We kept changing it until it took us too long to do and too far
from school. Also, Blackleaf had been sickly and he said it wasn't
fair to me, even though he got sick in the line of duty. Besides, we
had thirty-some dollars each and not the faintest idea of what to
spend it on. Maybe in Sears Roebuck catalog, or Monkey Wards.

What happened, though, was, I kept waking up early every
morning anyways, as though I still had a trapline. To stop this
waking up for nothing, I decided to put in a few mink sets along
the stony creek below the poison hemlock. On the first morning
out, just checking things over, I ran across some fresh skunk tracks.
Skunks are funny. Sometimes you can walk right up to them and
whack their backs near their tail with a stick and they won't
squirt you. Where do you think the tracks went? Right under
Manylips and Lala la's loghouse.

I told on the skunk after school. I went straight to the door
of the loghouse because I knew the skunk was still under there.
Skunks don't cruise at day, only at night. Manylips didn't tell me
to come in if I was fat, he just opened the door when I knocked.

"There's a skunk under your house!" I said first thing.

"Why hello there. Come in, come in," Manylips said, "What did you say?" Before I could answer, he said, "Oh, that skunk lives there half the time. I don't argue with skunks. Always keep on the friendly side of 'em. Come on in and make yourself homely. You ain't been around much lately. What is it, lots of school work? I never liked school and look at me now. Should've been a lawyer. They make lots of money. Always all dressed up. Always a suit and tie. That reminds me, sit down. You suppose your mother could sew me a suit? She's a good seamstress, your mother is, and I got me some material."

Lala la was rocking away in a rocking chair darning a sock stretched over a bottle. "I thought you gave up on that suit after you went bankrupt." she said.

"Hush up woman!" Manylips said in a rough way. "Damn it to hell, I'll use my money to see fit. You never bring any in."

"What money," Lala la said.

One of Manylips' eyes was twitching. He was mad. He had been reading something and still had on these reading glasses with metal rims. He had his head down, looking at Lala la over the glasses and it made him look like a bull ready to charge. "Cut off that backtalk!" he said. "Ever since the girls left, you been full of vinegar. If you'd brought 'em up right they'd still be right here in this house!"

"Well you drove them out," she said. "You and your 'get me this and get me that, hand me this and hand me that.' That's the only reason you didn't want them going off to school. They were smart to get out."

"Off to school nothing!" Manylips shouted. "You know what the state troopers said, found the youngest in a house. You know what they were telling us. Our baby is nothing but a whore!"

"Pa!" Lala la put down the sock and bottle and went to the kitchen and grabbed her coat.

The parrot and Manylips started talking at the same time. "Where you think you're going?" That was Manylips' voice.

"Tha-breh! Tha-breh! Tha-breh!" the parrot said.

Lala la didn't answer. She went on outside. Cooney was curled up in the middle of the floor snoozing through all the talk.

"I don't know what's got into that woman lately," Manylips

said, taking off his glasses and going over to the window. "She never used to say a word."

I was wanting to leave or, at least, talk about something else so I asked Manylips if he had sold his bow.

"Look at her," he said. "She's scooping snow. She's melting snow to wash clothes. She's a good woman. Gotta holler at her once in a while is all." He looked at me. "Ain't had much luck with them bows. Traded one off to Ox for some firewood. Money's getting scarce, I guess. They ought to print some more. Had some bad luck too. Remember when them Senecas came from Tonawandy and dragged that log across True Bugger's field and had that snowsnake meet? Well I been waiting for something like that. I had me a idee long time ago about them snowsnakes. I says to myself, I says, why not use a small iron rod, so I made one. All I did was sharpen the point and sandpaper it and steel wool it and wax it. It's small and round, don't you see? Less of it touching the ice. Not much to slow it down. I was right too. Got Soot-neh to throw it for me. Won forty-five dollars on bets and sold the snake right then and there for ten dollars. Should of got twenty but, well, don't you see, I won just about all the money they had. What do I do? I run out and buy my brother's axe sharpener and a bundle of iron rods at LeVans. Had 'em delivered right to the door. I was in business, don't you see. So I used up the rest of the money on some material for a suit. Never had a suit. Never in my life and here I was in business so I bought this material. Tried to buy a ready made suit but they didn't quite have the right fit. Couldn't of afforded it anyways. You know what they wanted? Thirty dollars and up. So I had to settle for the material. So I come home with my suit material and gets busy on my iron snowsnakes. Six, I made. All shiny and waxy. Put a tag of twenty bucks on each one. Tonawandy has a contest every weekend so I gets Knee-haw to drive me up. That's when the bad luck started doggin' me. Right off we get a flat tire before we're out the lane. So now we're late getting there. But that ain't the worst part. Soon's we get there Sundown come up with that iron snake he got off me and wants his money back. Says they been declared illegal. I hate to be thinking of that day. A bunch of them snowsnakers came crowding up around the car. They called my idee a white man's snowsnake. They called me a cheat and I don't know what all and

84

Knee-haw got shakey and drove us out of there. Then, course it didn't help none when I told him I was broke and couldn't pay him right then and there for hauling me to Tonawandy. Tell you the truth, I was glad to get home. Never even thought to unload my snakes from the car. I hear later, Knee-haw went and sold 'em for twenty-five cents apiece. Sold 'em for lightning rods."

I said, "Maybe LeVans will take the rest of the iron back."

After a while, Manylips said, "You know, maybe he would at that."

Later as I went out the door, he said it again.

"You know, maybe he would at that."

When planting time came, we got to monkeying around with doing that and I forgot all about Manylips and Lala la. Father planted the things rabbit and grackles might eat, close to the house because close to the house was where animals were shy to come to. When we got in what we wanted, I saw a package of peas, which were quite a few years old, being as we don't usually plant them. I put them in by the sumacs. They were barely out of the ground when I looked over one evening and, sure enough, a rabbit was already after them. I ran it into a hole and put up some trip snares. I didn't want to kill it in case it was a mother rabbit. The next day there wasn't any peas showing and the trip snares caught nothing. A few days later the peas were out again and so was the rabbit. This time I got mad and put out three steel traps. I woke up sleepy-headed and went to Sanborn with Father to get growing mash for the little chickens. I was at the Allen Milling Company when I thought of the traps. When we got back I went to look. Before I got to the hole a marsh hawk flew up. The rabbits were dead in two traps and partly eaten by the hawk. In the third trap was a crow caught by one leg. The crow pecked me so I stuck its head under its wing and brought it and the traps home. With its head still under its wing I pushed the crow up a coat sleeve so it wouldn't fight while I bandaged kitchen matches around its broken leg. I gave it the old turkey house to live in while it mended itself and fed it growing mash and cracked corn. I had ideas of teaching it to talk like Joss-hoot did to a baby crow but mine was too mean and old and pecky. When its leg got better

Mother told me to let it go because the guinea hens screeched so whenever they saw it. I told Mother that I would but first I wanted to see if I could fly it like a kite. I got a long string and tied it to its good leg and turned it loose. Twice when it came to the end of the string it crashed. On the third try it broke the string and never came back. I went into the house to tell Mother that you can't fly crows like a kite and who should be in the house having newspapers pinned to his clothes for a pattern but Manylips. He hadn't given up owning a suit.

Father was talking to Manylips in Tuscarora. Indians like to tease one another all the time. Father said, "Better not wear your suit or Lala la won't know you."

Manylips said, "Is that why you only change clothes once a year?"

Father said, "Better have two suits made. One for the baby. Your belly looks like it's got one in there."

Manylips said, "Three suits is what we need. I can see your second childhood. Au-g'yuh!"

Au-g'yuh means ouch in Tuscarora. He and Father had begun laughing and Mother had jabbed his skin by mistake.

"Let me play pin-the-tail-on-the-donkey too," Father laughed. Mother told them to cut it out or she'd make diapers for both of them.

The men were quiet until Mother was finished for fear of getting Manylips jabbed again. After that though, they sat and talked. Manylips said he was put out at having a-block-put-in-his-mouth and that he no longer cared what happened to the reservation. But no sooner had he said that when he asked what the council had decided about selling limestone to the steel company. When Father said it couldn't be done, Manylips began shaking his head and saying how the reservation could of been rich and how they could of had a lake to fish in. Father said the news had leaked out and all of a sudden everybody was scrambling to dig up papers or have some made to the property that nobody wanted all the years before that. Manylips continued to shake his head until Father told him that maybe some day his daughters and his grand-children would be looking for a place to live; that they couldn't live on top of water. Manylips was quiet for a while.

Manylips slumped in his chair. "I doubt my girls are coming

86

back," he said. "I was never too good at holding my feelings. Always wanted a boy, you know. Some people have all the luck but I ain't never had none. Ma and Pa, they had me doing all the chores because Dow-wed (David) was the baby." He wasn't talking so loud as he mostly did. "I guess I ain't been easy to live with." I had never seen Manylips looking so sad.

"Well," Father said, "the same thing happened to me but, look now, we can shift for ourselves. Your brother don't even have his own house and his wife can't even make fry bread. Your wife is strong and healthy and I don't know what we would of done without her when the children were born."

Mother poured some tea and Manylips perked up. "By gosh," he said, "I been thinking. My woman ain't complained all these years. She don't seem to have no wants. I ought to do something for her but, you know, I can't think of what."

"She likes flowers," Mother said. "I told her one time she could dig out whatever she wanted but she never did."

"I ain't much for flowers," Manylips said. "She's got plenty of them, but one time I seen something I know she'd get a kick to have. I was always gonna get it but I never got 'round to it. It's a stone. 'Bout that high." Manylips held his hand out about knee high. "Looks like a small bear. I just never got 'round to draw it out."

Mother poured more tea and Manylips was far from sad now. "I knew if I put my mind to it I'd get me a good idee. Steelplant," he said to Father, "if you ain't using that nag of yours this afternoon I could drag that stone out in nothing flat." He took a big drink of tea. "I could put that bear right in the center of the flowerbed. She'd like that. That's her clan, you know, bear. It's just down by the old quarry."

"Go 'head," Father said. "You be surprised what that little horse can do. You can ride in the democrat and chain the stone to the backend."

Manylips was barely listening. "We can name the bear Stoney," he said.

We went out and hooked Pony up. "Just drop the reins on her rump," Father said, "or she'll run away with you. Chain's in the back."

"I know animals," Manylips said and he dropped the reins

two times on Pony's back. She took off at a smart trot and Many-lips' feet lifted off the floor an inch or two. "Be right back," he said with a grin.

About two or three o'clock Father said, "Why don't you go help Lips. Then you can save him bringing the horse and rig back."

I ran to the creek and jumped across. Maybe Manylips was already bringing Pony back and I might not see him; I might miss him if I went around the spring path. When I got to the dirt lane I could see Pony's tracks going just one way: to the loghouse.

At the loghouse there was only quiet. Nobody answered the door and there was no Pony or stone bear. In the yard, though, I could see on the grass where Manylips had driven. I followed them. He had used Pony to drag in a few dead poles for cooking wood. Then I could see where he had headed off towards his brother's place. From there he could get to the quarry.

The edge of the quarry was the edge of the reservation. It was less than a mile away. I mean, in a straight line, so I cut down the hill at an angle. Maybe I could get there in time to help get the stone bear.

Near the quarry it was easier walking to go off the reserva-tion into the pines. Someone had started growing them for Christmas trees and had given up and just let them grow wild. They were big trees now and nothing much seemed to grow in the needles underneath and it was soft walking. At the quarry some of the huge pieces had been bulldozed off to the side and I had to climb up back around to the topside where Manylips would be driving in to. Right in my way, too, was this big blowdown tree and I stopped to look at it for the best way to climb over it. I was taking a small rest because maybe I had beaten Manylips getting there. But then, I thought I heard voices.

Lala la had her arm around Manylips and they were standing by the edge of the quarry looking down into it. Lala la was saying, ". . . when we used to come here. When was the last time? And that big woodchuck used to stand up and make sure we didn't come any closer. I wonder if he's still alive? The hole is still there, see it?" she said pointing. It looked like Manylips was trying to shade his eyes to see the hole when Lala la pushed him. He almost caught his balance and he didn't holler or anything and it seemed quite a while before he landed at the bottom.

Lala la just stood there looking around and once I thought she looked right at me but then she turned and looked at Pony. It appeared as though she might have been listening as much as she was looking around. I was quite a ways away from her but my heart was thumping like it seemed for sure she could hear it. Next she went and climbed up into the democrat. For quite a while she just sat there and it seemed as though I had never realized how small she really was.

I was getting ready to run when she got back off the democrat. Then she bent this small sapling down and stepped on it near the ground until it broke. She twisted it off and slowly broke the little limbs off it. What she had when she was finished would make a fine fishing pole.

All she did though was, she walked up and with one good swish, struck Pony on the rump. I knew Pony was no dummy and she was already trying to gallop before the switch hit.

When I left, Lala la was sitting under a young maple tree. She was moving that stick through the air in a poking motion. Probably she was cutting the web that a spider or army worm was hanging off of.

The Cucumber Tree

Naw'HRET-HRET (Sunfish) was probably the smallest Indian on the reservation for his age. When I was old enough to know him, he was probably forty-five already and had married a woman named OO'doos (wheat). She was shorter than he was but kind of fat. Naw'HRET-HRET could never have weighed even a hundred pounds. I don't know which one's fault it was but they never had any children of their own. They wanted one though, so they took over the upbringing of a boy named Dox. Dox was skinny. He was in the same grade as I was at school and he asked me to protect him against the bigger boys even though I was even skinnier than he was. We called him "Dox" because sometimes he made that noise, "dox," with his teeth.

One day after school I saw Naw'HRET-HRET at the store and he said, "Dox has been telling me about you. Why don't you come and visit him sometimes? We'd like to have you." So I did.

Mother and Father spoke quite highly of Naw'HRET-HRET and OO'doos. They said that even though they were poor, they had class. Naw'HRET-HRET had studied playing the flute and he played in the Shredded Wheat Band where he worked and made cereal.

Naw'HRET-HRET and OO'doos and Dox lived all by themselves in a tarpaper house with no other neighbors as far as you could see. Naw'HRET-HRET always seemed very weak, the way he moved and spoke. His voice was almost a whisper and I wondered how he could ever finish a song on the flute. Of the things that were planted around their house, none of it was anything that anyone else had, except maybe someone else might have a quince tree. Naw'HRET-HRET seemed to crave having something different than other people. He had asparagus and sugarbeets in the garden and a weeping beech tree. Nobody else had these things and even though I liked the weeping beech the best, Naw'HRET-HRET had another tree that he prized above all else. It was a cucumber tree.

OO'doos had extra-short arms and just as it often seems with short-armers like that, she could sketch very well and do paintings in watercolor. Even though everyone in the family was so small, I automatically behaved myself when I got there to play with Dox. They were getting ready to eat and even though I had already eaten, I couldn't get myself to tell them that, as though it would hurt them if I refused to sit at the place they had set for me. I had the feeling that they would all cry if I said that I had decided not to play with Dox.

We all had to stand up while Naw'HRET-HRET whispered grace. Then he had to keep standing to dish out the food because he was so little. Halfway through the meal Dox whispered something to OO'doos. She said, "Tell your father that he has taken all the asparagus and that, after all, you are his son and would like some of what is on his plate." Naw'HRET-HRET had four spears on his plate and he gave two to Dox. Dox put them both in his mouth. Naw'HRET-HRET glared at him and he spit them back out and cut them up. "You have company," Naw'HRET-HRET whispered.

When I left to go home I wasn't sure if I enjoyed myself or not. I never got to really play with Dox because Naw'HRET-HRET came out and supervised everything we did. It seemed as though he wanted to play with us but that he didn't want to lose any dignity doing it. Twice he showed me the cucumber tree. As it turned out, I never got the chance to visit Dox again to see if I would have wanted to go there again.

We got the news of Naw'HRET-HRET's death after it had been retold many times on its way through the grapevine. We heard that Naw'HRET-HRET had been killed in a gunfight.

When Dox didn't show up at school, I ran to his house that afternoon when school let out. Dox wouldn't let me in the house

when I got there because he said OO'doos had been crying and didn't want anyone to see her. He was going to be sent to Thomas Indian School and OO'doos was going to live with her sister. I said, "What happened to Naw'HRET-HRET?"

Dox was closing the door, but he said through the crack, "Oh, Billy Drumbeater came across our lawn Saturday night, drunk. He was singing a filthy song so Pa got his 10-gauge shotgun and told him to leave. I don't think Billy even heard him and I don't think Pa would ever dare shoot that gun because he never had ever dared shoot that gun before but do you know what Billy Drumbeater did? He went over and pissed on the cucumber tree!"

Dox stuck his head out of the doorway again and he sort of closed it on his own neck. Then he whispered like old Naw'HRET-HRET would have, "Pa shot Billy and Ma ran out and shot Pa by mistake." When Dox shut the door, I never saw him again. Before he shut the door he said loud enough for OO'doos to hear, "I'll see you."

The House that Song Built

THERE was a place on the reservation that looked like a picnic grove but it wasn't. Four people lived there in a shack that reminded me of a lazybird's nest. It was made around four trees that were alive and healthy and kept growing bigger and higher every year. This caused the shack to raise up and bits of lumber had to be added every so often. Oo'hrEE'wehh was the father. Oo'hrEE'wehh means, "music and words," or "song," so that's what we called him. He was small and dark and had a bony face. It seemed like he was always smiling but maybe the skin on his face was so tight he had to do that. I liked to look at him because he had these teeth that were like glass, like you could just about see through them. Big Melon was the mother. She was the biggest woman on the reservation. They had a boy that was thin and had dark rings around his eyes. His eyeballs were small or sunk into his head and it was quite hard to tell where he was looking. I often wondered if he was like that when he was born because they named him Glare. He had a sister that was quite a bit younger; probably my age but she never went to school.

This grove of trees that they lived in was part of a large woods and was all quite a ways from Shawnee Road. Only hunters would have any business ever going near their shack and if I hunted anywhere near there I would always swing over to see how high the shack had grown. I don't know how many people had ever seen Glare's sister because she never went anywhere except to play on her swing. It was made out of a long length of barbed wire looped through an old tire with the barbs near the tire hammered flat. Song had given her an old pair of men's leather work gloves to wear to make sure she didn't cut her hands while she swung. She was fat like her mother and had extra-long black hair. I don't think she could hear anything but she could see pretty good. Anytime she ever spotted me hunting she would take her gloves off and stuff them up into the top of the tire, over the wire, so if it rained they wouldn't get wet, then she'd hurry into the house. Sometimes Song would be outside scything the grove or Big Melon would be out singing on her stump chair. They would always wave and ask me what I had seen. When Glare's sister walked by them on her way into the shack neither Song or Big Melon would ever say anything to her; that's why I don't think she could hear and probably she couldn't talk either then.

Song never worked but he was a good hunter. He sold pheasants and rabbits and raccoons and muskrats to the other Indians. He was tricky about selling squirrels. He never sold them outright but he always threw in an extra one to get a better overall price.

One day I was hunting towards the swamp that we called Florida because it always seemed warmer when you got into it, and I saw Song standing with his gun, humming quietly and watching something. He saw me and smiled and motioned me to come quietly. He said that he had circled around a flock of pheasants and that they would soon be coming through the clearing. He said I could shoot what was left after he shot. He had a shotgun like I had never seen before. It was a 10-gauge lever action. There was no rust on it because he used it so much.

In a few minutes about nine or ten pheasants came picking their way out of the weeds. Song raised his gun. I thought that was very unsporting to the pheasants and I whispered, "You're not going to shoot while they're walking on the ground are you?"

"Of course not," he whispered back, "I'm waiting 'til they stop." With that he made a clucking sound and the whole flock stopped to look around. The 10-gauge blasted the middle of the flock to kingdom come.

"How come you didn't shoot?" he asked when the smoke cleared.

"Because," I said.

Now there was one thing that Song and Big Melon and Glare were all good at: music. They sang as a trio and they sang by themselves. They sang almost all the time at whatever they were doing except when they were asleep or when Song was aiming his gun. When it came to harmony, Song was no dummy. He could write music and he wrote the different parts of harmony that they sang. It all came out of his head and he wrote some very tricky sounds. The trio sang on the radio or at picnics or parties or at churches. That was how they made a living. They weren't very churchy but churches were places that they could sing so that was one of their favorite places. Some churches would not have them come back because they jazzed up the hymns.

Big Melon bought Glare a used guitar and soon he was playing in small night clubs. Pretty soon he bought some sharp clothes but he kept living in the shack in the woods. The next thing Glare did was buy a convertible and some boots. He needed the boots because there was no driveway from Shawnee Road to the shack.

Besides music and his new car, Glare took a liking to gin. One night he filled up on gin and drove his car into a concrete abutment and killed himself. Big Melon went into hysterics so Song bought her a dog to take Glare's place but it was too late; she had gone crazy. She stopped singing and started taking the dog to bed with her.

Everything went along fine until J.P. Morgan shot the dog. J.P. was an old bachelor that had a lot of chickens. That's why we called him J.P. Morgan, because he seemed so rich. Big Melon's dog got to chasing these chickens so J.P. shot it.

One evening when Father came home from work I heard him tell Mother that he had heard that Song was living all alone now. The next morning I went hunting and swung by Song's shack. He was outside humming away and skinning a raccoon.

"Where did you get it?" I asked, just for something to say.

"Right between the eyes," he answered. I had meant, in what woods had he been lucky enough to find it.

"Where's Big Melon?"

"She went away and left me but she was crazy anyway. I came back from hunting and saw a burlap sack outside tied up with red yarn. Before I could see what was in the bag she came out of the house with the girl and picked it up. I asked her where she was going but she wouldn't talk. She just went over to the side of the house and tore off a piece of cardboard. Then she took her lipstick and wrote C-H-I-C-A-G-O on it in big letters. The last I saw of them, they were headed for Shawnee Road. Ma was carrying the bag and the girl had the sign. The school teacher was telling me later that when he was on his way home he saw them by the side of the road. Ma was sitting on the bag and the girl was holding up that sign with CHICAGO on it. He stopped and gave them a ride to Barren Road. When he drove away from them they were waiting for another ride but they were on the wrong side of the road."

"That was a good shot you made on the 'coon," I said.

Song just laughed. I could almost see through his teeth.

Maybe three months went by before I checked on the growing house again. Snowflakes could, anytime now, be bouncing along the ground. It was that time of year. This day was extra nice, though, and I might as well tell you now, I travel mostly in good weather.

When I came to the house I stopped. Something was SURE different. The house had grown much bigger. Not up, so much, but sideways. A new part had been added on — to two more trees. The trees weren't exactly in the most convenient place so the house had gone into the shape of the number 7.

Another thing. The girl was in the swing again — and the swing had a new rope on it. While I was standing there, another thing, even more different, happened. The girl — I felt like calling her Little Melon, especially since she seemed to have lost some weight — got off the swing and waved at me. Then, instead of running into the house, she went and picked a branch of witch hazel. This is when it blooms, you know, late. Next, she came right up to me and handed me the blooming witch hazel and said, "Goohh" ("Here"). Things WERE different. SCAREY different.

Before I could come to my senses and say "Thank you" or anything, Big Melon came to the doorway of the house and said, "If you're looking for Song, he's at the Ditch, checking on if any fish are trapped in the pools."

"That's what I want," I said right away, and I took right off for State Ditch. Ten steps or so later, I noticed the witch hazel

still in my hand. I turned around and said, "Thank you," in English. Big Melon had her arm around the girl. They were both smiling and looking right at me. I felt "shivery" right in the sunlight.

It wasn't hard to find Song because I heard him singing before I got to where he was. The first thing I said to him was not "Hello." It was, "What's going on around here?"

"Grasspike," he said, holding up a nice long fish.

"No," I said, "I mean your new house — and your —" I wanted to say, "and your NEW daughter."

"Oh haven't you heard the news? Big Melon and I won the contest on the Ted Mack radio program. Did you see the new tarpaper on the house? How do you like it?" Song was all glassy smiles.

"I guess I saw the tarpaper but I know I saw the house because it looks like a 7 now."

"You know? — I never thought of that," Song said, "I'm glad to hear that. That's my number, you know — number seven. I was born on the seventh day of the seventh month."

"But what about Big Melon and— You said they went away."

"That's right too — you haven't been back since, have you. Sit down while I gut this fishy thing and I'll tell you about it."

I sat down quick.

"Well you know," he said, "I think Big Melon just had a bout of nervousness. I think that vacation did her good."

"Where? Chicago?"

"No. They got as far as Sanborn — then they got hungry. I guess the first thing they was gonna do was swipe some carrots off them German muck farmers but they ran into Heeengs beating them to it." (The muck farms are not even a mile from the reservation.)

"How did that stop them?"

"Heeengs is no dummy," he said. "She's a strong medicine woman. She took one look at the daughter and told Big Melon that there was a spirit in the girl — that's why she couldn't hear —

that's why she couldn't learn to talk. Big Melon told Heeengs that they were on vacation and had lots of time on their hands to get the spirit out. Well, Heeengs went right to work. I guess it took a couple days or better. Heeengs had to build a sweat lodge. Big Melon couldn't help either, Heeengs wouldn't let her — said she felt Big Melon was too jumpy — might disturb the medicine."

Song never stopped his teethy smiling. He talked right through it. "A funny thing happened through the cure," he said, "Heeengs was talking to the girl and telling her that she was going to give her a nice low voice. Big Melon told me afterwards that it was so exciting that her mind was right there too — sucking on every word of the cure. When Heeengs had the girl smoke on some purifying medicine, Big Melon couldn't help it — she took a few puffs too. What do you think happened?"

"What?"

"Big Melon got a low voice too. She ended up with a singing bass voice. I think that's how we won the contest — fooled everybody. We had 'em guessing who was who. But I want to tell you what else I think."

"What?"

"If Big Melon WAS crazy, I think she snuck right in on Heeeng's cure for the girl. Anyways, she got so excited with her new bass voice that she cut the vacation short right then and there. She couldn't wait to show me her new voice. She came right up to me and cut loose with, 'Rocked in the Cradle of the Deep.' Not to be outdone — after all, I'M the gifted one — I joined right in singing soprano."

"How much money did you win?"

"We got rich overnight. We won a HUNDRED dollars. And now we got a daughter that — in two weeks I'll have her singing the tenor parts."

"How much did you have to pay Heeengs?"

"Nothing."

"I bet you like your new house now. What do you use that new part for?"

"Nothing. Heeengs lives in there now," he said, slipping the gutted fish into his hipboot as a signal that he was done telling me how come things were "different."

As we started to go our separate ways, I thought of something. "Oh," I said, "I been meaning to ask you. What is the name of your daughter?"

"Melon," he said through his special teeth, "Same as her mother."

Hogart

ONE YEAR Chesta Raagit geh brought a white man onto the reservation to live with him among the pines. His name was Hogart. Not like his brother, Manylips, Chesta was fairly quiet in his relationship to the chiefs and churchy Indians of the reservation. Nobody questioned Chesta's way of making a living because he took odd construction jobs here and there, even when he was way past retirement age; he never had no birth certificate. Chesta also made lots of friends with people off the reservation, and for some reason, many Syrians. His big house was in a big grove of huge pine trees and every weekend was party weekend within the pines. Under the counter of picnic and party foodstuffs passed a fairly steady stream of moonshine or white lightning. Here's probably where Hogart came in. Maybe he knew the recipe for white lightning.

Indians like music. Only thing wrong was, unless they were drunk, the beat of the music had to be perfect or the Indians couldn't stand it. Being as there was a strong temperance society on the reservation, the biggest share of Indians didn't drink anything stronger than pop. Or if they did, they snuck it — from places like Chesta Raagit geh's. Hogart had a fiddle which he played good enough to make nickles from at the drunken Syrian parties. He was yet to learn that his playing wasn't good enough for sober Indians; even some drunk ones.

Gradually, Hogart got to meeting other Indians besides Chesta. He got to liking them. In fact, after a while he even began copying them. He grew to like the way they lived. Before he knew it, he began trying to BECOME an Indian.

How he found out that his fiddle playing wasn't quite good enough, he first got to be friends with an Indian named Clay-born. Clay-born played mouth organ, guitar, and bass drum all at the same time; or sang instead of mouth organing. Clay-born married my goo-sood (my mother's aunt) and she had a son named Char. Clay-born and Char used to play for me sometimes when I had a birthday. Char sang and played guitar. Clay-born was the boss and got to know Hogart through the parties in the pines. He also got to know the juice that flowed under the picnic benches. Clay-born, then, got Hogart to fiddle while the white lightning burned. Hogart, though, couldn't cut the mustard at any sober parties because he couldn't follow the perfect beat that Clay-born's fat leg laid down on the bass drum.

If Hogart failed to be Indian as a musician, he would at least LOOK like an Indian. He took his shirt off and came out of the pines to get a good tan on his skin. This move failed too, though, because all he did was burn and peel, burn and peel.

Next he tried to speak the Tuscarora language. Before too long, he made a big mistake. He liked this Indian woman named Bird. He tried to learn the Indian word for "bird" but instead he called her by a word which, although it is very close to bird, means a woman's private place. A good slap in the mouth sealed his Tuscarora word learning lips right then and there.

The closest Hogart came to being Indian while he was alive was, he became very poor. In order to stay alive, and being white, the thing he thought of was to go into business. He became a shoe and clothing salesman. What with the Indians sewing a lot of their own things and buying the rest at Dig-Dig's (secondhand stores like the Salvation Army stores and Goodwills) Hogart went broke. This puzzled Hogart because the Indians, in general, looked fairly fat while he was starving into a skeleton.

At first, he got pretty discouraged because lots of Indians planted corn and squash and stuff and he knew he wasn't cut out for hoeing, being as he was afraid of a sun stroke. Some Indians, though, didn't plant. Some sewed beadwork. Old women mostly. Hogart had big fingers and couldn't find a thimble to fit 'em and he quit trying beadwork because he kept getting jabbed by both ends of the needle.

The next thing he discovered on the reservation, though, did wonders for him. He discovered welfare. On the day his welfare check came you could expect to see Hogart on his way to Sanborn, pushing a wheelbarrow for groceries. This seemed to be a step in the right direction and probably he should have left well enough alone right then and there. That is, he should have quit while he was ahead, but no; Hogart wasn't satisfied.

All this struggling to be Indian was too much for his nervous system and his hair turned white as snow. All the tricks he used to dye it only made the Indians laugh so he gave up on hair color, even though white hair was a big setback.

Next he decided he might hunt with the Indians. Somebody on the reservation reminded him that a hunter needed a gun and exchanged a .22 rifle for one welfare check. The rifle turned out to have a hair trigger on it. Hogart no more than put a bullet in it when he forgot and set the butt of the gun on the floor. Bam! The bullet hit the ceiling and a good-sized piece of plaster came down and clunked Hogart's head. Also, on the way to the ceiling, the bullet cut the skin on Hogart's belly and mangled one of his ears. Of course it had to be the ear that Hogart used to rest against the fiddle when he played it. Worse yet, Chesta Raagit yelled at him for shooting in the house. Well — so much for Hogart's hunting experience.

The first time Hogart left the pine grove with the mangled ear, some Indian saw it and said, "You were about one inch from hell." This got Hogart to thinking. At the end of his thinking he decided that he better hurry up and join the church. He chose the Baptist church because it had a bigger membership and this way he figured he'd be more "in" with more Indians. The baptism was in February, right after revivals and when he saw the hole chopped through the ice he began changing his mind. It was too late. Oonook was too strong for him and force-led him to Thraangkie, the minister. A struggle took place but Hogart lost. Some say he wasn't properly baptized because in the struggle, some parts of him managed to stay out of the icy water. I saw the baptism and if Hogart could do anything, he could cough up a storm. I think he breathed in some water though, but just the same, he coughed until his face looked almost Indian color.

When communion Sunday came, Hogart was right there, waiting for his bread and grape juice. As he waited, he looked around. Here was lots of Indians fast asleep. So he went to sleep too. Suddenly someone jabbed him awake. Here was the plate of bread in front of him. "Thank you," he said, popping one of the little squares into his mouth and swallowing it. His face turned bright red as he realized that he was suppose to wait for the signal.

Finally, Hogart ran out of ideas on how to be Indian. Jeeks came to his rescue. Jeeks told Hogart that he needed to eat genuine Indian food. Hogart agreed and got invited to eat at Jeeks'. It was night when he got there. He had been invited to a supper of Nekhrehh soup. These are little brown tree frogs that have a dark brown streak trailing off their eyes to down their little backs. They are great jumpers during the day, even climbing rough barked trees. They hang out in big wet woods. How Jeeks' mother caught them, she would take a lantern at night and put it near the edge of a spread-out blanket. Then she would do with her tongue almost like a police whistle and tree frogs would come jumping from all over — into the blanket to see the light. Well, when she got back to hungry Hogart that night and when he saw her dump all these little Nekhrehh squirmin' and pissin' into her soup kettle of boiling water, he suddenly had to use the outhouse. He excused himself to go out but he never came back in to eat his Indian food.

When he got back to Chesta Geh (means Chesta's place) he told Chesta that he had given up trying to be Indian. "Once white, always white," he moaned.

Chesta took one look at Hogart and says, "No wonder! Look at yourself!" Hogart tried to roll his eyes inward to look at himself. Chesta says, "Go wan down to Dig-Dig's and get you some Indian duds."

When he got to Dig-Dig's he became confused. However, he did learn why the Indians call such places Dig-Dig's. Many people were digging into the secondhand clothing, trying to find whatever was at the bottom of the piles before somebody else got there. Hogart got bumped and pushed and ousted out of the scramble until he ended up with the leavings. Still, Chesta had probably unknowingly given him the secret that would solve all the tryings-to-

be-Indian that Hogart had messed up on without coming to Chesta in the first place. So he began picturing in his mind, just how Indians DO dress. He pictured Old Holland stomping through the winter weather with a long summer overcoat flapping unbuttoned behind him. Winter was coming but if Holland could do it, so could Hogart. So that's what he bought. A summer long coat with no buttons.

The next item of news on the reservation was that Hogart was dead. Pneumonia.

I give Hogart boo-coo credit for trying. But you know what? Even dead, Hogart failed. Instead of burying him on the reservation, the poorhouse stuck him in the ground someplace near Cambria.

The Sultan

ONE OF THE FIRST of many Indians to try to go to war was
a very handsome Indian we called the Sultan. What made him be a
sultan was, he had found a pair of shiny men's low-cut shoes but
they were too long for him. His toes never reached the toe part of
the shoes so they just curled up like sultan shoes.

Now here was a strange thing. The Sultan signed up to go to
war. He was told that he had a heart that wasn't any good; that he
might not live a year. The Sultan said, "Well, that makes me just
perfect. Doesn't it? Why send a guy that might live?" But would
you know, the man in charge of gathering soldiers told him, "No,
you can't go. That's the rules."

He wore, besides the sultan shoes, a black coat with a black
silk collar and a white shirt, but no tie. His mother got these
clothes from Mr. Pike. Mr. Pike owned Pike's Funeral Home which
was about three or four miles east of the reservation in a town
called Sanborn. The Sultan's mother was named Ya Fix, and she
was sort of the middleman between, if you died, the time you died
and needed cleaning or fixing, and when you got to Pike's, if you
were going there. So when Mr. Pike bought new clothes, he gave
Ya Fix his old ones for the Sultan to wear.

The Sultan had already shopped for a casket for himself. Mr.
Pike was quite large and tall but the Sultan was just a hair bigger
so he never buttoned the coat. All the women on the reservation
liked the Sultan and it was nothing for him to get his clothes
washed and ironed while he waited in bed naked. I think he had

black pants too. Sometimes the Sultan would say, "Looks means everything. Don't tell anybody but," then he would whisper, "I'm just a hobo." Then he would say, "You don't see everybody wanting to wash Double Ugly's clothes. Or Kidney Bean's. Or feed 'em." Then he would throw his shoulders back and stride out onto Dog Street with his head swaying from side to side and his nose up in the air a little bit; whistling to beat the band. Also he kept his hands in his pockets and it made the back of his coat, which was a foot longer than the front, stick out some, like a dumpy tail following him. Sometimes he would sing, "Death is just around the corner, oh, you crazy little corner. . . ."

The war, which was on the other side of the world someplace, had caused my father to prosper so we moved to Dog Street, which was quite crowded with houses. Some were even only a hundred yards apart. The Sultan lived anywheres. Quite often he lived at Kidney Bean's shack because that was a safe place to sell his dandelion wine from. People were a little afraid of Kidney Bean because of his wild looks and because of his wild driving. The Kid, as the Sultan called him, had several torn-down jalopies which he got a charge out of roaring the engines of, and spinning them wildly around his yard. His face was born with red blotches, of different shapes, like, you know, land areas on a globe. But there was one blotch on his left cheek that looked perfectly like a giant kidney bean. Also, his mother, Maa Bit, kept cutting his hair to make him look better but she might as well have left well enough alone. His hair liked to stand up and somehow it made you think of them things that grow out of the top of a pineapple. Other than that, he was good-looking.

The Sultan, in order to remain a sultan, had to keep adding new soles and heels to his sultan shoes and the Kid owned a hammer and an axe. The axe was to chop other shoes apart to get their soles. Also the Kid used it to chop whatever parts were not necessary on old cars so he could sell junk to the junkman. There was another thing that the Sultan and the Kid did. They were secret partners in poker games so they could live better. You would think that the Sultan would live at Kidney Bean's all the time but he did not. Sometimes he helped his mother in case she had new clothes from Mr. Pike or in case somebody died with change in their pockets.

110

Wouldn't you be wondering how Ya Fix took care of dead bodies? Well, that's what happened to me. I wondered. When I told the Sultan how I wondered, he said, "Good for you. I been asking myself, 'Who's gonna' take my place helping Ma when I die?' Look," he said, "it's a good trade. You get to keep any clothes Mr. Pike gives you and you get to see things you never saw before. Next time somebody dies even if it's me, I'll come and get you and you can help me and Ma."

At first I spent quite a bit of time thinking of how to back out of that but after a while when nobody died, I forgot all about it. Then one day the Sultan came whistling over. "Get ready," he said. I asked him who died. He said, "I haven't heard yet, but if they didn't, they're gonna'. I was talking to Three Eyes, hinting for him to fry me up some pheasant eggs, and a mourning dove came and started hollering on that apple stump."

Just then Grabber came riding by on his skinny-wheel girl's bike. "Bee Bi died," he said. He didn't stop because, being crippled, he had a hard time stopping unless there was a house or tree or something he could grab onto.

"Let's go in and eat first," the Sultan said, and we went in and told Mother who had died. I told her I was going to see if I could be of any help and she just said not to blame her if I had a nightmare. "I like nightmares," the Sultan said, as he sucked on a stew bone.

It was quite dark when we got to Ya Fix's. The kerosene lamp was on in the tiny house. As soon as we walked in I could see Bee Bi's half naked body laying on the floor. Half of her legs were under the bed because that's only how much room there was. "It's Bee Bi," Ya Fix said, "she's dead."

"Phew," I said, "she stinks."

"Bad breath," Ya Fix said. "We're gonna' wash her mouth out with soap and water. I went and cut her neck already." There was a big gash above her collar bone. "But I got to thinking, why rub her blood out of her face, she ain't going to Pike's."

"Oh shit," the Sultan said.

If the house was bigger I would have been standing farther back. I figured that Bee Bi was skinny but not that skinny. She was mostly bones, although she had a little round belly, like a basketball. One of her arms which looked like a bent cornstalk was up on a bundle of newspapers and the other was under the table.

The Sultan got a rag and some hot water and started washing her belly. "Let's take her pants off," he said.

"Shame on you!" Ya Fix scolded, "just reach down in there and wash as best you can. And see if she crapped."

The Sultan felt around in Bee Bi's pants and smiled. "Yep," he said and he pulled out a round dark ball like Billy goat dung. "Been eating bark again, ain't she Ma?" He flipped the little dark ball into the empty slop pail and it made the metal ring. "Hey!" he said to Ya Fix, "if there wasn't so much running to it, I might have been a great basketball player."

Just then Bee Bi's arm fell off the bundle of papers. Her wrist landed on the Sultan's shoulders and neck. He dashed out the door, leaving the wet rag in Bee Bi's pants. "She ain't dead yet, Ma!" he called through the darkness. "She tried to give me a hug."

"Get back in here and wash her mouth out," Ya Fix said, "and don't use the same rag."

"I ain't touching her," the Sultan said looking through the doorway. "I think she likes me. Anyways she don't have no money to pay us with, not even any relatives."

Ya Fix said that yes, Bee Bi had a beautiful daughter, Zillaphene, living with a Philippino doctor in Rochester. I was surprised how quick Ya Fix finished washing Bee Bi's mouth and went on telling that Bee Bi's teeth made her between eighty and eighty-five and that her daughter would be near sixty then. I looked around and the Sultan was gone. I went out and ran down the road after him. He heard me coming so he started whistling so I wouldn't run into him. "Well, did you learn anything?" he asked. I told him that I found out how little I cared for his job. "They don't all die without money," he said, thinking that I meant about not getting paid. "All Bee Bi had was two apple trees. Greenings. She was living in Old Cap's barn since her house blew down."

The Sultan was pretty sure that the army doctor was right, that he didn't have long to live. Besides having a heart that would pick up speed every once in a while, he also had sugar in his blood. Once in a while he passed out from it. He claimed it was quite restful. Nothing seemed to matter to him at all though and he went on sailing through life, however much he had left. As long as

112

he was going to die soon anyways, he began doing whatever nutty impulse came into his head. Like, he might go into a five and dime and go to the part where they sold goldfish. Even though he might be kicking the bucket at any minute, he did everything nice and slow; you could even say gracefully. Slowly, then, he would go in front of the fish tank. With his coat over his arm, he would carefully roll up his shirt sleeves as far as he could. Then, gently, he would ease his whole arm in among the fish. All of a sudden he would woosh the water around and around and make a wild whirlpool out of the water and the fish. If any fish slopped out over the top he would say it was their fault for not watching out for such emergencies. As long as he was going to die anyways, I wondered why he bothered to roll up his sleeves.

Next he might go over to where they sold mouse traps. Maybe a hundred or a hundred and fifty of these little wire and wood traps would be just laying any old way in those sectioned off counters. The Sultan would reach in with such a smooth natural way that no one paid any attention. He would pick up a trap and carefully set it. Then he would put it neatly in some far corner so as to make the most room for all the traps that he would set and replace all over the whole mouse trap section.

One day I looked down Dog Street and there was a small crowd of people admiring a nice-looking convertible. Who should be sitting at the wheel but the Sultan. He had his arm around Mayflower just as though they were wheeling along on some turnpike. "Give us a ride! Give us a ride!" the kids were hollering.

"I can't," the Sultan said, "it ain't got no motor in it." After a while one of the kids that was hollering opened the hood and sure enough, no motor. Come to find out, Kidney had just towed it in from the woods. Someone had stolen it, ditched it on the reservation, as quite often happened. Then they took the motor out and left the empty shell. Kidney came up with two buckets of kerosene. He was getting ready to set fire to the car, then cut it up for junk.

Before Kidney could throw the kerosene on the car, Old Three Eyes hollered from his stump chair, "You can't burn that jitney there! You'll kill the walnut tree." The Sultan told Kidney why didn't he hook onto it again and tow it back of his shack.

"We can't make it," Kidney said. "I had to put my three

tires on it to get it out to the road. Now two leaked away." The Sultan told him we'd all help push but he stayed behind the wheel with Mayflower. We got going through the field when all of a sudden the Sultan cut the wheel over and both cars went into a muddy little ditch. "What's the matter with you!" yelled the Kid.

"I don't want you burning this junk near my grave," the Sultan said. I looked over and saw a round hole in the ground with fresh dirt beside it. I went over and looked into it. It wasn't all that big around but quite deep. The Sultan climbed out of the car and smiled proudly. "How do you like it? I got to thinking how I want to be buried and standing up seems best. No casket."

Kidney couldn't get his jalopy out of the ditch so he goosed the gas pedal. He went forward but still in the ditch. Then he got out and burned the convertible. It was a big fire at first but then it died right down. The kids went home and Kidney said to the Sultan, "Now you gotta help me get my jitney out of this ditch."

I went over to the dry side and got ready to push, never thinking that the Sultan would help. To my surprise he got right into the mud but off to the side, so as not to be splattered when the wheel spun. However graceful the Sultan was, this time he was not. Maybe it was when the Kid had it in reverse by mistake, or something, but whatever it was, he spun the wheel on the Sultan's foot and tore the shoelaces and tongue to smithereens. The Sultan just kept right on pushing and as the jalopy came out of the ditch he leaped aboard and they went back on to Dog Street and on towards the store.

A couple days later the Sultan was still limping, so Kidney got after him. "Why don't you do something about your foot? Come on, let's have a look at it."

"Yeah, we might as well," the Sultan said, "I didn't want to look at it so I been going to bed with my shoes on."

We crowded around as the Sultan took his shoe off. There was a big scab mixed right in with his black sock. "Jesus Christ," the Kid said, "You gotta get that sock off." The Sultan went into Kidney's shack. In a little while he was back. What he had done, he had taken a scissors and cut the sock off from around the scab. Later on, he had a nice oval dark spot on his foot because the sock just grew right on into his skin.

I would say that it was just about a year from the time that the Sultan was told that he had a year to live, that he died. In fact, he probably kept track of that date. So on or about that date, he expected to kick the bucket. I'm no detective but I'd say he drank his wine so as not to feel anything if he died when he was supposed to. A teacup of it sometimes put his sugar overboard and, as I say, he often passed out.

Why I say this: when I went over to see his body, there was two empty mason jars on the scene. One was in Kidney's shack and the other was next to his grave where his body was; dead standing up. Double Ugly was there in an argument with the Kid. Double Ugly had an awful harelip that went right up into one of his nostrils. He was having it out with Kidney as to who got what of the Sultan's possessions. Double Ug was claiming to be a distant relative of the Sultan's because they were both of the Turtle Clan. About the only thing that the Sultan owned, besides his clothes, was an old battered army bugle. He had salvaged it somewhere and kept it as a reminder of his near army days. The Kid thrust the bugle into Double Ugly's hands and told him to get off his property. It was tricky to think of the harelip and the bugle together. It was the maddest I had ever seen Double. His lip was almost purple. He stood there just shaking. Finally he let out a beller. "KIDNEY!" he hollered, "YOU GOT A DEAD MAN'S COAT ON!"

116

Old Claudie and Bullet

CLAUDIE came back from the war half crippled up. A bullet had hit his knee and gave him a fairly good limp. He had been hit somewhere else too and wherever it was, it caused his hair to turn white. Of the Indians on the reservation, even the old ones, it was unusual to see anyone with white hair so Claudie became known as Old Claudie. He was easy to talk to so people used to ask him where he had been hit. He would say, "In the epiglottis." No one ever knew just what that was and he liked to watch the way people acted after he said that. Some would sort of smile while others took it very soberly.

Old Claudie took to drinking as soon as he came back to the reservation. He drank hard cider or wine or just about anything he could get ahold of. Why he got to drinking was because of what he saw when he came back. Before he went to war he lived with his mother, Miss-Moose; just the two of them in a shack of a house on her property. There was a hundred acres all around the house. Old Claudie planned to go back living just the way he did before he went to war but when he got back to where the house should have been, with his mother in it, there was nothing but a great big cornfield.

What had happened was that when Claudie had left, his mother took ill and needed money so she sold the land to Bullet. Bullet had a fairly big farm but he was always trying to make it bigger. When wintertime came, Claudie's mother froze to death so Bullet tore the shack down and made a chicken house out of it.

When Claudie asked around what his mother might have done with the money, he was told that there didn't seem to be any money; that Miss-Moose told around how she was going to spend the money as soon as she got it. When Claudie asked Bullet, all Bullet said was that he didn't know what had become of the thousand dollars or the bushel of apples or the bag of potatoes that he had given her.

Bullet was tricky. One day he came to our house and gave us a dozen eggs and a basket of grapes. Then he asked my father if he would sell the fifty acres that was near his farm. "Of course," he said, "I'd have to clear out the hardwoods before I could farm it," implying that the woodlot would also go along with the fifty acres.

When my father told him no, that he was saving the land for me when I grew up, Bullet asked for the basket that the grapes were in.

Bullet was also lucky. Like, out of his seven children, six of them were boys and they were the ones that did the work on the farm. But even before that, before Bullet got ahold of the place, it seemed as though there would someday be a fight for the farm. Bullet had two brothers, and Old Shotgun, his father, owned it. Then all in the span of fourteen months, the old man died, one brother was found to be full of TB and put in the county sanatorium, and the other brother drowned in the Lower Niagara when he speared a sturgeon and wouldn't let go of the spear handle.

Our house was less than a mile from Bullet's farm. Whenever my mother let me I'd go over and ride the pigs or feed the chickens or chase the cows in. One year during summer vacation Bullet rounded up a bunch of kids about my age to pick his raspberries. I was one of them. In a week we had them all picked. It was Saturday when we finished and went to the house to get our pay. Bullet said, "How would you like to go to the show and see Tarzan?" I guess we all knew that if we said no that we wouldn't get any pay at all. When we got there, there was a sign that said, "Children under 12 free." Bullet didn't have to pay anything.

I hung around the farm all I could when Bullet started building a new house. It didn't take very long either. All he did was make a house right on top of the old one; like a big shell when it was finished. There were a lot of braces between the old part and the new part and it was just perfect for us kids to climb around on.

It was here at the farm that I got to be friends with Old
Claudie. Bullet must have felt sorry or something, or guilty, because he asked Old Claudie to come and live there. Bullet said he
could work there and for that he would always have a place to
sleep, although Old Claudie slept in the barn. One thing, Bullet
never told Old Claudie what to do and he just seemed to putter
around.

How I got to be friends with Old Claudie, I helped him carry
a bushel of rotten elderberries out of the kitchen. We dumped
them out by the woodshed and Old Claudie called the chickens.
It wasn't long before they were drunk. They'd stagger around at
first, then they'd plop down on their elbows and start rocking.
Every once in a while one of them would think of the berries
again and try to get back at them. Usually they would get up off
their elbows and fall right forward on their face. Then they'd lay
on their side for awhile. When the urge came to go to the berries
again, they'd just start peddling the air with their feet, still on their
side, and maybe with that bluish skin sliding slowly over their eyes
and back again.

Then one day I saw Old Claudie carrying an armful of straw.
Pretty soon, there he was again carrying another armful of straw.
He looked just like a bird building a nest. I kept out of the way
and followed him watching him go around the barn and around
the silo. Sure enough; there under the big burdocks and hollyhocks Old Claudie was really making a nest. Pretty soon he went
down cellar and came up with a couple of two-quart fruit jars. He
put them in his nest. Then he started whittling on a piece of old
dead sumac. By now I was getting so interested in whatever Old
Claudie was doing that it wouldn't matter if I got hollered at for
getting home late. I could even take a spanking.

What Old Claudie made out of the sumac was a sort of
hollow plug: a spout. He put this in his pocket and went into the
tin shed. Out he came with a marlin spike and a hammer. He went
into this shady nest under the burdock leaves by the silo. Anything that ever grew in the old manure back there grew to giant
size. I could hear a pounding noise but Old Claudie never came
back out.

Finally I could stand it no longer. I crawled into the nest

119

with Old Claudie. I was sure he would yell at me. Instead he just grinned. What he had done, he had pounded a hole in the silo and tapped it like a maple tree for its sap. He had tapped the silo for its corn squeezings. Alcohol dripped into one of the fruit jars. I could tell that Old Claudie knew I wouldn't tell anyone about this even though he didn't say anything.

Old Claudie began to sometimes invite a friend of his named Groover on a Sunday evening to his nest. Old Claudie had a lot of friends among the drunks on the reservation but the only one he trusted was Groover.

When cooler weather came, Old Claudie moved his nest into the house. That is, he moved it into the space between the new house and the old house. One weekend Old Claudie threw a party and invited Groover over for a house warming. When Old Claudie woke up in the morning, Groover was not in the nest. Even though it was fall and the grapes picked, there were many warm days yet. Something began to stink around the nest so Old Claudie got a lantern and looked around. What he found, he found Groover all bloated up, floating in the old cistern. He had gone to take a leak because when they pulled him out his dink was still out.

Old Claudie went into mourning. Bullet thought it best to leave him alone but probably he shouldn't have. How Old Claudie went into mourning, he went on a big drunk. That was the weekend that the annual circus came to town and Bullet's family had become very circus-minded because that was how Bullet sort of paid his children for all the work they had done all year. While they were gone, Old Claudie threw the biggest party he had thrown so far. He invited all the drunks to mourn Groover's death. Somebody knocked the jar of corn over. John Bunker lit a match to find it and save it. In a second, the alcohol and straw were all aflame. It was all the drunks could do to save themselves. There was nothing the drunks could do but watch, first the house and then the barn and woodshed and finally the chicken house all go up in flames.

That happened on Saturday night and Bullet had his family sleep in a neighbor's barn. I remember thinking, "I have the feeling that Bullet has taken over that farm already."

In the morning Mother made me go to church saying, "And don't you be going to the fire in your good clothes. In fact, I don't

want you going over there today. They'll feel bad enough without you blurting out everything you always do. Everybody will be there telling them that everything will be alright."

In the afternoon I began begging to go there anyways. By evening I was near tears so Mother said, "I guess you can run over for a little while. Everybody will be gone but don't stay after dark. Be careful and hurry back and tell me what it looks like."

I climbed the rail fence and ran across the fields. Rain clouds were blocking out the setting sun so I was all out of breath when I got there. At first there didn't seem to be anybody in sight. Then I heard voices. They were coming from right out of the black rubble of where the barn was.

I recognized Old Claudie's voice so I went closer. It was getting darker all the time and I knew in a few minutes it would rain. I got up as close as I dared. Old Claudie and three of his friends were squatting right in there where the fire had been. They were eating a burnt horse or cow and finishing up the party for Groover.

Digger was there. He dug all the graves on the reservation. He had buried Groover under the butternut tree. Digger was talking. He was talking about the bulldozer operator, Bob Staats. " . . . so Bulldozer Bob and his old lady and old Dooh'doo left Buffalo Raceway in the brand new Olds Ninety-Eight. Bob and Jersey Bounce got to scrappin' in the front seat. Jersey was going to jump right out of the car while it was driving fast. The Bulldozer yanked her back in. She kicked the front windshield and broke it. About that time they came to the toll booth at the bridge to Grand Island. The Jersey Bounce was yelling and screaming, 'HELP! HE'S KILLING ME.' I guess the toll man called a cop or else the cop was parked along the side. Anyway the big Olds is doing over a hundred across the Island when, '—BANG—BANG—BANG,' a cop car was chasing and shooting at them. Bob yanked the Olds off the road to see what was all the commotion for. Him and Jersey Bounce chewed the two cops out royal — told them to stay out of their business and quit shooting up their new car. The cops didn't know what to say so one of them said, 'What about that old man in the back seat? Is he all right?' Dooh'doo was all scrunched down on the floor of the back seat. Bob says, 'DOOH'DOO! Are you all right?' Well you know how slow Dooh'doo talks. He says, 'I don't know — what does blood smell like? — If it smells like shit — I'm shot.' "

There was a big roar of laughter and at the same time, a long streak of lightning wiggled across the west. Then the laughing and the thunder mixed together and I felt the first few drops of rain.

Thraangkie and You-swee(t)-dad

ON SUNDAY I was to get myself down to Cow Hole — to Lake Ontario, to be baptized into the Baptist Church.

On Saturday, Thraangkie, the minister, came over to talk about it, to remind me to be there. We went into the shade of the russet apple tree. I was ten in April. Now, little green apples were on the branches.

No more had we got there when we caught sight of You-swee(t)-dad poking his way down the lane. I mean, he was using a cane. You-swee(t)-dad is the name of a title. He was chief of the clan of the bird that sat at the top of our totem; the Snipe. In a minute, him and Thraangkie were talking in Tuscarora about the weather. I figgured You-swee(t)-dad had come to talk to my father about Indian medicine. After about ten minutes, though, I wasn't sure WHO he had come to talk to because him and Thraangkie got going and after a while, they forgot all about me.

"... and I'm sure the boy would be happy too, if you could ask yourself to make the effort to witness his baptism into the Baptist church — his receiving of the Holy Ghost. And you know? I don't know if you've given this much thought but I have a feeling that one of these days you yourself will get the call and join the church too. Maybe this is why the chiefs' council is always tabling this and tabling that — you know — you carrying the highest title among the other chiefs — and they are, just about

125

every one, members of the Baptist church. I'm sure the council would pull together and work together if you let God's spirit into your heart — if you had the power of God to guide you in council."

You-swee(t)-dad was leaning forward, resting, with both hands on his cane. I liked his cane. It was an upside-down little sumac tree because it was gold color. He had carved the roots into what looked like a big bird hand clutching a ball. The trunk part had been spiraled by a bittersweet vine. He spoke very draggy Tuscarora. "You and I don't get to talk very often. Maybe we have reasons, maybe not. Not many visit and talk together anymore — that was the old way. Always. Now, I come to your house, your wife is home alone, I go home. You come to my house — you come at revival time. You have revival people with you. Something is wrong. Something is wrong more than you say. Yes — the council does not often decide, in one evening, what to do. In the old days, I have heard, the council did not go home at midnight because the chiefs were sleepy — sometimes it took days to make the right decision. Nor would they hold council after sundown. Now we meet at night with no patience. This is not right. Now the clock moves faster and we run behind it. Of the delegates to your revivals, from Cattaraugus, from Osweken, from Red House, even from nearby Tonawanda, they are becoming fewer and older. From what I see, you cannot be so sure that the Holy Spirit alone will mend these things. From what I see, the Great Law of the Iroquois cannot mend these things. I have read the Bible. It is a great and wonderful book of words. I have studied the Great Law. It is good too; not evil, not wrong. From what I see, I see no living examples of the Bible OR of the Indian way. What I see, I see confusion. I can even feel it. It is in my bones — in my guts. I have told my own children, 'Go and get a good education,' but what I really was saying is, 'Become SOMEbody, but be prominent — be rich. It doesn't matter if your guts spill over with bile, as long as you are these things.' But it is not the Indian way — NOT the Indian way. Now I am older. I see different now."

"You-swee(t)-dad, I want to tell you something. I want to tell you that I feel your kinship in the color of our skins and in the language that we use. We are brothers in creation but I feel that I have been amiss somewhere. Somehow I have failed to open

126

your door to a new life — the life that Jesus lived. Wait now — wait until I finish. It is easy for me to bask in the glory of the Lord — to overlook that there are others who have yet to know this peace — have NEVER known this peace. It is true — the problems in THIS life are many. And they do not solve themselves. I am not without problems but by myself I would be helpless. BUT. One does not say, 'God, do this for me. Do that for me.' That is the same as saying, 'SHOW me first.' That is the same as a child saying, 'Daddy, GIVE me some candy because I like candy.' You might say, 'Bring in the kindling first,' but God does not say that. All He asks is your FAITH; your sincerity. Now — once you place your faith in Him, He will help you. Believe me, brother, you will KNOW that He is there, with you. You will FEEL his power within you — You-swee(t)-dad — you look at me with cold fish eyes. I cannot do this thing FOR you, but I can pray for you. If you will but put aside your pride, which is by no means a disrespectful pride, and ACCEPT what IS — God and His Power — I think you will come and tell me about it, because it will seem, at the same time, both such a simple thing, but a miracle too. I say this because, that day, for me, the day that I discovered the Holy Spirit in accepting God and Christ, is a day I shall never forget. I wanted to run about and shout to everyone what had happened. I felt as though all of my life before that had been wasted — trying to do so much all by myself. I even feel as though I am allowing myself to be carried away again by that feeling, but I can't help it. That's how it WAS on that day. Perhaps I see you, You-swee(t)-dad, the image of myself, in confusion — just as I was before I opened my door to God. Or else it's the excitement of that, plus knowing WHAT can be yours RIGHT NOW even though the choice is all yours. Yes, the choice is all yours — and I feel the Power of God touching your heart. I am happy to know this, but we both — together — will feel GLORIOUS if you accept Him today. NOW! If you can but open your heart, my brother."

In the blue of the sky, to the north, one small cloud was being dragged by its feathery tail in the direction towards Ransomville.

"Today you call me brother. You say I can feel — this — glorious. You say that you feel that God is near my heart. Perhaps He is always near my heart, then, because I do not feel different

128

now or yesterday. I do not feel any different now or as I did on that day when you rode to my house with a deacon of your church to borrow my axe for your chopping-bee. On that day, when you saw me chopping my own wood and could not let you use the axe at that time, you did not call me brother. When later I came and split many blocks of wood, you did not call me brother. Wait. Wait as I did to hear you speak to me. This glory feeling. I have known it. It is not always good. Two autumns ago, my small daughter was dying. For two days and almost two nights we stood by her bedside. I saw Dr. Plane close his black bag and I knew what he did not want to say when he placed his hand on my shoulder. 'I can do nothing more. I am sorry. She is in God's hands.' I wept, and I entered the feeling of despair. My feet were no more on the ground. My mind was empty. I could not see. At this time a voice came at the door. It was the voice of a white man. It was a loud and hollering voice. It said, 'You-swee(t)-dad IS A GREAT DI-AM! He is a GOOD man! He is a KIND man!' I went to the door and found old John Bunker standing there. The smell of rotten fruit was strong on his breath — but he felt no despair as I did. He felt the feeling of the want of food. I told him my daughter was dying but I let him in. His walk was a weaving walk but his feet were on the ground. He saw my daughter and turned and went out the door. 'She's dead,' he said. 'I will get Steelplant for you. I will get Saw-gwaw-hree(t)-thre(t) for you.' I felt the cold skin of my daughter and comforted the shaking crying of my wife with louder crying. I did not hear Saw-gwaw-hree(t)-thre(t) come in, but I saw him throw the Indian tobacco under the bed. And the Blue Skullcaps and the Solomon's Temples in his hand — I saw him make the medicine and rub my daughter's arms and neck — and I saw her suck the medicine from the wet rag. I could feel my feet now. I had stepped from my despair. My feet were standing on the ground again. My mind was free again — and I helped Saw-gwaw-hree(t)-thre(t) stroke the Indian medicine through the throat of my daughter. Yes, my feet were on the ground — then — as they are now as I speak to you. But then — but then came this glorious feeling of which you speak. It came because at that moment, the eyes of my daughter fluttered and her lips became a smile — and in this same moment — so great be- came my joy from this miracle that my heart pounded my blood into my brain until I knew not where my feet were. My arms were in my daughter's puke but I — I was in the glory place. My head was shaking up and down — YES, YES, to Saw-gwaw-hree(t)-thre(t)'s instructions about the Solomon's Temple medicine but I heard not a word he spoke. NO, not a word — for in the morning my daughter was again in coma and the Solomon's Temple lay on the table untouched. During the night my feet had crept from the glory place and now, at morning time, with my wits about me once more, I rushed to prepare the medicine. My daughter was spared — is alive today — but not because of the glory feeling — and so now you can tell me that I am wrong. That the feeling I had was NOT the same feeling of which you speak. That it was God's will that my daughter should live. But had she died — then THAT too, you would tell me, was God's will. So I say 'no' to your glorious feeling. I say 'no' to a feeling that perhaps the members of your Baptist church possess on the seventh day of the week. On Sunday. Because on that ONE day, dressed in their best clothes, on their way to church to praise God, they never wave to me, or call out to me when I am out in my yard. No, Thraangkie — there is something wrong there. There is something wrong when people see me for six days — then suddenly — on the very day on which you practice your life's calling — they go blind. And I get the feeling of something being upside down, or inside out. Or backwards. Or whatever it is that has grown people suspended from the earth for one whole day."

"Who is without sin?" Thraangkie smiled. "I wouldn't want you to come to church just to receive a wave or handshake. You-swee(t)-dad, it is good that you speak out. I hear you well. I hear you speak of confusion. I find you seeking excuses. I hear you say you have read the Bible. I hear you say, 'There is something wrong.' And without the guiding Hand of God I might not have heard you. I might not have seen your plight. I might not have recognized the Devil's handiwork. It is the Devil's way to turn you against your fellow man. And HE IS sly. The Devil is VERY sly. No man wants to be accused of associating with the Devil, and he will rant and rave and swear a hundred times that this is not so. But the Bible says we are BORN in sin. I'm sure you will find it hard to admit that the Devil has caused you to speak out so bitterly. But that's the KEY, don't you see, the very thing that God is

130

asking me to point out to you. But you have spoken OUT, my friend, and in doing so, much of that bitterness and confusion has left you. It was but the Devil clanging a cymbal to scare me away. But now you see how God has helped us both understand what has been the root of your troubles — has been robbing you of the peace which you seek — the Devil. And here you stand, You-swee(t)-dad, just an inch away from shedding the Devil and accepting the Lord Jesus Christ as your own personal Savior. Will you pray with me? Let us say the Lord's Prayer together."

"Thraangkie — you say that you hear me. You say that it is with the guiding hand of God that you hear me. Perhaps you hear me from the glory place. What you have done — you have swept my words under the blanket of the Devil. You believe me to be in great misery. Of myself. But the ball is not in your lacrosse stick. You have missed it — and now you make ready to score a goal with empty stick. So now I ask you to release your stick. Release your God for a moment and become Thraangkie the real man. The Indian [ehgweh hehhwehh which means, 'real people']. For as we are; as we have been — but the length of my cane from each other — we are not together. One hears not the words of the other. You see not what I see. I feel not what you feel. So let me speak. Hear me. Hear me not as a sound but as a person. Look at my words and taste them. Then tell me what you feel. And what you see. And what you hear. And then — when we have touched each other's words — when we have felt the weight of each other's words — THEN, we will have spoken to each other. THEN, we be together. So then, I speak. And I say first, that I would have you hear me say that I do not ask you to reject the God of whom you speak. I think He is the same God that our forefathers called the Creator. Why I ask you to release your God for a moment — I wish to speak to YOU, Thraangkie, without an interpreter. Wait! I will do this." He pushed his cane into the earth so that it stood by itself. Then he moved over and sat down. Thraangkie and the cane and You-swee(t)-dad now formed a triangle. "Let the cane take my place. Let the cane be You-swee(t)-dad. I will be a neutral being — and the neutral being speaks, saying, once this land we stand on was stood on by Indians only. Ships came across the Great Waters bringing people from another land place. They came seeking freedom to practice their religion. In the same boats were

Bibles and guns; hope and anger. In their Bible it was written, 'THOU SHALL NOT STEAL. THOU SHALL NOT KILL' but by the time they were through stealing the land, many Indians lay dead. The Indians still alive were frightened. They were told to go to school and learn a new and better way of life, that they were pagans who worshiped idols. THIS was spoken by the people who came seeking RELIGIOUS FREEDOM! In their Bibles were the words JUDGE NOT THAT YE BE NOT JUDGED but they judged the Indians to be inferior. They did not learn the Indian language or the Indian way of life, the Indian law, which does not separate church and state. Even today they think wampum is money. Can you picture the President of the United States taking a week of his time to make a string of wampum so that he could say to you, 'Thraangkie, this string of shells is yours to keep — as a symbol of my good faith — that I will not let U.S. Highway 104 be built across your cornfield.' Or picture how quickly a net would be thrown over you if you had presented Abraham Lincoln with a string of black shells saying, 'Mr. President, these shells are proof of my dream that Booth will shoot the back of your head.' No. These Bible carriers did not try to understand the Indians' ways. The seekers-of-nest-people judged. They judged that the totem pole and the False Face and the song and dance ceremonies to corn, beans, squash, medicines — to life — because they were a mystery, were evil. They did not try to discover that these things were the Indian's way of teaching — not by books, but by the eyes and the ears — the feelings in the belly. Not just of the past, but of the now — and of the future by dreams — a way of life — a way of life that recognized that all things were to be respected. That no man could hold the burning embers of tobacco in his hand; but a stone of the earth could. It had that power. Not a power to be feared but to be used — as one uses cornbread for eating. And the tobacco, itself a growing symbol every spring, of earth, water, air, and fire, to be used like wampum, to vow and give of the feelings of thankfulness that grew deep in the guts — the little voice in the guts of every single thing that the Creator created. The voice within the oak that says, 'I feel your need for my wood.' The voice within the real person that says 'take some of my precious smoking tobacco in exchange.' The voice within the belly of the night which speaks to us in dreams — in pictures — that we may see the

132

medicinal plant we need — that we may see our very hand, in the picture, sprinkling the tobacco — and hear our lips bequeath our body, when it dies, to the earth — that it may rot — and fertilize the earth, to feed the seeds, of medicines yet to ripen. A simple way of life — a peaceful way of life. No guns. No gunpowder. No bullets. A simple way of life that had, in its language, no words such as 'primitive' or 'uncivilized.' No need for words like 'faith' or 'believe.' No need because of a WAY of life beyond faith. A way of life — of peace of mind such that spawned no need for the invention of alcohol or liquor to dull the mind, to falsify the mind. And so — from across the great waters came the seekers-of-nest people, seeking more than just a nest. They came seeking a way of life, which, they claimed, was in a book that they brought called the Bible. And now, after close to three hundred years later, that way of life appears to still be only inside of that Bible. And I hear you say that I need faith and I can have this way of life which is still being sought. Thraangkie, you and I were told that there is a law which says we had to go to school until we reached a certain age. We went. And we learned to speak, and write, and read a strange language. We read that Indians were becoming civilized. We read that science is making great advancements for civilization. Lately I have read a strange thing. I read in the newspapers that science may soon discover the secret of dreaming into the future. That they stumbled upon some Indians in Mexico doing that. I was at John Roman's when I read it. I was waiting for him to butcher a pig so I could have the blood and guts. [John Roman was a white man who lived off the reservation. He was the preacher at the Presbyterian mission on the reservation. He also was a butcher.] You know what John Roman said? He leaned over close to me and said, 'I'd be headed for the racetrack if I could do that.' I guess that's all I have to say. My cane will be a cane again and I will be You-swee(t)-dad."

"I have heard you, You-swee(t)-dad, and what you say is all very well. I FEEL what you say too, and I feel that it comes from a time which is past. I hear you speak of science, which says we were once monkeys. It also says that as the generations go past, those parts of our bodies that we don't USE will fade away, such as our monkey tails. Maybe that's true of our brains too then. And perhaps it is true of God's plan — and the Bible. Don't we see that because the Indian no longer USES the elm bark for a house, the elm trees do now fade away — just as the Great Law of the Iroquois does so fade. But the Bible does not fade. The Baptist church does not fade. Don't you see? Don't let your brain fade too. This is the time of changeover for us. Sure, the old ways die hard. But we don't see a locomotive pulling its cars with a horse harness. You and I are not here to stop the ways of science. But it does seem fearful — these changes. Unknown things. But the Bible predicts these things. I think you fear the Bible. I think you fear God. That is alright. That is good. For when you do NOT fear, you do not respect. I see that God IS an unknown to you. You speak of the people who came across the Great Waters and you say that they judged the Indians. At the same time, I hear you judging them; yet, just as the people of science, you seek proof of God. You seek proof, first, of what is written in the Bible. You-swee(t)-dad, you and I — everyone — came from our mother's womb yet unable to see. Before our eyes had vision, we KNEW we had a mother. We felt SECURE because of that. The growing up — the growing AWAY from that secure place in our lives was frightening and we always will want it again. But hear this, my brother, it CAN be had. You can be born again. I know because it happened to me, and just as I accepted my mother without seeing her, so did I accept the Father, and the Son, and the Holy Spirit. From that day on, I KNEW I had been reborn. I KNEW my life had changed. I KNEW the power of God, because without it, my life was headed nowhere. And now I KNOW — that when my work on earth is finished, when God takes me, there is a place waiting for me in heaven. Before I was reborn, I feared death. That is all gone now. Knowing that the heavenly Father has a place for all who accept him comes only after we have been born again. This, I feel, you do not know, my friend, and time can be so short. Death knows no age and our choice is heaven — or hell."

"Thraangkie, it is good that we talk together. It is better yet that we hear each other. You say that you are going to heaven. Now I say that I am going to the Happy Hunting Ground. I, too, do not fear death. I believe that I will hunt in the Happy Hunting Grounds and you, Thraangkie, will do whatever is done there, in heaven — because this knowledge is in our hearts. I do not say, 'Thraangkie, you are wrong. MY way must be your way.' Now, though we are both here on earth. And I confess — I do not understand the god of which you speak. Not because I have not seen your god with my eyes. I see YOU, Thraangkie, born again in the religion of this god — peaceful — not afraid of death — not caring that your children do not have shoes, yet you yourself HAVE shoes — believing in your god but not believing Olive when she told you that your children stole candy and bubblegum from her store. If your god comes before your children, this I cannot understand. My children tell me they have given some of their lunch to your children in school, when they come with nothing to eat. Again, I say, I have read the Bible which is called the Word of God. In that book I liked the story of the man called Jesus Christ. Those that follow his teachings are called Christians. They seem warlike people to me. In our history books at school we read of these Christians forming Christian armies. Instead of preaching the words of their teachings, they attacked the Moslems, calling this killing the Crusades. It is the FEELINGS I get from these warlike ways. It is as though the feet of the Christians were not on the ground. I mean, Thraangkie, if a person of this Moslem place put a rifle to your temple and said to you, 'Since you do not do my Moslem way, I pull the trigger in the name of MY God,' surely you would wonder if that is right to do. It does not seem right to me. To me, war is killing. It is one thing to stand and protect yourself, or your country, or your property or your home and family — but to march forth into somebody else's land — THAT, to me, is wrong. To march forth to kill, singing what is called the Battle Hymn of the Republic — 'mine eyes have seen the glory of the coming of the Lord' — THAT is crazy. They are in that glory place. Do you see the confusion of it, Thraangkie? My feet are on the ground but you do not hear them. You can hear the sound of the marching feet of soldiers or crusaders but those feet are NOT on the ground. I cannot tell you how many of these Moslem people became Christians but I have been told that there are more Moslems than Christians in the world. But then, I do not know what this word 'crusade' means. Is it like witch hunt? I wonder; because when the Christians came here seeking a place of religious freedom they soon began hanging some of their own tribe. This was called witch hunting. Is that not judging others? To seek religious freedom but to not allow it feels to me as though the golden rule is

but a dream. Do not these things cause confusion of the mind?
You remember the missionary who taught us to read and write in
school. I brought a husk doll to show how it was made. I was told
to take it home immediately — to get rid of it — that I was a pagan.
I argued that I did not pray to the husk doll, and neither did ANY
Indian — no more than the missionary prayed TO the Bible or to
the church steeple or to the cross on top of it. I was punched in
the ear and sent home until I was old enough to learn. And looking back, now, it still feels like a part of the crusades, or witch
hunts. So does the burning down of our Longhouse. In the name
of God. You say, Thraangkie, that it is good to speak out my
anger. I believe you. I am feeling better already. And yes, perhaps
I do fear your God. But I feel it more as though by becoming reborn, that I might become blind to the needs of my family, or become part of an army that wants to fight — even as I saw two
Baptist church members, last week, fist fighting in the churchyard
over a woman. Thraangkie, all these things are like bad dreams
that I would like to forget — but they come back in new happenings, like omens. Even now, the picture is, of you with your arms
out, to your sides, holding back an army. And when you say to
me, 'You must be born again . . . ,' this army continues your
words, 'OR ELSE!' " You-swee(t)-dad swayed his head slowly. No.

"After the rains, my friend, you don't reject the delicious
mushrooms just because the poison Amanita — which looks so like
the mushroom — is growing there also. You don't require yourself
to eat the cornbore (corn worm) living within the heart of the ear
of corn. You do not become angry with all of your tomatoes because some have dry rot. The husk of the walnut is bitter but the
meat is sweet. We have the gift of choice — to accept our fellow
brother. Or of accepting God. Or the Devil. If Jesus Christ came
walking by, right now, along this dusty lane, we might say, 'There
goes Jesus Christ, the Son of God — but His feet are dirty.' Oh, my
brother — Satan never gives up. Satan never gives up and I don't
say that taking the first step to God means that you can lie in the
shade, free from Satan. Just as we had to learn to walk, we don't
just step into the divine footsteps of Jesus Christ and take this
trail for granted. Oh no — man on this earth is just flesh — and the
flesh is weak. The flesh of man is so weak that it didn't stop at
telling Christ that his feet were dirty. The flesh of man CRUCI-

FIED the Son of God. Oh how the Devil must have smiled on that day — but Jesus Christ AROSE from the dead. I am not saying to you, 'You-swee(t)-dad, join the Baptist church so you will be better than your fellow man.' I do not say, 'Accept God so you can snub your neighbor.' I do not say, 'Accept the Holy Spirit so you won't see the dry rot or the cornbore in the cob.' I DO say — that WITHOUT the power of the Father and the Son and the Holy Spirit — you are powerless — you are at the mercy of the Devil — just as those very men were who THRUST that spear into the body of the SON of GOD as he hung from the Cross. NO, the Devil tempts us all, and many people listen. The newspapers wouldn't have much to say if this wasn't so. Thievery, rape, murder, deceit — and of these deceit may be the worst, brother, because we only deceive ourselves. And I can see the Devil smiling at you, You-swee(t)-dad, as he must smile so often when his work is being done — when you deceive yourself into believing that you can do without God — that you can do without the POWER OF THE HOLY SPIRIT — that you can fool Satan all by yourself."

"You speak well, Thraangkie. Many Indians cannot do that. To me, the finest of words are a thing of beauty — just as the notes of the song sparrow strike my ear. But as beautiful as that song is, it BELONGS to the song sparrows and not to me. And no matter how beautiful that song is, the song itself is not the bird itself; merely the song OF the bird. More yet — that song belongs TO that bird and not to any other kind of sparrow. The songs — the voices of birds and animals and men are different but their wants —their needs—are the same. A home, food, sleep—and a need for freedom as they go about getting these things. But just as there are different kinds of birds and animals, there are also different kinds of people — even different kinds of plants — trees. The oriole does not waste its time scolding the cuckoo-bird for building such a flimsy nest. The beaver does not scold the otter for playing on his slide, that the otter should be cutting wood instead. Nor does the ash tree criticize the oak because the acorns do not have wings for spinning and flying. Nor the bedbug boast of a better home than the spider. These creatures of creation go about their business, guided by the spirits and instincts within their beings. Not people though. Of course not—not people. PEOPLE have highly developed BRAINS! — PEOPLE, Thraangkie, like me and you. We cannot leave one another alone. 'My child is smarter than your child because she was talking at one year old.' Yes — my baby can talk. She says, 'My doll is better than your doll.' Oh if we have anything, we have BRAINS! We are not like stupid trees. WE can conNIVE!'" You-swee(t)-dad lay back now, looking up at the little green apples above him. "I have a friend in Niagara Falls," he said. "He is Japanese. His son makes pictures on Main Street. For forty years and more I have known this friend, and in that time I have yet to hear him speak an unkind word or do an unkind act. For many hours we have spoken. He has told me of his religion — Shinto. Never once did he say that I should believe what he believes. He spoke of another people who he admired. They were mountain shepherds. Their religion was Zen. They believed that God was within themselves — that their way of life would show that. He spoke of another religion — Janism. These people forbid themselves to harm even the smallest insect. I told him what Mirror Jack's son had learned at Niagara University — that people called Greeks had a god named Abraxas — one half good, one half evil. I told him of our Creator. I told him of the strange man from Ona-DUK-gyeah, Ta-hra-DA-ho. How, during the evil half of his chieftainship, snakes grew from his scalp instead of hair. How he used supernatural powers to stop every attack by his own people to take away his title. How Degonawida, the Huron, and Hi-ye(t)-WA-the(t), the Mohawk, came upon this evil leader. Ta-hra-DA-ho, as they visited and preached the uniting of tribes to form a Great Peace [the Iroquois Confederacy]. How, instead of attacking the evil and powerful Ta-hra-DA-ho, they came singing the Peace Song. How this attack of kindness defeated the evil monster — and how he changed into a wise and good and peaceful leader. How this once evil name, Ta-hra-DA-ho, is now the title of the Onondaga chief who sings the Great Peace Song, the Hi-Hi. And when I finished, my Japanese friend, Kondo, wanted me to tell him these things again, but he did not wish to be an Indian — or a Greek — only himself. He only smiled and spoke of how our wonderful brains could both be a blessing and a curse. He spoke of the evil among the professed followers of Shinto. I told him of how the Tuscaroras were taken into the confederacy of the Great Peace by the Oneidas. Of how the Tuscaroras obtained a reservation through the good will of the Senecas. Of the war between two Christian

138

nations over our land. Of the Tuscaroras ignoring the adoption laws of the Great Peace — refusing to even adopt other Indians, whose ancestors adopted the Tuscaroras. I told my friend that the Iroquois Confederacy may not have read the golden rule but that they had performed it to the Tuscaroras who have read it but not performed it. 'Yes,' my friend said, 'the superior mind of Man!' And so it is." You-swee(t)-dad stood up. "Thraangkie," he said, "I think the golden rule is a good rule, and what I have done unto you is — I have spoken my heart — and that, my friend, is the greatest kindness we can give. If our words bump each other — if we bump our heads on the doorway going into the house — let us not blame the house." You-swee(t)-dad picked up his cane. "I must go now. I must speak with a deacon of your church. He will give me some tobacco. The ghost of my grandmother — my clans-mother — comes in the night, rattling the silverware to awaken me. She wants to fill her pipe again. We, you and I, must talk again. We WILL talk again. It has been a good talk, Thraangkie." Thraangkie and You-swee(t)-dad shook hands.

"Yes," Thraangkie said, "It has been a good talk. I, too, must be on my way but we must not close this open door between us. You may have closed the door to the way of some people who pose as Christians but the way to the Kingdom of Heaven is always open — through Jesus Christ our Lord."

You-swee(t)-dad shuffled off towards our house. I was still laying against the russet tree. I was thinking of how smooth the talk of two people could end even though they did not agree. Just then, You-swee(t)-dad stopped and pulled out a cigarette lighter and lit his pipe with it. Thraangkie called out, "That fire-making tool that you use came from the minds of the people that you just spoke against, You-swee(t)-dad. So did the telephones that your friends on this reservation are beginning to put into their homes."

You-swee(t)-dad started walking again. He did not look back. "And don't forget the clap," he said.

Around three the next afternoon, Thraangkie was standing in Cow Hole up to his waist. It wasn't raining but it was thinking of it. The water was up to my neck almost and Thraangkie was holding my hands and the back of my neck. We helped steady one another as the waves came in. I was saying br-r-r-rrrrr and Thraang-kie was saying, ". . . in the name of the Father — and the Son — and the Holy Ghost." Next thing I knew, I was over and back and under water. When I came up I could hear Edna's powerful alto voice above everybody else's ". . . when Je-sus waaashed — my sins awaaay. . . ." Her voice had a powerful quiver to it and I thought of the way Soot-neh described it in Tuscarora, "gwinnee(t) you-tho(t)-hraw'gause" (you can even hear the fat rattle).

As I waded back to land I happened to look down at my shirt. I could see through the wet pocket. I had forgotten to take out my fuzzy caterpillar. It had been baptized too. Before I went to get dry and change clothes I couldn't help throwing a perfect skip-stone that my eyes saw among the seaweed and the dry, curly shiners. I wheeled the stone out flat, onto that long saggy part between waves. For some reason, what with the Holy Spirit in me now, I expected the stone to set a new record for numbers of skips. Instead, it went regular — maybe eight, nine skips. Then it went into one of them swirly things that skip-stones make in water before they sink.

On my way back, all dried up and ready to skip more skip-stones, I met Oo-nook. He was done leading people into the water. His shoes were going "squeeg, squeeg, squeeg, squeeg." I felt like I needed to tell somebody that I was disappointed because I didn't feel any different now than I did before I was baptized. I told Oo-nook because he was a strong-looking man and maybe he would give me a strong answer. He grinned his regular big grin and made a little nod, "yes." Some of his teeth were missing. "Nobody is MAKING you feel that way," is all he said.

The Feast

I WAS TOLD by the oldtimers on the reservation that the New Year's Feast used to fall more near the end of January or the first part of February, whenever the fifth day of the New Moon fell, and was called the Midwinter Festival. Maybe it was strictly Iroquois custom, but if so, the Tuscaroras latched onto it and dragged it up closer to Christmas. In fact, I went farther than that and celebrated Christmas and New Year's as one whole big ball.

I guess almost everybody did, in a way, because it took just about a week to get ready for The Feast.

I had no more got used to shooting the .22 rifle in a kind of guessing-type shot so's I could hit moving game when under the Christmas tree appeared a long double-barreled 12 gauge. I was a little scared of it, to tell the truth, because I hated loud noises and was barely used to the rifle. The new shotgun wasn't new. In fact, its barrels were shiny from use. Maybe it was third or fourth hand and I think it was made in England. The name Hopkins and Allen was barely readable on one of the barrels.

I had the feeling of needing to try it out more than I was scared of it so I opened the shells and took one and picked the gun up. Man, was IT heavy.

Father was looking at me, grinning, and I says, "Thank you, Santa Claus," to him.

He quit grinning and said, "Since you got two guns now, how about Santa Clausing that .22 rifle to me."

"Not yet," I says, lugging the shotgun into the kitchen, "this one might not even shoot straight."

Brrrrr. The kitchen was cold. I didn't have no shoes on neither. I opened the door and opened the gun and put a shell in the left-hand barrel. There was a mound of snow out by the rose bush so I clicked the safe off and swung up on it. KA-BOOM! The kick spun me sideways and the gunbarrel hit the door. My ears rang and I quick shut the door to kind of keep the sound out. "Sort of loud," was all I could think of to say. Really, it was very, very loud.

"I'll say!" Mother said in the living room.

I went to the window and stuck my tongue on it to make a hole through the ice to see if I had hit the snow hump. Yep, I had. And guess what was under the snow hump? My football. Dr. Jingo, my cousin, had given it to me. He had made it from a cow's bladder when they butchered. Oh well, when Pony dies maybe I'LL make one. If horses have bladders.

"Maybe you can have the .22," I told Father as I put clothes on to go outside with. "But first I have to see if I can balance on my skis with that shotgun. It weighs half a ton. And loud."

"Don't forget to learn your piece for the Christmas program tonight," Mother said.

"Oh that," I says and went outside.

We got to the church early, which was about half an hour later than last Sunday's announcement time for starting. As others got there, all the kids and men helped bring in the bushels and boxes of presents and started dumping them in the front of the church and trying to get the boxes and baskets back to their owners.

If any Indians only went to church once a year, it was on this night. And most everybody brought from twenty to sixty or more presents and pretty soon only tall men could heave the box or basketful of presents to the top of the pile. Mostly, they slid back down. If people brought glassware, we were usually pretty careful about picking up the broken pieces and sneaking them out the back way.

The programs were pretty much the same every year and we

tried to rush through that part to get at the presents. A few tunes like "Silent Night" by everybody kicked it off and I always tried to work my way next to Bee-land to hear him pray. He had a command of the Tuscarora language like an English professor does of English only Bee-land was like a poet too. Like, he prayed poetry. After that, girls and boys of different sizes and shapes got up and said pieces. I'd run up and say something. It didn't matter much what you said because, what with babies crying and everybody making noise, nobody could hear good anyways and they'd clap even if you got scared and cried. Then we'd do the play of the manger scene. One time I was one of the good shepherds and in the back room I tripped over the overflow of presents and broke my ironwood staff. Lucky it was ironwood or it might have broke clean through and as it was, when I went up next to the doll in the crib, it looked like I was giving it a great big question mark for a present. Another time Bedbug's mother sent him to church because she said he needed it and Bedbug said he wanted to be in the Christmas play. Lulu was the director and she was so scared that Bedbug would swear on the stage that she told him just to bring a bushel basketful of hay. That would be his part. When he got to the church he had trouble getting the basket through the doors. Just then Melchy Henry, the visiting minister, came up behind him and said, "What's the matter son?"

Bedbug says, "I brought this hay for Jesus Christ and I can't get the goddam door open."

Next came the giving out of the presents and here's how that was done. Every present had to have the name of who it was for, shouted out, before it could be taken to that person. So two women were appointed to yell until their voices gave out. Then some man referee let in a substitute.

It was my habit as it was most others, too, to give trick presents. Like, I might transfer the label from a tin can of peaches with the pretty pictures of peaches on it to a can of surplus meat and give that away. Once I found a lead brick that weighed seventy pounds and I painted it gold and put a red ribbon on it and gave it to Jumbo. I had to have Ju-gweh carry it up the back stairs, it was so heavy. Or, for instance, I happened to look up as the names were being called out and Goth-hoff (give me) was holding up a toy bugle and yelling, "Lye Man." Lye Man had just

143

been in a car accident and had all his front teeth knocked in. Another time Mars was holding up a pair of four-runner kids' ice skates and yelled out Annie Dink's name. Annie Dink could hardly walk because she weighed, maybe, two-fifty. Naturally, it was late by the time that these mountains of presents were given out, even though there was a steady stream of kids taking arm loads 'round and 'round the church. It was almost impossible to hand anyone their present and mostly you had to throw it at them. I was delivering presents and had both arms pretty well full when Nicknick, who was delivering also, threw a pair of socks, which were to me, at me. He was a fair distance away and the socks flew good, because they had a long blue ribbon tied to the top. When I let them hit me on the head, BONK! I found out a better reason why they flew so good. There were two Brazil nuts in each toe. Another time I was really loaded down and somebody gave me one of my presents in a huge box. Finally I struggled around with this even bigger load and opened the big box. I kept unwrapping and unwrapping and unwrapping and unwrapping until I came to my present. It was five black jelly beans with a note, "Take one a day. With love, Jumbo."

After all the presents were all finally given out, Bee-land would pick his way through all the ribbons and unwrappings and wave his arms around for silence, which never came. He would be trying to make the announcements about The Feast. Everybody knew what they were because Bee-land was nearing a hundred and he had given the same announcements every year for so long that I was never able to find anyone who ever heard of anybody else ever giving The Feast announcements except him. And talk about mumble. On a clear night, if every frog and cricket was dead, you still couldn't make out what Bee-land was trying to say in English. He liked children and he spoke English for the benefit of those that might not know Tuscarora which, of course, for sure, now, they didn't know what he said.

All he was telling about was when The Feast was, what day The Hunt would be, who would be collecting food donations on what road, what game was legal in The Hunt, who all the cooks were, who the captain of the young men in The Hunt contest would be, who the captain of the old men would be, who would make the corn bread, who was going to debate for the young men, who for the old men (which, he always named himself), what the rules were to be on the old men's team, and so on and so on. You know, things like that. It may seem like a lot of important things not to be hearing but everybody knew what had been going on for years and years. Probably why Indians don't have a written language. Barely spoken. At least every word seems dragged out to me.

The next thing I know I'm under the covers and I can feel Bluedog next to me kicking and dreaming and chasing a rabbit. Then, Bump! Bump! It's my father poking the ceiling of the kitchen under my bed, telling me it's morning. I reach out and rattle my shoes as though I'm getting up but instead I just move into a better sleeping position.

"Jaaaaaaa! Hoooooo-Ahhh! HAW! HAW!" That's right too! It's noo-yaw he(t)-gyeah(t) (New Year's time, isn't it). I can't be sleeping! I hear Sir William driving his oxen after food donations.

I jump up so quick it scares Bluedog and he comes out the bottom side dragging all the covers with him. He had been sleeping upside down. However scary it was to Bluedog to be waked up like this, I don't know; but he recovered pretty fast as he was dashing past the hot-air register on his way to someplace less scary. Bacon smell was coming up from downstairs and Bluedog went back and sniffed it.

Outside, the yelling of Sir William to the oxen was getting closer. I hurried up and got dressed for outside to help load the jars of pickled crabapples, sturgeon, serviceberry jam, venison, all kinds of fruit, some in two-quart jars and others, like Northern Spies, in bags from the straw bin in the cellar. There was pig guts (blood sausage), pies and cakes and I don't know what all. In the straw in the big sled were strings of white corn and squash and cheese and a whole bunch of stuff that Sir William had already picked up. Next came my mother who was one of the cooks and Sir William threw her into the straw like a sack of potatoes.

"Ghiih-niih-huh (Turkey Little) got sick so you are the captain of the young men tomorrow," Sir William said. Before I could ask any questions he swished the blacksnake whip, CRASH! and yelled "Yaaaaaaaaah HOO(T)!" I already had my hands over my ears. The oxen leaned forward and the big snowback turned into spray.

"Tomorrow is Hunting Day and I'm the captain of the young men. Tomorrow is Hunting Day and I'm the captain of the young men," was all I could think of as I dug out my short flat skis. The fronts of them weren't even turned up at all, only sandpapered upwards. I made them myself. I found the maple boards for them in the attic. In fact they were still supposed to be up there, bracing the joists. Every so often I looked at the roof but so far it hadn't sagged any. You could only drive square nails into that wood and I had to drill through the skis to screw an old pair of my father's shoes to them. I could get right into my father's shoes with my big me(t)-me(t)s (moccasins) on. [Note: when you see a (t), like in me(t)-me(t), it means you pronounce it like "met" but just as you are pronouncing yourself through the "t," stop. Chop the "t" in half.] My mother got my big me(t)-me(t)s from Jeep-Boy's mother Mea-Neese, who made them from moose neck leather which she chewed (tanned) herself. Plus, on the inside, she lined them with beaver fur with the fur against my feet. My feet were as warm as the beaver was when it had that fur around IT.

Father was by the woodpile making kindling when I went in to get the Hopkins and Allen to see if I could balance it on the skis. I couldn't find either gun. I went back outside. "I can't find my gun," I says.

"That's funny," Father answered. "Maybe boogyman took it."

"HEY!" I yelled. "You did it!"

"That's part of the rules of The Hunt. Anything goes — captain," he called back. I looked around. My skis were gone. I think my face got red. I went into the house to talk it over with Bluedog. He was finishing his dream by the fire. "Hey Blue," I says, "what do we do now?"

One eye came up but that was all. Not even a thump of his tail. Like, "What do you mean WE."

The rules for the contest of The Hunt said that if you had one or more children, THAT put you on the old men's team. Bluedog probably had some kids.

146

The captain of the young men went to bed that night without Bluedog. I had found my skis. They had been tossed from where they lay through the hole that Bluedog used to get under the house. But I never found the 12 gauge or the .22 rifle. One thing, Father had not gotten to my bow and arrows and I had them in bed with me instead of the dog. They didn't give out much heat. I had put out half a dozen snares at different holes along the north ridge but on four of them I had to poke the hole open because of drifts. Once, before I fell asleep, I thought I heard a noise and just to be on the safe side, I opened up a window and yelled out. "Get away from them snares!" It turned out I was just jumpy because I heard my mother and father laugh in the next room.

It wasn't quite light yet when I woke up to the sound of the silverware of my father eating downstairs. I had all my clothes piled near my bed and when I was dressed I was ready to hunt. When I got downstairs Father was going out the door. He had a big horseblanket safety pin pinned to his sleeve and the .22 rifle. One thing he didn't know was that in snooping around for the guns, I had found the box of .22 bullets in his mackinaw and had exchanged them for cracked corn from the chicken house.

"Have a fine day sir," he smiled, reaching for the door.

"Where you gonna hunt?" I asked foolishly.

"Maybe Nova Scotia," he said, closing the door.

What that big safety pin was for was to catch rabbits with. Father'd be glad he had it when he opened the box for bullets. What you do with the safety pin is, first you find a brushpile. If it has a hole going into it, good. If it don't, you make a hole in the snow where it was before it drifted over. Then you take more snow and build, like, a tube to aim the rabbit through. Then you take the big safety pin and safety pin the cuff of your coat sleeve shut and fix the coat so the rabbit will have to run up the sleeve. Then you stomp on the other end of the brushpile. Bingo! Rabbit pie! At least that's the way it's supposed to work. Sometimes a rabbit

147

will come out someplace else. Sometimes there won't even be a
rabbit at home. Or sometimes they just refuse to come out.

I cut two thick slices from the raisin bread Mother made
with my hunting knife. Then I took my bow and arrows into the
cellar and opened up the roaster and cut off a slice of ham. This
was where we kept our food, like an icebox — not cold enough to
freeze things. Half a hog hung from the snowapple tree, froze solid.

On the way to check my snares I passed the frozen half-hog.
A snow drift had built up on the hog side of the big tree. It was
high enough so dogs could jump and bite the meat so I stomped it
down. I had the shoes on the skis more to the back so the front
wouldn't dig in on a downhill run.

Out of six snares I got two rabbits; both from holes that I
had made. Snares work pretty well in snow if you can make the
hole shaped like a keyhole so the rabbit's feet go under the wire
instead of stepping on it and knocking the loop flat or out of the
way. That is, if the loop don't get freezing rain or snow on it and
freeze stiff.

Well, I wasn't skunked anyways but as captain of the young
men's team I was wishing now that I had set more snares, because
drifting snow don't make the best hunting. There might be tracks
in the bushes but they would disappear if they led into a field.

Just then I heard the crack of a .22 rifle. Either my father
had fooled me or it was someone else.

I struck out west, working around behind people's houses
that lived off Upper Mountain Road. Rabbits like to hang around
where people live. I wouldn't have much chance on pheasants with
a bow and arrow.

Just the same, when I saw these pheasant tracks I followed
them into Manny's corn field. I was just wondering what kind of
arrow point would be best to use if I did see a pheasant, when one
stuck its head out of fallen corn stalks. I just grabbed any arrow
and shot fast. It was a close shot, maybe only fifteen paces, but
when the arrow was about halfway the hen pheasant took off.
Some feathers came off its back near its tail but it just went into a
nice glide all the way to the next bushline. Just by habit, I
watched it go. Sometimes shotgunners will wound a bird and it
will catch a few BB's and crumple a couple hundred paces away
or so. And that's just what my pheasant did right now. It started

148

beating its wings to clear the bushline and suddenly somersaulted into the snow. I went to get my arrow. It had a broadhead point on it. I had been saving it in case I saw a deer. I had seven arrows, all told, with three different kinds of blunts. To this day I still don't know what kind of an arrow point is best on pheasants.

I went and got the pheasant and slide-walked back to where I first picked up the pheasant track. You can make good time on skis in the open. The area I was in now looked good for rabbits but there was very little sign. I thought of trying the coat sleeve trick but lots of Indians were using oil stoves now instead of cutting wood for heat. Brushpiles were old and hard and if rabbits were under them you couldn't shake the pile enough to budge them.

I was thinking of stopping and taking a bite of my sandwich when I saw a grey squirrel's nest. Around here, every squirrel's nest has a wild grape vine growing up to it because the squirrels use the stringy bark of the vine to line the nest. Three jerks of the vine and a fat squirrel was acrobating on scant limbs over my head and I got my skis crossed trying to turn around. By the time I turned around the squirrel was zipping along this red oak limb and I took a desperation shot because mine weren't the kind of skis you could kick off and run after squirrels from. The blunt caught the squirrel in the throat and picked it off the limb as though I had planned it that way, which is what we like to say when something tricky happens by luck. I wished Su(t)-neh was here. He is a better shot than me with a bow. Maybe I should throw my guns away.

About noon or better I ran into Duck Soup. He had three rabbits hanging off his belt and something else in a bag and no gun.

"Ferchrissakes," he said, "ROBIN HOOD!"

"What about you," I came back. "What do you do? Scare 'em to death?"

"Give the animals a chance," he went on. "Use a spear next time."

"I will if YOU use a flute and a bag over your head," I said.

"Damn poor pickings," he said, sitting on a log. "I'm going home."

"How about letting me take your bag then," I asked, "I

gotta have one before I get to the Council House tonight. I gotta be our captain tonight. Turkey got sick."

"I know," Duck Soup says. "He's having his tonsils cut off and he likes cornbread the most of anybody. Why don't you come home with me? I ain't got no other way to carry my ferret, 'cept in the bag, and then you can HAVE the bag."

"How come you ain't got more rabbits if you got a ferret?"

"Oh I don't know; not too many holes and lots of them's drifted over. This weather is bad hunting all around. I seen quite a few guys so far and nobody has much."

"I know the holes," I said, getting worried about the lack of game count. "Let's walk along the hill."

"Naw, I gotta get home," Duck Soup said. "Stinky ain't all that good noways. He's too wicked. He gets in a hole and kills the rabbit and it's hell to get him to come out. No matter how much I feed him. I tried taping his nose but then all he does is back up."

"Come on, let's try it anyways," I pleaded. "I'll give him the rest of my ham sandwich."

"Even if you give the rest of the ham sandwich to me, I still gotta go home. I'm wearing Turkey's boots and they're so ploppy I got me a pukey blister on my heel. I'll do well to make it to the Council House."

I was a little disappointed but not enough to carry Duck Soup on my back along the limestone escarpment. Also, Father knew all the holes and he had a way of getting the rabbits out without a ferret. He used a half-inch rubber hose which he poked down the hole. Then he stoked up his pipe with Skwa-hree(t)-Nu(t) leaves and blew it into the hole. Then he used the rabbit-in-the-sleeve trick. But he told me smoking was bad for my lungs.

"O.K.," I said to Duck Soup, "I'll go to your place with you."

"When we get there we can eat," he said, brightening up. "Then you can take my 20 gauge and try back of the muck."

We took off.

As we neared Duck's house I said, "What about your old man? Can you trust him not to run off with our game?"

"Oh hell," he says, "he twisted his ankle yesterday morning

150

on his second trip to the backhouse and it's big as a puffball. He
had the backdoor trots from too much Jenny at the Marlboro.
Ended up using even the back cover of the Sears catalog. If him
and I go to the Council House together, it'll look like the blind
leading the blind."

So after a bowl of corn soup, I took Duck Soup's Iver
Johnson 20-gauge single and about six or seven shells, which was
all he had. I just got past the backhouse when, WHIT-R-R-R-R!
Up flew a hen pheasant. It went straight up off to my left and
flew broadside in front of me. I could see its legs tucked in and its
yellow eye looking at me. It even dumped once as I led it perfectly
in my mind. What a beautiful lead I had on it too, as it flew out of
sight. The captain of the young men hadn't put a shell in his gun
yet.

I threw a shell in and slapped one ski a few times and waited.
Nothing flew up. The pheasant had been a loner. I crossed its
track and headed towards Song's shack. In a short distance I came
to somebody's tracks headed towards the muck. Then I heard a
beagle back of Mocks'. Duck was right, every place was pretty
well hunted by now. I swung out along state ditch and through
the old picnic grove. If Bluedog wasn't on the old men's team he
might have come in handy. He was good on pheasants. Or rabbits.
The 20 gauge felt nice and light and I felt like traveling.

That's about all it amounted to, too. Like going for a walk.
Walk, walk, walk, walk. All the squirrel nests had been shaken and
brushpiles jumped on and cornfields zig-zagged. The sun was on its
last legs. A C-47 was groaning along, close to the clouds with the
sun always reflecting off of some curve of the shiny metal. Every
hunter has felt this feeling. It says, "Waaaall . . . better start back.
You can come back some other day."

It was probably four, four-thirty, so I struck out on a line
for Duck Soup's. I was sailing along on the crusted snow on the long
fields behind Miss Mooses when, Goo-gug! Goo-gug! Goo-gug! A
big shiny cock pheasant rose up out of the crabapples right near
Miss Mooses' house. It was probably ninety yards away and it was
heading for the cattails for the night. That take-off sound always
makes me cock the hammer or flip off the safety latch. A big

horned owl took off, just then, to go to another tree and suddenly the rooster banked and started down in a low glide. I decided to shoot and gave it an extra long lead. POW! The light gun whacked my shoulder and stung my hand and the rooster spun sideways like a helicopter blade into the ground. It was hit but it ran like a turkey for the bushline. And the bushline looked about a mile long and at the end of that was the edge of the cattails. "Good! . . . BYE!" I thought to myself.

I looked at my hand. A drop of blood was forming in that webbing of skin next to my thumb. The latch that you break the chamber open with had jabbed me. Ducky could HAVE THIS gun.

I looked out towards the cattails. A lone figure was coming out of them. It didn't matter who it was. I sucked in a deep deep breath and sent a war whoop echoing into the cattails. Then I pointed to the bushline and started taking long slide steps towards it.

I hadn't gotten down the bushline very far when I heard a single shot near the other end. Good luck, whoever you are, I thought to myself.

As I got closer to the end of the bushline it got thicker and blacker with wild grape vines and thornapple bushes and big stones. And right in there, sitting on a stone, was the guy that got the ringneck. It was Song.

He was never not smiling. He had the kind of teeth you could almost see through. "Gaaaht-NIH! Oot-thraw-hraw'd!" he said. It means something like, "Well I'll be! Something rugged!"

"Chweaaant" (hello) I said, dragging it out like Song spoke the language. He hated to use English.

"Gwehh-nik-gwehh-tha-skihh-nihh(t)" (It seems as though you are well).

He threw the big ringneck to me. I told him it was his. "You'll starve to death at the rate you're going," he said in Tuscarora.

He picked up a bag and dumped it out. Nine pheasants and one rabbit fell out. I looked at his gun. It was a 12-gauge double-barreled Hopkins and Allen. I though I was the owner of the only one in the United States.

"Neeow-weh-hoih(t)" (Thank you big) I said to him. He was

still smiling on the rock when I started taking long easy strides towards Duck Soup's house.

As I passed Saphronie's house it was dark already. She lived way back in the woods all by herself. I saw there was no lamp lit in her house and for a second got the feeling that she might be dead. She had to be close to a hundred; maybe more. Then I remembered that Saphronie was one of the cooks. Also, she loved to pound the white corn into flour for some reason.

Ducky was stretching when I got to his place and I could tell from his eyes that he had taken a nap. "What time is it?" I asked him.

"Oh you got long time yet," he said. "Maybe two, three hours. Sit down and eat."

"Nah," I said, wanting to start collecting the young men's game and worrying about the poor hunting weather — also that Song, all by himself, had whipped Duck and me. "I better get going. I can eat at the Council House."

"WHAT? And waste my time cooking for you?" It was Duck Soup's mother. Her remark was typical in Indian homes.

"Ouch!" I said loudly, "You're twisting my arm off." I took my coat off and Mallard put a huge bowl of venison in turnips, onions, carrots, and white corn in front of me.

"If you want more, help yourself," she said. "If you can't eat what you got, dump the rest back in the pot." There was a kettle steaming away on the stove. Mallard went back to some sewing.

I told Duck Soup what a wallop his gun had. He looked at my hand and laughed. He showed me a scar in the skin webbing of his hand too. I started to tell him about Song.

"If you'd eat instead of talk, you'd have a little more weight to back that shotgun up with," he said. "I'll go to the Count with you. My heel's O.K. now, I drained it. Nobody brings their game in 'til about eight-thirty anyways. You know, make that dramatic entrance."

Duck's father, Ra-boo, had been sleeping on the couch. His ankle didn't look too bad. He had both shoes on, except one wasn't laced up. He coughed and sat up. "Salamander," he said, looking at me. Quite a few Indians had started calling me that. "Did you ever get that 20-gauge loaded?"

I told him about Song giving me the pheasant. Ra-boo called Song a traitor. I said, "No. I think he was just rubbing it in. He had nine other pheasants and a rabbit." Ra-boo smiled and closed his eyes and wiggled back into the couch.

It was after eight when Duck and I approached the Council House. We could hear the sounds of things going on, mixed with yells and laughs, from almost a mile. In the long low shed that used to be for horses and buggies, there was much activity. Three mammoth black iron cornbread kettles were firing up. It was funny how the excitement started so early. I mean, the cornbread loaves wouldn't be going into the water for a couple days yet and here they were starting to heat the water already. Boiling water, then, is just as exciting as Bee-land praying or a little child playing with fire by the kettles or a hen pheasant and an empty shotgun. That's what The Feast was all about.

The area was well lit up from the poppy flames under the pots. Flashes of shiny axe heads flew and chips flew and jokes flew. A couple hundred Indians were in sight and I yelled, "HEY! WHAT'S GOING ON HERE!!"

Somebody yelled back, "We ain't celebratin' Columbus Day!" Probably it was Digger, the grave digger.

If things were in high gear outside, then things were in over-drive in the Council House. Or they were stripping the gears.

The Council House was a jungle of long tables full of food in different stages of readiness. Indians of every sex, size, shape, color, smell, sound, and description were swarming like doctors and nurses; each performing the most important operation ever performed at each table. In the kitchen, where the baking took place, it was 90 degrees in the shade and windows were open.

At one end of the Council House a single table had been placed for The Count. Bee-land was there with his old gold railroad watch, which, regardless if it was off fifteen minutes or so,

one way or the other, IT was the official time. The Count was set
for nine o'clock. The Count was the most single of events, that I
ever heard of, on the reservation, that ever started ON time.
Bee-land's time.

Under the table was straw, and quilts that the Indian women
had made. Many Indians never went home and slept there. They
slept there and kept fires going and turned the drying corn or
stirred the eyes out of the corn in the hardwood ashes or told
ghost stories or brought in more wood or ate or emptied garbage
or made more or kicked dogs out or let them in or chased kids
away from a cake so they could lick off some frosting themselves
or slept or pounded corn or shelled it or fought over the backhouse or did nothing. Indians came and went and much food
came in, prepared, for the workers. Some of it was cooked in the
kitchen and you might see a woman busy with one hand holding
her baby, who was, in turn, busy sucking on a tit, and with her
other hand, the woman might be putting pigs feet into the corn
soup so she could eat. Or some woman might take time out to
HAVE her baby.

Buck-Buck came in with a heavy-looking bag of game and
for a while I wasn't sure which team he was on. His first wife had
died and his second wife was ready to have a baby any minute. He
came up to me, much to my relief and added to my bag which was
near full. Je-dah, meanwhile, was starting to fill his second bag. He
was at the other end of the table. He was the captain of the old
men's team.

Asa came in. He was carrying a terrific fat raccoon. He would
be sixty-six on New Year's Day. Little kids were surprised when
he put the coon in my bag. He had never married.

Lloydy came in. The kids went wild. He was carrying a jack
rabbit and they had never seen one. He had been to Canada where
he was born. He was on the old men's team.

Song came in, and from the crowd of oldtimers, cheers rang
out in Tuscarora. They had been a little worried because the bag
that Je-dah filled up before mine filled up, was smaller. Now I was
worried.

Bee-land held up his watch. "Quarter to nine," he announced in Tuscarora.

There was a buzzing in the crowd and the word went outside. Now people began streaming in to the already full house and those hunters who like to cause last-minute excitement began coming in.

The Flu-Flu boys came in, each with a bag. Duke, Fill, Balls, and Err. They came to my side of the table.

There was a roar at the door and a lot of pushing and shoving as Gare came in dragging a big buck. Its horns were floppy because his .303 had caught it a little high, between the eyes.

Tea-Eye unloaded into one of my bags. He had shot a partridge that was blue-grey and white with some red trimmings. "Hungarian partridge," he said. "The 3-F conservation club in Lewiston released them and this one found my old buckwheat field."

Many of the hunters had gotten only one piece of game. Au-gyen-hu(t)-gyeh-hath oo(t) (Long Summer) came in. He was about fourteen or fifteen. He took his squirrel to the old men's side because he had gotten married and his wife, Ooge, had given him a daughter just before Christmas.

"One minute to go," Bee-land announced. Very little English was now being spoken. This was strictly an Indian thing and the Tuscarora language flowed in the buzzing crowd. The game was all in bags now and Bee-land yelled, "Oo-nih!" (now).

I reached into a bag and laid a squirrel on the table. Its guts were hanging out. "Ehh-jeeh" (one) I said.

Je-dah touched the deer and said, "Ehh-jeeh." Everybody laughed at the difference between the squirrel and the deer.

And so it went, with the game piling up at each end of the table. A number called at one end, and the echo of it at the other.

"Naag-deeh" (two).
"Naag-deeh."

"Uhh-siih" (three).
"Uhh-siih."

"Hih-duhhk" (four).
"Hih-duhhk."

"Weeesk" (five).
"Weeesk."

"Ooo-h'yuk" (six).
"Ooo-h'yuk." As Je-dah dropped the rabbit to the table, it
banged kind of hard and we both realized, when the crowd
laughed, that this would be fuel for The Debate.

"Jo(t)-nuhhk" (seven).
"Jo(t)-nuhhk."

"Naag-khri(t)" (eight).
"Naag-khri(t)."

"Neeh-h(r)eh" (nine) (to pronounce this you roll the *r*).
"Neeh-h(r)eh."

"Whuth-hehh" (ten) (*u* pronounced as in *us*).
"Whuth-hehh."

"Ehh-jess-skuh-huh(t)" (eleven) (one-teen).
Echo.

On went The Count with much comment from the crowd at
pieces of game, especially towards provoking something to be used
in The Debate. "That looks like the squirrel that lived in Bee-land's
attic" or "That should only be counted as a quarter of a point because three-fourths of it is shot away" or, when the Hungarian
partridge came out, "Whose guinea hen is that?"
On The Count went. "Naag-dees-skuh-huh(t)" (twelve or
two-teen); "uhh-siihs-skuh-huh(t)" (thirteen); "hih-duhhk-skuh-
huh(t)" (fourteen), and so on.
The Count hit twenty, "Naa-wuth-hehhh" (two times ten).
Then thirty. "Uhh-siih-de wuth-hehhh" (three times ten).
Then forty. "Hih-duhhk-de wuth-hehhh."
The pile of game at each end of the table would soon grow

158

bigger than the table would hold. But each year it was the same way. And never would it change. The sight of such a pile of game, ready to overflow a table, was good for the hunter's heart. It could be pictured again when game might have a bad year and hope would flow through his veins.

Forty-one. "Hih-duhhk-de wuth-hehhh-ehh-jeeh."

Now two more small tables were called for. The small tables were placed next to each end of the long table. And The Count went on. It came to fifty. "Weeesk-de wuth-hehhh."

Then sixty. "Ooo-h'yuk-de wuth-hehhh."

Then seventy. "Jo(t)-nuhhk-de wuth-hehhh."

Then eighty. "Naag-khri(t)-de wuth-hehhh."

At this point, I could only see Je-dah's head over the pile of game of the old men's team. And that's all he could see of me. I was getting worried because it felt to me that I was about out of game. Maybe two or three things was all I had left. Once before, when I was at about the count of sixty-five, with two or more pieces of game left, I thought I was finished. But my team was only teasing me and they pushed out this other bag which, now, was about gone. I looked at my team and they were worried too. They didn't have any more game hidden on me.

Once before, too, when I was feeling around in the bag that I recognized as the one I got from Duck Soup, I felt a bird and started to pull it out. I looked down and saw that it was a crow. Ra-boo had snuck it into the bag while Duck Soup napped. I had a hard time keeping track of this illegal bird. Right now I thought of using it as a final count, just for laughs, but I was wanting to win. I was getting desperate.

At eighty-one, I put a rabbit on the pile. When Je-dah said, "Naag-khri(t)-de wuth-hehhh-ehh-jeeh," I put the same rabbit back into the bag.

Deer-eyes, who was about seven, but small too, saw me do that. He had brought in one rabbit, which he had trapped, and to Deer-eyes, all his hopes were riding on that one rabbit. It might as well have been a rhinoceros. It was for those members of my team, with feelings like Deer-eyes, that I was worried. I should have gave Deer-eyes more credit. He went under the table.

159

When I said, "Eighty-two," there was a pause at Je-dah's end of the table. Deer-eyes had caught Je-dah doing the same thing that I was doing.

Rather than wait for Deer-eyes to expose him, Je-dah said, "Oo-nih, wa-guhh-nook-ni(t)" (Now I have run out).

There was a big roar at my end of the table. When it died down, I reached into my bag and pulled out a Blackduck and yelled, "Guy-yus-steee!" (one hundred) as much as to say, "We've won!"

Some members of the old men's team had been told, by Ra-boo, about the crow; to watch for it. They came storming over, crying "FOUL!" and before I could somehow get rid of the bag with the crow in it, they found it. Whether they thought the duck was the crow or not didn't matter. Duke had found the duck, frozen to ice by its breast feathers, in the swamp back of Old Shrinkable's. It was the only black duck I had ever seen at The Count.

"SU(T)-UH!" (look!) Bee-land cried, pointing to the crow which was now being displayed, "AW(T)-AW(T)!" (crow!).

Much laughing and noise was going on. My face was red as a beet. Then Mick Mick hollered at the other end of the table. "SU(T)-UH!) (look!), he yelled, picking a bag off the floor and jumping right up on the table. "H(R)OOOS-S'GWAAH-NI(T)!" He tipped the bag upside down and a little dead mouse fell into the old men's pile of game. The laughing and hollering signified the end of The Hunt and the end of The Count for that year but The Debate, which was really supposed to decide the winning team, would be held next year, which was a few days away. Bark rattles and willow drums and turtle rattles came out from nowhere and amid dancing and whooping, Bee-land chanted some poetry to thank The-Great-Spirit. The game and the tables and the dancers and drummers moved out of the Council House to the fires by the monstrous kettles. Here the game would be cleaned and bagged and hung in the cold night air; ready for pot pie.

Back in the Council House, Saphronie had one of the oo-hruh-nehs. Here I can only describe the oo-hruh-neh. It looks like a long wooden dumbbell, in a way, and it is about five foot tall. It's made from a four- or five-inch seasoned elm or maple log with the ends tapering slightly. The middle, which is the handle section,

160

BLOWER MASK

(CURES BY BLOWING ASHES)

is about one and three quarters inches in diameter. It is used to pound the white corn into coarse flour. Saphronie was pounding the white corn that was dry enough to pound. She was trying to show the younger children how to pound the corn without having it fly out of the oot-de-guh-neh. The oot-de-guh-neh is made from a twenty-four to twenty-eight inch section of big seasoned buttonwood. One end of the section is hollowed out by fire until a nice deep bowl is formed. This is what the corn is pounded in. It is quite a trick to pour some corn into the oot-de-guh-neh and keep some of it from flying out with the pounding hits until the kernels began to break up.

The cornbread makers were Big Man, Digger, Short Shot, Jumbo, Klark, Beulah Land, and Owen Green. And they were watching and making sure that only the best hardwood ashes were being used to separate the black eyes out of the kernels and that the corn had swollen to the right size and that the drying corn had dried to the right dryness and that the corn was not pounded too fine.

The cornbread that was being made to feed the food preparers was being made in the kitchen. Digger was mixing the big, almost cooked, red kidney beans into the rough flour. Klark was wetting this mixture and forming the loaves. They were about ten inches in diameter and looked like a pancake would if it rose five or six times what it was supposed to. Or if you cut a loaf square down the middle, the cut part would have the shape of a flattened football. Beulah Land was slipping the raw loaves into a kettle of boiling water on the stove and Owen Green was keeping track of which loaves were cooked or half cooked or raw. All of the cooks switched around at times and all of them got a chance to test the loaves to make sure if they were cooked and all of them got to eat quite a bit of cornbread and all of their bellies showed it.

Goods that needed to be kept from spoiling were hanging from trees and rafters in the carriage shed. The food was placed in big squares of qud-deh-hoi(t) (government alloted cotton big) with the corners tied at the top to form socks.

Mother was one of the pie makers and she was seasoning the pots of elderberries and sour cherries and strawberries and pump-

kins and squash and thumbleberries and whatever else was on the
stoves. She used sugar and maple syrup and molasses and cinnamon
and nutmeg and ginger and cloves and oh I don't know what all.
Others were peeling Greenings and Russets and others were lining
deep pans with pie dough.

Vernon Jack was starting to decorate the cakes and he was
using a hot water bottle with the syringes that come on it.

As fast as any donations of pig guts came in they were pretty
much fought over among all the food preparers. The large guts and
the stomach (sausage) was filled with seasoned blood and suet
and the little guts were just braided and all was cooked about the
way the cornbread was.

As the day of The Feast arrived the ovens went into full
production of the deep wild game pot pies. By the time the last
fire went out, the old hewn rafters of the Council House would
have soaked up enough Feast smell to last about a year.

Now when the day of The Feast arrives and it's time to get
out of bed, do the Indians jump up and start eating up The Feast?
NO. Do they jump up? YES. They jump up because not only is it
the day of The Feast, it is also New Year's Day too. In every home
on the reservation, somebody has something ready like apples, or
cookies, or carrots, or maple sugar candy, or walnuts, or pears;
things like that. Families dash about from house to house yelling
"Noo YAAAAA'AH!" Some are on foot, some in cars, some might
hook a couple horses to a big sled and three or four families
might jump aboard. It's best to yell as loud as you can so whoever
is in the house can come to the door with the goodies, otherwise
you might lose time and not finish the whole reservation. Also,
don't forget, when you come to the house of the clan of your
father, which in my case is HRAU(T)-GWEEESE (Turtle), you
holler, "Noo YAAAAAAH-OO'WEE H(R)eh!" Here, you will get
a gingerbread doll. Oo'wee-h(r)eh means doll. Noo-yaaaaaah, I
think, comes from the English words New Year. So The Feast
really lasts for two years and when the new one comes, you gotta
let people know about it, plus you get paid for yelling.

So on the morning of The Feast, the whole reservation is
noisy from the Noo-yaw'ers. Sometimes, in a car or sled, the driver

never really stops and the Noo-yaw'ers run crosslots between houses. And quite often, several from the same bunch will be hollering, "One for the driver! One for the driver!" And even more often, the driver never sees the cooky, or whatever. Nobody is fooling nobody, though, because everybody has been Noo-yawing at some time or other.

Dogs, too, get in on the act and will chase the kids and bark and hope the kids will fall in the snow and spill their eatables all over. This might even happen at a dogless house, though dogless houses are extremely rare on the reservation.

If you're Noo-yawing and you ain't done with the whole reservation by noon, forget it. Because everybody will be at the Council House or on their way to it.

The Feast itself is just plain eating. If you get full while you're eating, and you see something better that you didn't get a taste of yet, don't think you can go outside and run around the Council House a few times, to settle your food, and then come back in and eat more. Eat more right away, because others are jammed at the door waiting for the next serving.

If you're late, though, don't worry. The stories and jokes that you will hear while you're waiting in line will make the time go fast and before you know it it'll be dark. Servings go on until everyone that wants to eat, eats.

If you happen to get into the first serving and you're a fast eater and you get done too soon and don't know what to do, don't worry. There's always a sporting event planned for such people as you. Whatever you do, don't go to bed yet. The main attraction is still coming.

Outside it's pitch dark but in the Council House it's not. The gas lamps have been fueled and pumped up and hooked back up with the long hook-back-upper pole and they are sizzling and sputtering away. The tables have been folded and put away and the food divided up by everybody and the folding chairs in place. More chairs have been borrowed from the church and the mission. Every chair has somebody sitting on it and every standing space against the wall has somebody standing on it and the two long balconies on each side of the long building are so full of people that they spill on down the stairs going up to them. Maybe it's around eight o'clock. The Debate is about to begin.

Each debater speaks three times.

I-ee-sog is the spokesman for the young men and Bee-land for the old men. I-ee-sog gets up first. He looks pretty much like the Indian on the Indian head nickle. He is wearing a red sweat shirt under his tattle-tale grey white Sunday-go-meeting shirt and he has the white sleeves rolled up. This is about the way he dresses for both indoors and outdoors, except outside, he might roll the sleeves down if it's extra cold. His black baggy pants had perfectly matching oval pin-stripe patches on each knee and he had army-colored suspenders holding them up. It looked like he had tried to put shoe polish on his work shoes and had said, "Oh to heck with it." He was never married. Both speakers were masters at the Tuscarora language.

I-ee-sog stood and looked slowly about the crowd, nodding his head in a lazy manner. "I want to thank all you witnesses," he said, "for showing up at The Count. And as you saw, with your own naked eyes, we simply out-hunted, and therefore out-pointed the old men again. I think we young men should take pity on them and during the summer we should take them by the hand and lead them out of their houses and take them to where the game lives and say, 'THIS-IS-A-HUNTING GROUND!' and actually take our finger and POINT it out to them: 'THIS-IS-A-SQUIRREL.' Maybe that's all we should tell them for this summer, lest they forget by Hunting Day." There was great laughter. "LET'S HONOR THE WINNERS!" he shouted. "LET'S CLAP ALL NIGHT FOR THEM!" He let out a war whoop and danced around with his hands clasped and shaking above his head while the young people clapped and whooped. He sat down but the noise went on for about ten minutes.

Bee-land stood up. He shuffled up to the front with his hands clasped behind his back. He had on his oldest son's dark suit which hung open because there were no buttons on the coat of it. It fit him pretty well except he had had to roll the cuffs of the pants up. The suit was a bit wrinkled and the coat pockets were sagged out of shape from him keeping his hands jammed down in them so much. The bottom part of the pant legs were smooth because he wore his knee boots underneath. He had made

165

them from leaky hip boots. Under the coat he wore his undershirt. A long red bandana was rolled and snugged up around his neck with a hollow bone carving of a beaver. His hair was halfway between long and short and the bottom half of it, from the line where his hat had been, swung outward in jabby spikes. There was a few white hairs here and there. One of his eyes was lower than the other which he kept squinted shut all the time. The other was barely open. His mouth was slanted the opposite from his eyes, probably from trying to push the low eye up. He was chewing tobacco at high speed until he adjusted his pockets, at which time he spit it out. He pulled one hand out of one pocket and blew his nose and moved his feet over about three inches to make sure he was in the middle of the room. Then he cleared his throat in a long clear.

"We have had a wonderful Feast," he said, clearing his throat again. "It is a fact that nature has provided us with that Feast." He let that sink in. "We have the sky and the trees — the sun, the northern lights, the graceful arc of the swallow — we have snowflakes." Here he took out a rag and wiped his bottom eye. "We have music — swarming bees — geese — the singing brook — the laughter of the loon. And then, my dear brothers and sisters — we have these other things — wind funnels or whirling dervishes — strange monster pictures in the clouds." As he took his hand out of his pocket and pointed his pointer finger roughly at a forty-five degree angle in front of him, he said, "And tonight! You have witnessed THE-MOST-PHENOMENAL FREAK THAT NATURE HAS EVER DARED PRODUCE!" and he dropped his finger at I-ee-sog. "HERE is a man born with TWO TONGUES!" There was thunderous laughter and applause and war whoops from the old folks. "And what's more," he said, striking his finger out in different directions on each syllable, "I'm gonna let you see him again with your own naked eyes." There was more laughter. Beeland clasped his hands behind his back. "But first I must tell you a story." He looked at the gaslights as though he was trying to remember something. "Yes," he said, looking back down, "the middle of August — about the fifteenth — I had just pulled out that rotten fence post at the end of my driveway. I was eating my lunch and I happened to look out the window and you'll NEVER guess what I saw." He stood there shaking his head. "I saw the

166

freak of nature setting a snare in the post hole." The old folks
went wild again. When they quieted down he went on. "Now I
have seen stones shaped like animals and different species of trees
grown entwined and drinking each other's sap but — oh —" Here
he put a hand over his brow and looked down and shook his head
from side to side. "— so I went to where the pride and joy of the
young men's team was, and I asked him matter of factly, 'what are
you doing?' And he answered rather sharply, 'It's mine! *I* found
this hole! And I'm gonna get that fox too!' " Again, the old folks
went wild. "I might have believed him if he had mentioned a crow.
At least a crow might have fit in there. And speaking of crow, let's
give a big hand for that illegal crow that nullified any pieces of
legal game that the young men's team might have counted." The
old folks made as much noise as they could, and that was plenty.
Bee-land started for his seat. About halfway he stopped. "I guess
THAT settles THAT," he said, and went and sat down. The old
demonstrated their approval with roaring laughter and war whoops
and hand clapping. The women with children squealed with delight and some stomped their feet.

Now it was time for round two of The Debate. I-ee-sog got
up and reached down and pulled each pant leg up until his bare
legs showed at the bottom. In this position, he high-stepped to the
front and as he went, he made like a manure pile was getting
deeper. The whole crowd laughed. "When I was in the war," he
said, "we had gas masks and I wish I had brought back enough for
everybody here tonight." He held his nose with one hand, for a
moment, then with his tongue, he made a noise to mock Bee-land
blowing his nose and then snapped the imaginary snot into the
imaginary pile of manure. There was more laughter and I-ee-sog
made quick motions like brushing dust off his hands, then struck
a pose with his head up high. "I'm not the best doctor," he said,
"but I can EASILY tell you what happens to a person who eats
mice. They pick up a disease called, 'born loser,' and for some
reason, they can't see or hear anything after that." I-ee-sog was a
medicine man. "But the worst thing about the born loser disease
is that the mouse later yaps all the time, 'YAP yap yap YAP yap
yap' and a terrible odor of manure can be smelled for miles."

I-ee-sog put one hand aside of his mouth, and lowered his voice as though telling a secret. "I don't care to talk about sick people or use names," he said, straightening up, "but one day I was way out by the stone quarry gathering medicine when I smelled the smell of a born loser. It came from the other end of the reservation and this smell got stronger, if you can imagine that. Finally, I passed out. When I woke up the sun was near the west and this person was standing down wind from me. His initials were Bee-land and he had the born loser disease something fierce. He begged me to help him but it was too late. He had eaten too many mice. He was tired-looking, too, so I asked him why and he said that he had been chasing J.P. Morgan's white leghorns with a heavy can of brown shoe polish. Now any fool knows you just can NOT make pheasants out of white leghorns. Just the same he kept on begging me to help him so I at least made him feel better. I told him that bad breath was better than no breath at all." The young folks laughed and cheered. "And now, dear people, what do you think has happened. The old men's team went and chose this sick person to be their spokesman. And what does he DO? He brings a mouse to The Count. OH HE'S TRICKY. But I knew he was sick so I watched him. AS SOON AS HE SAW that his team had run out of OBJECTS, and I use THAT word loosely, why he rushed to our side of the table and I SAW him pull a crow out of his pants and you all saw him TRY TO DISCREDIT THE WINNING TEAM! To the one or two honest hunters on the old men's team, I offer my sympathy. But it's up to you two men, wherever you are, to try to stop losing, year after year. I say it's HOPELESS — because it looks as though your team has become ADDICTED — to EATING MICE." I-ee-sog went to his seat to the cheers and whoops of the young people. Everyone was enjoying themselves and many women cheered both speakers. Just before I-ee-sog sat down, he again held his clasped hands aloft and gyrated to show victory.

Bee-land jumped up and pointed at I-ee-sog. "Did you see that swimming stroke?" he shouted. "That is the swimming stroke of a drowning man — just before he sinks out of sight. That signifies the desperation," Bee-land went on, as he walked to the front, "— of the young hunters, if indeed they hunted at all. And I know that it did not sit well with anyone here tonight to hear the words

168

born loser." Here Bee-land smoothed out his voice and gestured
far off. "But just as in a dreeeeam — there is NO! SUCH! THING!!
— Just as sure as you are born, The-Great-Spirit would NOT permit
ANYONE to be BORN a loser — BUT — there ARE occasionally
born — HARD losers." At that point, when he said "HARD," he
drew laughter by raising his arm up and out and jabbing his pointer
finger down towards I-ee-sog. With his other hand he pretended to
sort of shield the pointing hand. Then he folded his arms and
smiled. "Young people," he said in a fatherly voice, "if your
spokesman has caused you to have a drowning feeling, don't let it
make you angry. Try to take it like grown men. Try not to be
HARD losers. If you feel like crying — go right ahead — there's
nothing to be ashamed of in crying — you might even feel better
afterwards. You are young yet. I cannot really blame you for
going to the Oppenhein Zoo with those wire cutters and obtaining
two pheasants and a guinea hen — you will learn where reservation
boundary is; where you can shoot legal game — and when you
learn to shoot — it won't be necessary to walk the roads at all
hours of the night, picking up game flattened by automobiles —
and in conclusion, dear babies, remember — one — have a good
cry — and, two — if your spokesman hurt you and you feel as
though you WERE born a loser, always remember, there's a step
lower than that — to be a HARD loser — and THAT — is pitiful."
Bee-land swayed his head sadly. "—JUUUUUUST PITIFUL!!"
he said loudly. As he went to his seat, he pretended to be wiping
his eyes in sorrow for the losing young men's team. He received a
standing ovation for his performance.

Round two of The Debate was over. Some Indians had come
from some other reservation to sing an Indian song of thanks. The
Tuscaroras had forgotten the songs of their ancestors. In order
that the visiting singers might get back home at a decent time, it
was decided to do the song and dance at this time rather than
wait until the full debate was finished. (As it turned out, they
stayed late anyways.)
Jay Claws and Snake Powless went up front and very slowly
began walking around in a circle. Already up there, and sitting on
short, fat, sawed-off legs were Old Snapping Turtle and Nicodemus

Hawk. Old Snapping Turtle had on buckskin leggins and a light blue breech clout. His shirt was purple and over that he wore a buckskin vest with about twenty white weasel tails decorating it. He had a very skinny face and long grey hair which was not braided but wrapped with strips of weasel fur. His eyes were sunken and his eyelids were always open to bare slits. He had a snapping turtle rattle with the neck and head stretched and dried for the handle. Every five minutes or so he struck it, once, against the palm of his right hand.

Nicodemus Hawk had on a black shirt with a bib that ended at his belt in three sharp points. The bib was solid white with porcupine quills. Long white horse-tails hair hung in three bunches at the bottom. His pants were made of cotton big, dyed purple by wild grape skins.

170

Claws and Snake wore red shirts and dark leggins. Long bunches of buckskin thong hung from pink shell buttons from their tan breech clouts and from a line sewn across their backs. They wore narrow buckskin sweatbands and Nicodemus wore a wide one because he was fat and sweated more. By this time, Snapping Turtle was hitting his palm with the rattle about every two minutes.

All four Indians at the front of the Council House had beaded flower and vine designs around their pant cuffs and up the side and on their moccasins.

Snapping Turtle's bottom jaw always hung open and you could see a few long yellow teeth. His bottom lip hung loose and quivered a little. He had the tempo picked up now and all of a sudden a low gravely wail came out of his lips. It was a jaggedy sound and sort of got to your spine. Nicodemus had a big tom-tom in front of him called a water drum. There was water inside of it. Without warning, the big drum and his voice came thundering into Snapper's beat while the dancer's feet came on like drums too. Soot-neh was up in the balcony and he let out a terrific war whoop. He had lungs like a buffalo.

The left or right shoulder of each dancer was slowly dipping and rising in smooth arcs as their whole bodies turned in full or half circles, then reversed. At the same time the pounding feet were doing movements that were almost a blur while still taking

the dancers in that big circle that they had traveled in such a slow walk.

Each dancer had a separate style all his own and Claws had a way of turning his feet in little jerks which suggested the reversing shuffle of the women's dance. He worked it right into the style he had of placing each down-coming foot at erratic spots on the floor. Snake, on the other hand, had a great variety of little steps and movements that he worked in at different times. He was Onondaga and probably the best dancer I have ever seen. I had seen him dance before at The Condolence when my father was raised as Sachem Chief of the Turtle Clan. Snake's name may have come from a spectacular step that he did which is hard to describe. On the down step, his heel hit the floor and sprang back up in a twisting motion as though it had exploded off the floor. It was as though he had killed a snake by twisting his heel on it, then, to avoid its poisonous strike, he had jerked the foot away. On that up-spring, he could snap that foot to any wild place in the air; even while his shoulder might be in a low crouch. Every once in a while they gave a yell.

Suddenly Old Snapping Turtle gave a shriek and Hawk dribbled the drum into the sound that a partridge makes when IT drums. Then Snapper yelled, "JAWWWW!" and the dance of thanks was over. I think the Great Spirit liked it.

I-ee-sog had changed his clothes during the dancing. He now wore cotton big leggins. They were about the color of a Vick's vaporub jar if you held it up to bright sunlight. Discs of double conch shells hung all over the bottom of the leg pants and they gave off the sound of sleigh bells when he walked. His breech clout was a light wine color and it was decorated the same as his moccasins: white beaded flowers and snipes. Other than that, all he wore was a white doeskin vest and a choker on his neck. The vest, along all visible edges of it, including the arm holes, had a design of a small winding vine of purple beads with fern-like leaves of the same color. Here and there along the vines were small lavender beaded flowers. All the choker was, was a huge pink shell disc with two bear claws in the middle. He was not fat and when he moved his arms, the thin muscles moved like water and when he spoke, his stomach did the same thing.

"What I have done here tonight," I-ee-sog said soberly, "is

deliberately refrain from pointing out the most glaring defect of
the — er — er — glimmer of humanity — that the old men's team
has chosen as their spokesman. The reason is — it has become
evident all by itself. It was beginning to become evident a few
minutes ago when he began speaking to his youth as soon as he
realized that he was in his second childhood." The young folks,
knowing that this was the last round of The Debate, put on an
extra loud display. "And as all you witnesses saw this man walk up
here and talk to himself, you saw that he was having great difficulty walking — no! — he is not getting old. It's his toes that are
bothering him. Now, nobody else in this Council House walks
with such difficulty, and for a very good reason. Nobody else
liiiies like he does." As I-ee-sog stretched the word "lies" out, he
pushed his head forward and opened his eyes as wide as he could
to emphasize how unbelievable it was. Then he paused for a
moment and grinned. "All of us have caught fish and added an
inch or two to its size after we've eaten the evidence, but NO-
BODY says 'I caught one THIS big!' " As I-ee-sog said "this big,"
he stretched up on his toes and, grimacing painfully with his face,
he leaned sideways and strugglingly reached one hand as high
into the air as he could. Then he clenched his teeth and made
another greater-looking effort. And amid screams of laughter, he
appeared to fall down and clutch his feet and writhe with unbear-
able pain. EVERYBODY had to laugh at his antics. I-ee-sog got up
with mock difficulty and hobbled comically a few steps. "See!" he
said. "See what can happen from stretching the truth? There is the
evidence, then, that fish stories are very very poor excuses, especially when the old men's team has already lost, to use to try to
cover the shame that they have heaped upon themselves. And this
is what was most shameful of all. Not only did they not have
enough pieces of game to win, they did not even HUNT. Ordinari-
ily, after The Count, the old men sit around and watch the young
men clean the game. But did you notice how they rushed out this
time. And they began what they called 'gutting' as far from the
fire as they could, so that we couldn't see that half of their rabbits
were nothing but skins, filled with sawdust. And you can still see
the sawdust out there, where they tried to kick it around and hide
it." There would be hoots and yells from the young folks and
some boos from the old folks every time I-ee-sog made a point.

Sometimes he stopped and sometimes he went right on talking. "But that's not all. Nine of them pheasants that were counted out on the old men's table were not hunted at all. They were POISONED. I'll give you a hint as to who did this. His wife had a baby around Christmas-time. While his wife was having that baby, this SO-CALLED hunter had to do the cooking for the family. His corn soup was SO BAD that the family had to throw it out and nine pheasants died eating it, where the corn soup landed. But with nine poisoned pheasants and WHO KNOWS how many sawdust-filled rabbits, PLUS a mouse and a crow — it's no wonder they feel so much shame. And, SHAME ON THEM TOO. They deserve it. They deserve it because, first of all the young men's team still had at least two full bags of game when the old men's team captain had only empty bags. THAT, first of all, is the deciding fact." I-ee-sog held up one finger. "Second," he held up two fingers, "crows and mice are ILLEGAL — AND ALWAYS HAVE BEEN!" I-ee-sog swung his arm slowly around so everyone could count the two fingers. "That means of course, that the young men's team need only have brought one single count of game to The Count because illegal game causes a forfeit of ALL their game. And THIRD," he held up three fingers, "the old men hunted on the WRONG day. They tried to HOG THE HUNTING GROUNDS on the day BEFORE The Hunt. But STILL they lost. THEY CHEATED!!" he roared. As he said "THEY," he pointed towards the center seats where most of the older Indians were sitting. This naturally caused this section to become sober-faced. "And SEE how GUILTY THEY LOOK! It must be a sad feeling to lose that way. But I am HAPPY to be proclaiming the VICTORY for the young men's team." This caused the younger folks, many who were in the balconies, to cheer. "And SEE the happiness of victory!!" he said, pointing to the balconies. "and it is a SWEET VICTORY — to hunt over already hunted hunting grounds and THEN — to defeat the old men by HEAVY COUNT!!" The young people were still cheering. Over the sound of the cheers, I-ee-sog shouted, "LET THE WINNERS SHOW THE HAPPINESS OF WINNING!" While I-ee-sog had changed clothing, he had instructed members of the young men's team as to what he would say and what he would do. So at this moment, various members of the young men's team suddenly produced

174

bark rattles and tom-toms and with Big Egg leading the beat,
I-ee-sog went into a victory dance. His feet were a blur as he
doubled, with his feet, the beat that Big Egg was laying down.
I-ee-sog's upper body twisted and gestured in thankful motions.
He was one of the best of dancers and the impressive finish to his
part of The Debate was viewed with enjoyment by all. He had
given one more instruction to be passed around to all the young
people and as soon as a loud war whoop signified the end of the
dance, all of the young folks pretended to leave the Council House.
"WAIT!" I-ee-sog pretended to beg. "THERE'S A CLOWN ACT
FOLLOWING TO HELP CELEBRATE OUR VICTORY!" Even
the old folks clapped as I-ee-sog received a standing ovation. More
like a jumping ovation from the young men's team. Little Deer-
eyes was jumping the highest.

When the Council House settled back down again, everyone
looked forward to Bee-land's final rebuttal because he was never
to be headed. I-ee-sog was almost to his seat. Bee-land spoke as he
started from his seat. "When the spokesman for the young men's
team was doing what he called a victory dance, what he was doing
was the ST. VITUS DANCE! No wonder the kids got scared and
began running for their mothers. *I* even started looking for a
NET!" Now it was the old folks' turn to clap and yell and stomp
their feet. "When I was between the ages of two and four, I believed everyone and everything. HERE," he raised both hands to
both balconies, "we have young MEN believing what I believed
when I was TWO! — ANYONE AND ANYTHING! Right now,
we must TRY to be patient with them. Perhaps one day they will
awaken — when they are older — and HOUSE BROKEN — washed
a few diapers — THEN there might be a CHANCE — and they may
discover the DIFFERENCE between dreaming — and what is real.
Let me illustrate," Bee-land shook his head. "Right in the
MIDDLE — of my fifty-acre field — on HUNTING DAY — a
young man was seen — carefully spreading a two-foot loop of his
mother's clothesline on the snow — and tying the other end to his
waist — and after shivering for two hours, he decided not to WAIT
for a rabbit to snare itself. I say RABBIT because of the clever
thing that he did next. He tied a carrot from a string on a pole —

175

but THEN — he was seen later, trying to lure my WHITE CAT to
that clothesline — with a CARROT on a string." Bee-land shook
his head while his team laughed with glee. Then he went on. "At
about the same time this was happening — over on the other side
of the reservation, Ra-boo, who had decided it was suicide to be
outside while the young men were, er, hunting — looked out his
window and saw a young man looking up and running zig-zagged
through his field. 'I could barely believe my eyes!' Ra-boo said.
'He was chasing a flying seagull — WITH A BUTTERFLY NET!!' "
As the older people noised their approval, most of the young folks,
realizing that The Debate would soon be over for another year,
began laughing too. Bee-land was smiling his crooked smile. "Now
you might be thinking," he said, "at this time — that these are
RARE and ISOLATED cases — but THAT'S NOT SO!! As the
pot pie was being prepared in the kitchen — and the cooks were
relating their family ups and downs — two mothers were talking.
'I sometimes wonder what my son is going to become' one mother
said. 'Most likely an inventor. He's always daydreaming. He can't
even remember to empty the slop pail,' she says. 'What I mean is,
like on Hunting Day — he was out almost all day — and when he
came back — he wasn't hurrying at all. I HAD to rush up to him
and say, HERE, son, you forgot your gun!' " From the laughing
crowd, someone in the balcony yelled, "Was it YOUR son?" There
was more laughter. "And the other mother said," Bee-land went
on, calmly, " 'Gee that's too bad. I'm not worried about MY son.
HE'S going to be alright. Because he's healthy. He ALWAYS takes
a nap at noon. Before noon, on Hunting Day I happen to notice
that he had forgotten his teddy bear so I sent his sister out with it.
And guess what? She came back and told me that MY son was
aiming at a squirrel — but when sister reminded him it was time
for his nap, why, he just curled right up with his teddy bear and
went right to sleep.' " As Bee-land talked, he mimicked some of
the action of his stories and the crowd loved it. "Now you can see
why most of us stayed in our cellars on Hunting Day. It wasn't
SAFE to be out with these young men afield. Of course, the BEST
hunting spots were the safest and I KNEW that only members of
OUR team knew these places, and as you saw, at The Count, the
old men brought in LEGAL, full-grown game, and everyone SAW,
that these fine specimens of game were all killed by ONE perfectly

placed shot, whereas, the young men's captain would pull out half a squirrel or rabbit, and some young man would remark, 'good shot — blew the whole hind end off that one.' Then out of another bag, the young men's captain would pull out and COUNT the OTHER HALF of that same animal." Here Bee-land mimicked the voice of a small child, " 'Good shot! Blew the head right off.' " He paused and acknowledged the laughter. "As I was saying — most of us remained in our cellars KNOWING that it would only take a few of our team members to defeat the young men. It was DANGEROUS to go outside. But I took a chance anyways, think-ing that if I was careful, I could water my horses. So I cracked the door open and peeked outside to make sure first — and WHAT did I see!! A young man crawling on his belly. He was SNEAKING UP ON A BIG STONE! The stone in NO WAY resembled any known bird or animal. So I watched — FASCINATED by the young man's stalking ability. He would CRAWL — head down, for three or four feet — then stand up quickly to see if the stone had run away yet. Now I thought the young man was seeing something that I DIDN'T. But WHEN the young man crept to a distance which he decided was within his shooting ability — ABOUT SIX OR SEVEN PACES — he suddenly DASHED into the woods and returned with a small tree crotch which he quickly jabbed into the snow to rest his gun on. Now — mind you — the young hunter was READY to shoot. He aimed carefully and shot. BUT HE MISSED!!" Bee-land made a helpless shrug and gesture, to delight the crowd. "And when that young man DISCOVERED that he had STALKED a STONE — why he became ANGRY! There was no need to kick the stone and throw down his gun angrily! After all, the young man had done ONE thing RIGHT! He had put the CORRECT end of the gun to his shoulder!!"

Everyone in the Council House could feel that the Midwinter festival was almost over with, for one whole year. The Hunt and The Debate were all part of the celebration and whoever brought in the most pieces of game, young or old, didn't really matter. So, now, the young, too, joined the laughter. Bee-land had stopped for a moment because his mouth had become dry. He went to the drinking water and dipped out some water from the pail and drank from the dipper. Then he went and squared himself up in his dead-center speaking place and wiped his nose on his sleeve. "Yes

it's been a great feast," he said. "Some of it is still on my face."
Then laughter again because everyone figured that Bee-land had
probably forgotten that he had a suit on and to keep that spirit
going, Bee-land pretended to smell his sleeve. "Serviceberry jam,"
he announced. Next, he squared himself up again and put his
hand up to quiet everybody down. "Now," he said, "it's time to
point something out to everyone here. The purpose of The Hunt is
to provide the meat of The Feast. Let's forget about the crow
found in the young men's bag. Let's forget about the young man
who leaped up on the old men's table with A mouse in A bag. Let's
forget about all those cat scratches on his hands. WE KNOW it's
not easy to take a mouse away from a cat. Let's just forget that.
Let's pay attention instead, to the team that brought in the
MOST meat for The Feast. Now we all know that the whole pile
of game brought in by the young men's team did not weigh as
much as the FIRST piece of game counted by the old men's
captain. I'd say the deer ought to be worth a hundred pieces of
game. Without being a hog — let's say fifty then. Fair enough?"
Lots of noise came down from the young folks in the balconies.
"Oh alright then," Bee-land said, "we'll let nature decide." He
stepped back and stood up on one of the stump chairs. "I'll drop
an object to the floor," Bee-land declared. "If it touches the floor
the young men win. If it doesn't, the old men win." So much
interest was created in what he had said that everyone fell silent
and craned their necks to see better. Bee-land pulled his hand out
of his baggy suit pocket and held his arm out and dropped an
object to the floor. It never got there. It was a small bird, and
halfway to the floor, it swooped up into the rafters. Bee-land just
stood there and smiled his crooked smile. The Debate was over.

    As Bee-land made his way back to his seat amid the noise of
the approval of the people in the Council House, Big Egg joined in
with a light, rapid beat on the water drum. It was not really notice-
able until everyone else quieted down. The first person to make
any movement was Beulah Land, the cornbread cook. She pat-
tered out in her moccasins into the area that Bee-land had just left
from. She twirled around a couple of times and her apron, which
she still hadn't taken off, fluttering, she broke into the drum beat

with the swish-swish noise of the women's dance. Several whoops broke out as other women danced in behind her until there was a full circle. The side-to-side movement of their feet sounded like dry leaves, if dry leaves could dance in time to the drum.

The women received great cheers and when they finished, some of the front-row chairs were folded and from then on, everybody danced that wanted to dance. I danced or drummed or rattled until I was pretty well winded. Suddenly I remembered my skis. They were still at Duck Soup's and I was thinking about how Duck's dog chewed everything chewable up. I hurried out of the Council House into the night. But then I slowed up quick because I couldn't see anything and I realized that Chewer would already have chewed my skis if he was going to. Behind me, coming from the Council House, I could hear two voices starting to sing the happy wiganawdeeyoot song and before cheering drowned the voices out I recognized who was singing, I-ee-sog and Bee-land.

I was just beginning to see better when something began banging me on the leg. It was Bluedog's hind quarters. He had come to the Council House with Father and was coming home with me. "Come on!" I said to Blue, "I'll race you." And I ran as fast as I could. But as fast as I could run, I didn't have a chance. But then, after all, we were on Dog Street.

The Reservoir

I T'S a son-of-a-gun to monkey with the kids in big families. Some are fighting while others are playing, but any minute the ones who seem mad enough to kill each other are both on the same side, beating up on the ones who just got done helping them fight or have fun. But, of course, the worst thing is to not belong to that family and jump in and try to rescue a victim getting beat up. The whole family jumps on the rescuer with the victim jumping on the rescuer the hardest. The reservation is like that; like one big family.

In fact, if the United States is at war, the Indians from different reservations enlist like it was an attack against their family. But then, they are just as ready to fight city hall or the state or the United States. At this time, the Indians unite as a separate nation, which nobody seems to know if they are or are not. Also, a lot of Indians don't worry about that, as long as there is a bit of excitement in the family once in a while. Also, just as Indians are not sure how much of a separate nation they may be, there are Indians on the reservation who are not Tuscarora and who defend, sometimes better than some Tuscaroras, the reservation. At other times, they might kick up a ruckus at feeling not accepted, and often for good reason.

If the State of New York is like a big brother in one big family, one day big brother wanted a bite of little brother's candy. More like sister's candy because the women on the Tuscarora Indian Reservation outdid the men in many ways.

What happened was that big brother got the bright idea that the Niagara River should do more than just create something to look at at Niagara Falls. It could be making boo-coo more power. What the idea was was that as long as the Niagara River made a bend just before it fell over the Falls, why not dig a channel and take a shortcut to Lewiston. Then as the water wants to pour down the gorge into the Lower Niagara River, why not let it pour through electricity-making machinery? Better yet, why not let the water rest up first at the top of the gorge in a lake or reservoir? All that water could REALLY make electric then, couldn't it? Well, this is what happened. But as big ideas often pop up in beautiful weather, they sometimes don't look so good in bad weather.

Weather, in fact, did have something to do with one of the things that big brother forgot about. Six or seven years later, when all of the hassles that big brother's idea caused were all worked out and the idea was starting to work, ice came from Lake Erie and jammed the channels to the reservoir. Dynamite was tried. Nothing happened. Probably a good-sized sturgeon would of done more. So now icebreakers or tugboats are needed or the Big Idea of big brother isn't so big.

How the Tuscarora Indian Reservation happened to find itself part of the Big Idea was that part of the reservation was where the reservoir would need to be. Another, bigger, part of the reservation was where a beautiful state park would be which, in the Big Idea, would surround the reservoir. It seemed like, one day nobody knew this, the next day EVERYBODY knew it.

The news was like an explosion on the reservation and it traveled about like the fuse on a firecracker. It was like looking out your window and seeing a stranger pulling boards off your house and saying, "I bought your house last night, didn't you know that?"

Big brother's name was The State Power Authority and many eyes were on his scalp. The war was on. The name State Power Authority was shortened to SPA and some Indians got the letters mixed up sometimes and said "ASP or SPCA."

The first SPA "troops" were the poor surveyors. I say poor because they got the worst of it. Though it was not a real war it

182

was very much like a real war with privates and sergeants and generals. Sometimes rank came in handy and other times, I suspect, a "four-star general" wished he had taken up some other sport.

In the old laws of the Iroquois, the chiefs were called lords and since the clan mothers chose the lords, the Tuscarora Indian Reservation had some fairly high rank monkey farting among the privates. Much higher than the SPA realized at first.

Believe you me, it ain't easy to see what's going on all over the place at the same time at a shindig like this.

Nor could it be known what was going on at different headquarters where, likely, headquarters didn't know, and would like very much to stay out of the fields. The action was where the best and bravest of the Indians were. They were women. Of course, during the day most men were working, but when they did come off the jobs they still weren't often the most active.

One man didn't stand still, though. G-By came charging through the bushes because he didn't like to see these surveyors sighting along his land. He had a stout cane and in about a minute he gave some free lessons in how to cross-check with a lacrosse stick. The surveyors picked themselves up and took on off out of there. The reason G-By wasn't on a job was because he was over seventy years old.

As fast as the surveyors put stakes into the ground, the women gathered them up for fire to cook donated food on. One small girl held a large American flag and stood in front of a surveyor's transit.

Just the same, it was a simple thing for a surveyor to stand on the spot where the first hole for test borings into the rock would be made. And here came the huge bulldozer towing the drill rig. It came rumbling up Garlow Road, and to the worried surveyors, it probably felt like help in the form of a General Sherman tank. It never got off Garlow Road. Jeet-niiht (bird) went and met it and threw herself right in the way and the big diesel Cat ground to a halt.

The drill rig had been rented from Kroening who had drilled wells for Indians for drinking water.

By this time some men had drifted in from jobs and Oxen was one of them. He was small but powerful. He stepped up to

Kroening. Kroening stepped back. "Don't be afraid of me,"
Oxen said, "I'm not afraid of you."

"What's the matter?" Kroening asked. "What's going on
here?" There was two, maybe three hundred Indians as far as you
could see.

"If you find your drill rig upside down tomorrow morning,
it might pay you to find out," Oxen said.

Different other things like this were happening but it was
what can be called the first few skirmishes. Now it was time for
the SPA to put a stop to this nonsense, and in the morning air a
chorus of sheriff car sirens wailed from the substation to the
reservation. Sheriff Murdock had just been elected.

Now here were real bullets. Some of the oldest Indians who
could hardly walk began to cry. In a little while the deputies were
out in the fields keeping order while the surveyors' sledgehammers
began pounding on stakes. I looked out across the field and there
was only one Indian moving. But, man, he was moving. The dust
balls behind him were ten feet apart. It was Fox, and he was running like foxes run across a big field, in a straight line. Fox was the
grandson of Babymind who was the fastest runner at Carlisle, and
Fox was no slouch either. I figured he had discovered a nest of
yellowjackets.

The next thing that happened was, there was a cloud of dust
at the far end of Garlow Road. Pretty soon you could see that a
car was leading it. Out of the car jumped Fox. Turquois was chairman of the chiefs' council. He came out of the other door wearing
a Bear Claw Necklace. Fox had driven the car up the left-hand side
of the road and had stopped just short of Sheriff Murdock's front
bumper. Murdock was standing by his car door with his hands on
his hips, near his gun. The dust caught up now and went all over
both cars. This drew all the Indians and some of the deputies like a
magnet.

The wind blew the dust off to the east. "Get your men out
of here and you go with them!" Turquois boomed at the sheriff.
The chief had a country preacher's voice. His thumb was up,
pointed towards the substation.

184

"I'll do nothing of the kind," Murdock said, leaning comfortably against his car.

The chief didn't look much different from any other wrinkled old Indian with long hair and the sheriff didn't look much different from any other sheriff in uniform with big rosy cheeks. Together, though, even they were both medium size, their looks was saying, "I'm on the opposite side of you!" Only one thing was in common. They were both wearing cuffs. Murdock's was black leather and part of his gloves. Turquois wore beaded cuffs. They were light blue with white flowers.

"You're trespassing," Turquois said.

"I'm the law," Murdock said.

"This is the Tuscarora Indian Reservation," Turquois said. "This land is under federal jurisdiction. You better go get a federal marshal before I have you arrested." Turquois put his hand on his car door. "You better hurry," he said, "I'm drafting an injunction against the State Power Authority." Then he got in the driver's seat and drove away.

By then all the deputies had gathered nearby. "Let's go," the sheriff said, jumping into his car and gunning it around in a half circle. "The chief's up to something," he called out the window as he stepped on the gas. In a few seconds it looked like chickens do when one gets a worm. There were no sirens though, and out near Gill Creek I saw an Indian girl running with her hands above her head. She had both hands on a stick, and a spool of yellow ribbon was unreeling off it in the breeze. It was the ribbon that the surveyors used to mark the trees. It wouldn't be hard to track her until the ribbon ran out and she jumped Gill Creek.

Like the tides in the ocean and the tides in war, so did the events of the battle for Indian land go. The newspapers had a picnic. It didn't matter to them if they reported the tide in when it was out as long as there was matter to be printed. And there was plenty to print; enough to last through any lulls in battle when the battle fields waited to be taken into court. Also, the never-ending family squabbles that the reservation seemed to enjoy never let up either.

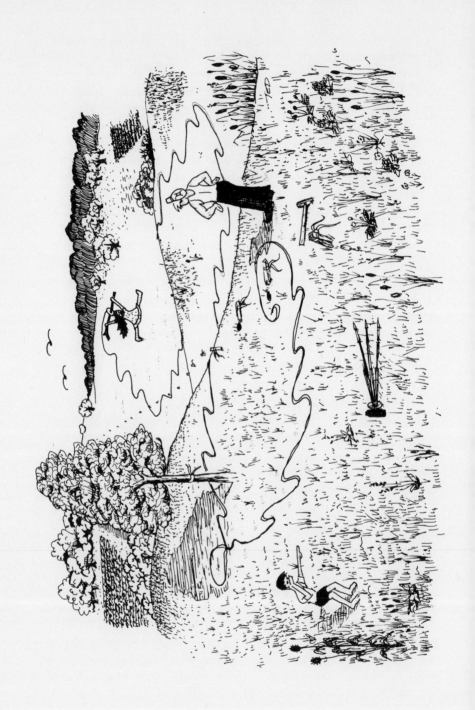

The Power Project was the name of the Big Idea and it was the SPA's pet baby. The SPA wasn't going to let this baby die although it was going through the mumps and the measles and the whooping cough like any other baby.

If the Baby was having these short-lasting diseases such as hundreds of contractors fighting over bids and then trying to back out when they found out how much limestone lived in Niagara County, then the illness of the fight for Indian land might better be called the seven year itch. In order to stop the seven year itch the SPA began using many "doctors" with many ways of cure. One of the best medicines expected to do the trick was called the Bribe. Nobody knows how many doses were given or if some was swallowed or spit out. The Tuscarora Indian Reservation, as a family, had enough squabbles within itself to show that some of the medicine probably got into the bloodstream.

When the federal marshal arrived, surveying and test boring began and Indians felt powerless to stop the work, and here's where the squabbles began. Some Indians, needing work and seeing the work being done anyways, went to work. Trees were being cut and Indians were good at it. Others, who had factory jobs already, called them traitors. Those Indians, including chiefs, whose land fell within the part where the reservoir and the park would be, began to give up hope. Some of them began to see dollar signs if they owned large parcels of land. Then along with the medicine called Bribe, another medicine might be called Shock Treatment. At least, it had to be pretty scary for those men, women, and children whose home, favorite trees, and playground fell in line with these little stakes with the yellow ribbon on them. They might find it easy to start looking for the next best spot on the reservation before all the best spots are already taken. But those that moved out had to face the "boos" of those that didn't have to move and more so from those that wouldn't move. A lot of Indians were involved because the outside edge of the park was a deep bite into the reservation.

Some never gave up and many were women. The army to harass never seemed to get smaller even though now they were facing jail sentences and fines. The chiefs, meanwhile, had not really allowed any moss to grow under their feet either, although the wheels of justice of the courts seemed to be lacking in grease.

187

The chiefs held meeting after meeting to decide who could be trusted and who could not, especially of lawyers; and when to use stalling tactics and when to hurry; if it was best to listen to one lawyer's advice to hold out for a big, big price or to never give in; what, if anything, to tell the newspapers; and decisions on endless questions and pressures from the Tuscarora Reservation family. Many other meetings were also taking place in homes and fields and woods. Into all this, the doctors were trying to feed Bribe medicine and Shock Treatment.

Very Bear, of the Bear Clan, whose mother was clan mother, was one of the fiercest of fighters of Indian right on the Tuscarora Indian Reservation or maybe of any reservation. During all this struggle, he seemed not to be doing much. Some wondered why, while others knew what was going on. Very Bear's reputation was well known and the U.S. Marshal was well informed that here was a dangerous Indian to be watched carefully and thrown into jail for the first false move he made. Very Bear, though, figured on this and during the day he sat in a car in plain sight with his lawyer. A .35 Remington pump was also in plain sight in the car. Now this automatically caused the marshal to post some men near-by and while they were guarding Very Bear, the Indians whose meetings Very Bear had sat in and made plans with were that much more free to go about their harassments.

Some Indians just naturally thrived on the excitement and practically lived on Garlow Road. Others went home and tried to think of ways of stopping the taking of Indian land and hunting grounds. There were photographers around and sometimes these Indians would return to Garlow Road with signs and banners hoping to have the papers carry pictures of their messages for public sympathy. Sometimes it worked. Sometimes non-Indians joined the harassers, or owners of stores donated food to the Indians who continued to resist. Usually, though, the photographers would not take pictures of the signs or banners or if they did, the papers would not print them; sometimes because the words were unprintable.

Just the same, many pictures were printed and if you just read the papers, the Indians seldom won. Also, in those pictures, the pictures of whoever might be familiar to local judges or sheriff's deputies or state police would be pointed out to the marshal as being a ringleader and watched more closely. On one particular morning, Hoodoo and Crane were listening to the eight o'clock news on the radio and they heard that they had been arrested on Garlow Road that very morning. So they went out to Garlow Road to show the other Indians that the radio report was a lie and at nine-thirty they DID get arrested.

Moonflower was big and strong and beautiful and had long black hair and big white teeth. She was mad enough that the reservoir would replace the new house that her husband and she had built. Then she heard that a state trooper had knocked her husband flying through the air with his car as he flagged traffic near the Stauffer Plant in Niagara Falls. The news was that the trooper claimed Warwhoop was struck by another car; that he, in fact, chased the hit-and-run because he thought Warwhoop was dead. But Warwhoop never died at all, even though his legs were mangled, and he told Moonflower the truth. Now she got madder.

The thing that looked the worst to her was the drill rig drilling holes in a line with her house. The men on the drill rig had huffed and puffed to remove a huge stone out of the drill bit's way. With what looked like no effort, Moonflower picked up the huge stone and heaved it into the hole as the drill bit came down. WHAM! The drill bit bent like a flybeard on a big carp's back. The men ran to the marshal to tell on her.

The marshal's name was Cranden and he itched to catch the harassers and have them jailed because every contractor was crying the blues and scared to death of bankruptcy and so far the harassers were hard to catch. He said, "Even the old women can run like the devil."

"This one's a mean one, I think," said one of the drillermen, "I mean she's strong and she's right over by your car waiting for you."

Cranden says, "I'll handle her," and he started off with long steps. He was well over six foot.

At Cranden's car, Moonflower was not alone. Pheebee Willy was with her. Pheebee was so old she was almost dead. She was one of the ones that cried quite a bit. Moonflower had a long stick and was standing lazy-like near the back of the car. The end of the stick was letting air out of Cranden's tire s-s-s-s-s-s-s-s-s. She had asked Pheebee Willy to stand in the way so Cranden couldn't see what she was doing. So now here came Cranden.

Pheebee Willy says, "Stay right where you are, you boogeyman, or I'll witch you."

Cranden never paid any attention to her and started to walk right around her. WHAM! Pheebee Willy came across with a terrific haymaker and it flattened Cranden's nose. Pheebee said later, as though she had been the one getting punched, "I don't know where that punch came from."

Cranden went around Pheebee and blinked back the tears. "All right," he said, pulling out a pair of handcuffs. "You're gonna have to come along with me."

Moonflower reached in her pocket and pulled out a long, scaly sand lizard. She put it on her palm, holding it by the tail with the other hand. She looked at it. "You got deadly poison, haven't you?" she asked the lizard.

She squeezed its tail and it answered by sticking out its long tongue and hissing. And then she threw it on the marshal's chest.

"Yeow!" he said, running backwards with his eyes popping. Next, buttons were flying all directions as he ripped his jacket off, not knowing where the lizard was and probably imagining it to be running all over his back or something.

Actually the lizard had streaked off in another direction, Moonflower in another, and Cranden was dancing around for nothing. Pheebee Willy just stood there. She was crying again. But this time it was because she was laughing so hard. Pretty soon Cranden took off in his car to get another jacket. "BEH-BEH-BEH-BEH-BEH-beh-beh-beh-beh-beh-," went the flat tire as he drove out of sight.

Moonflower went home to change clothes and do her long hair up under a straw hat so she wouldn't be noticed so quick when Cranden came back. She got there just in time to see a brush-cutter cut off the little walnut tree she had planted when the house was finished.

Now she was running but she was running kind of zig-zaggy. Why she was zig-zaggy was because she was so mad she was wanting to find something to pick up to hit the man that cut the tree down with. Of all the things she could get her hands on, what do you think she grabbed? A PITCHFORK! And before you could say "Pretty blue skies," that man turned into SOME kind of runner.

Now both of these runners had terrific reasons for speed. In Moonflower's mind, she was going to run this man so far away that he'd starve to death trying to get back. And him, well he just wanted to live to a riper older age, that's all he was running for.

The man had a pretty good start on Moonflower and he was headed towards the bushes, hoping to lose her. She cut off to the opening to the right of the bushes because the bushes were made of prickly ash. YEOW! The man had hit the bushes and was fighting his way back out of them. "YEOW!" he said again. There was a slight downward hill starting at the opening and the man saw it and began shifting gears.

Moonflower's house was right out in the open on Garlow Road and most of us had seen her take after the brushcutter. We were also running at high speed too, thinking he might have stolen something or something.

The man hit the opening at full throttle and so did Moonflower. Just as he broke over the hill he glanced back. Here was the pitchfork starting downward and aimed perfectly for his butt. Now I'm sure you can understand where he got some extra speed from. The same place that Pheebee Willy got her haymaker from. The man was a little heavy but it didn't hold his legs back any and what with Moonflower's hair blowing in the wind I thought it looked a little like Moby Dick and Captain Ahab.

ZING! The pitchfork, from where I was, looked as though it struck a rock and bounded upwards. The man, though, went downwards and out of sight.

When we got there Moonflower was just standing there looking at the man. There was blood all over the place and the man, white as a ghost, sitting there, was staring at the blood squirting out of his ankle. The pitchfork had gone all the way through his ankle and through his shoe, which was still stuck to the bent fork of the pitchfork.

I could tell that Moonflower was worried but she put her hands on her hips as though to give the man a stern lecture. But all she said was, "Don't cut any more trees." Then she went back to her house to change her clothes and left us to take care of the man who had received some of the Shock Treatment that was going around. He was, in fact, in a perfect state of shock.

In the harassment meetings it was many times agreed on never to hurt anyone. Strictly harassment. And probably the pitchfork thing was about as hurty as it got, except for some fistfights that were pretty evenly matched and nobody was hospitalized. As I say, it was about impossible to know what was going on all over, but in general, the women were capable of Moonflower's courage, except maybe they couldn't pick up that huge rock. And maybe now, she couldn't do it either.

If it wasn't for the harassments, much more of the reservation would have been destroyed. The work was going slow; sometimes even stopped. Sometimes workers would quit, either from sympathy or from fright. That was one thing. If the Indians were frightened, so were a lot of the workers. A lot of them tried to get on other parts of the power project. Many had even gone to school with some of the Indians and for that reason would not work there, or else they would offer money for food for the harassers. Some though, were strangers to the area and sort of thought of Indians as most history books tell about them. I mean, maybe these workers liked to read paperbacks about Indian fighters. Like this one surveyor helper. He was thickset and never wore a shirt, maybe to show off his muscles. None of the Indians paid any more attention to him, other than to let the air out of his tires or whatever the children were doing to any other worker. How he was different, was, he began making remarks like, "I'd like to smash one of them redskin's teeth in," or "I'm gonna take me a couple of them good-looking squaws home to bed with me sometime." Or, "I ain't ascared of these dumb injins, what the hell's the matter with you guys."

So the surveyor boss sent him in on G-By's property. Not much had been done on G-By's land because a lot of Indians liked G-By and had harassed the surveyors pretty badly in that area. Maybe it was more like because G-By himself sat on his porch with a full-choke double leaning against the railing and nobody knew if BB's or double OO buckshot or slugs were in the chamber.

Anyways, a few of us Indians went along to see what we

might do to slow down the surveying on G-By's land. Pretty soon we see the surveyors put on shirts and so did the tough surveyor helper. Pretty soon we can see why. There were lots of mosquitoes and pretty soon there was just me and Fox left because the others said, "They won't last there long and even if they do, they're getting harassed anyways."

I was sort of thinking the same thing except I wanted to get a line on where they were going to set the stakes so we could come back to the right place and pull them back up again. The surveyor's helper had a stake in his hand and a surveyor had another. They were working furiously and it looked as though they'd be getting in a lot of stakes. Just as the helper put a stake down on point to drive it in, a .270 exploded from about two hundred yards or more. The stake blew up in the helper's hand and the echo vibrated through the swamp. In the moment that the surveyors and the helper froze before they ran, another .270 bullet roared and the other stake that the surveyor held blew up. The bullets were hollow points and there wasn't anything left in either stake carrier's hand. And by the time the second echo died out there wasn't any surveyors or helper left in sight either.

There were a few Indians that shot like that but only one or two used a .270. And maybe just one could shoot that fast. Oxen's brother, White-Corn. If meat got low on the reservation in the late fall, White-Corn would spotlight some deer at night and pass the venison to the needy. If there were three or four deer standing up to three hundred yards off, the biggest one would get it between the eyes. The rest got it in the lungs.

Offhand now, I'd figure that most or all of the SPA workers that sort of had that Indian fighter feeling like the helper I was using for an example, might quit or go to another contractor on another part of the Power Project. In this case, the example did not. He did not come back the next day but probably he was getting a permit because on the day after that, he came back wearing a Colt .45. And bullets.

This raised a few eyebrows, including Marshal Cranden's. He knew of the disappearing stakes and he didn't tell the helper not to wear the Colt but he did get everybody together. "No more shooting," he said. "Harassment is one thing, but shooting is something else. We don't want anybody getting killed here." Five workers had already died on the Power Project, but from work accidents. One had fallen into a huge cement pour. He was from the state of Oregon and was now buried under thousands of yards of Portland cement.

"O.K. I won't shoot," Hroo-saa-noo said. She had never shot a gun in her life and she was about fifty-five years old. Her feet were bare and she was curling her toes in the sandy dirt.

"Young lady," the marshal said, looking at Hroo-saa-noo, "I'm going to ask you if you won't personally do me one big favor." He had learned that she was Very Bear's aunt and had singled her out as a ringleader, which, by the way, he was right. She had pulled off a few pretty good tricks after a bulldozer had gouged a big ditch right across her long driveway for no real reason. "I want you to promise me that you and your friends won't take the yellow ribbon markers off the trees," Cranden said. "Do you think that you could promise me that much?"

"Yes I can," she said.

"I mean, would you, please?" the marshal pushed.

"Yes, I'll promise you that," Hroo-saa-noo said.

The next day all the trees that had the yellow ribbons on them still had them on. But so did every other tree in the area.

The surveyors' helpers and the surveyors were there too and they finished up another small job before going in among all the yellow ribbons and mosquitoes. So it was quite warm then, by the time they got to G-By's property. This time they brought hand pumps of two-gallon size to spray the area of mosquitoes. Right away they pushed themselves through the nu-heehk bushes, spraying them as they went. Then one of them said, "Hey John, did you shit?"

"No, but somebody did," came the reply.

Come to find out, Hroo-saa-noo and some others had dipped into some backhouses and, walking backwards, had mopped all the bushes with a watered-down paste of ood-gwe(t)-hreh. All of that surveying crew quit, including Colt .45.

Gradually, now, even though the harassments continued, the work went on and it began to seem as though there really wasn't much use fighting the SPA. Patience was running low towards the

chiefs and rumors flew left and right. Homes were being moved and new homesites were being bought. Some of the Indian women had infiltrated engineering and project offices as secretaries and much information came from that direction. There had been an effort by the marshal to starve out the harassers because some contractors were falling farther and farther behind schedule. All stores were asked to refuse food to Indians, and police or sheriff cars were placed near store entrances with a lawman there to pressure the storekeeper. So food had to be gotten from farther and farther distances. Some stores and restaurants brought food out at night but probably some of it never got to anybody because the person bringing the food would not know where to bring it to and any cars cruising on Garlow Road at night might be stopped. So despair began to creep into the ranks of the resisters.

And no wonder. The injunction to stop work, which the chiefs had obtained, had been overridden by a higher court. The surveyors had been granted permission to survey but that was all. Twenty-five or thirty state police had also come around at the time of the injunction but they respected the injunction and stood back. The sheriff had not.

Hiring a lawyer is usually fairly easy. But when the legal matter involves a versus-the-United-States, many lawyers shy off. Of those that don't, it then becomes a case of who to trust. The chiefs settled on a man named Laws. However good Laws was, or regardless of how many times he gave advice to accept the most money that the Tuscarora Indian Reservation could get, he stuck it out through all the courts and all the appeals, winning a few and losing more. Now I can't tell you how many decisions and appeals or reverses there were because I'm not a lawyer. And all I knew was, SOMEBODY was taking over Gill Creek, and I wanted to stand by the water, every springtime, next to G-By, and watch for pike and listen to the Hhu-deg-Khroth (frogs). So that's where I was, in the fields, not the courts. That's how I can get goofed up on exactly what was going on in them. Or when.

Very Bear knew, though, and about this time he said, "Them rich Jews in New York City that floated out them bonds for this project ought to be getting a little itchy and worried. They like to get a project like this moving on schedule. The courts are holding them up and so are we."

196

Almost as a prediction, we got word that a group from New York City and Albany wanted to meet with the chiefs. The meeting was for Tuesday night.

On Tuesday night the chiefs went into the Council House and locked the door. I was standing outside with the crowd when these big black limousines pulled up. A picture of the state seal was on each car door.

First, the driver of the first car rolled down the window and asked if this was the Council House. Someone told him it was and all the men in suits got out. They went up to the door and one of them knocked. Nobody opened it. The man knocked again, as loud as he dared without hurting himself too much.

After a while you could hear some shuffling and the latch rattled. Chief Tom Isaac stuck his head out. "What you want," he says.

"We're the delegation from Albany," the knockerman said. "We're the people you want to see."

"That's just it," Old Tom says. "We don't know yet. We're having a meeting to see if we want to talk with you." He pulled in his head and locked the door again.

"See here!" the man shouted, "We've driven all this way, ..." but the door didn't open. The men in suits went back to the cars.

No sooner had they got settled down when my father came to the door and let them in. He was a sachem chief now and his name had become Saa-gwa-hree(t)-thre(t). He let the men in and everybody else that could fit into the building with the door open.

The meeting itself was not much except maybe the end of it. Laws, the lawyer, was there and sat with the chiefs. Some of the chiefs, like Chew, didn't speak English the best but they understood.

At one point, the main speaker of the suited ones was telling about the benefits of the project to the Indians. He was saying, " . . . and on the whole east side of this dike will be a huge sign, TUSCARORA INDIAN RESERVOIR. . . ."

June Bug jumped up and interrupted him. "Maybe you should have brought some beads," he said.

The man, I think he was introduced as a past Lieutenant Governor, got red in the face and raised his voice, "See here. I didn't come here with that frame of mind!" he said.

All the talk that went on during the meeting didn't mean anything. When it got late and nothing was agreed to, the main speaker got up again. He was through bargaining. I don't remember what the first offer in dollars was for the Reservation property. Maybe one or one and a half million, which I don't know the meaning of anyways. "Well," he says, "we're not getting any- wheres and we've all got some important business to conduct tomorrow. I have to hand it to you Indian people. You drive a hard bargain. And a good one." Here he paused to let that sink in. "I have," pause, "in my power," pause, "one final offer." Pause. "You'll have a short time to decide this and then we're leaving. And I know — and I know your attorney knows — that you don't have much chance in court." He paused again and looked around. Then he pulled what he expected to be his ace up his sleeve. "Ladies and gentlemen, I offer you eight million dollars for said property on this reservation!" He sat down.

He had said that we had a short time to decide and Turquois used it right away.

"You don't understand," Chief Turquois said, standing up. "The land is not for sale. It is not for me that I speak, it is for my children's children and their children's children." The meeting was over.

After the meeting I sat up all night and talked with my father. We had talked before but I had to tell him I was getting the first of a giving-up feeling and it took most of the night to dare to tell him that. His clan was Turtle, mine was Wolf, after my mother. One of my chiefs was in the position of having to move, it looked like, and he then became one of the ones who was caught in that die-if-you-do and die-if-you-don't feeling. His name was thqwah- hree-nih-huh (Wolf Little) and often he was furious at any Indian who would work for the SPA and cut trees on the reservation and yet he himself was forced to give in to the SPA and to prepare to move and accept a new home. I asked my father what he thought was going to happen.

He said, "You're big enough to understand what can happen. Some day there might not even be a reservation here."

He talked slowly. "Whoever is President of the United States can have a lot to do with it. Now take this Power Project. At the first smell of it, Chief Turquois went to President Eisenhower's inaugural. It seemed like a good play. Turquois usually attracts the newspapers and here was a chance to see what kind of a President Ike was. Turquois asked him to uphold the Treaty with the Tuscaroras if the State of New York tried to take some land. Ike passed the buck and turned the matter over to the Department of the Interior. The Interior turned it over to New York State and the chiefs' council fought that. Before we could bring our case up, Harriman went ahead and condemned the land that the SPA wanted. Maybe some money changed hands, maybe not, but the condemnation was processed on a Saturday. The chiefs didn't get a letter about it until Tuesday. On Sunday, the day after the condemnation, some SPA men were already spotted on Garlow Road. The letter of condemnation with a permit to survey came around one o'clock in the afternoon on Tuesday but the surveyors had already started in that morning."

This was all going over my head so I ran out towards Garlow Road in the wee hours of morning. It was up to me to give up or not and I so much did not want to give up that I was running like the wind. Only I wasn't sure where or what I was running to.

Big noises of big engines could now be heard for miles. Some came from as far as the gorge where drilling and rock removal was going on. Those big machines made me feel so small. It would soon be hraw-thek-gyeh-huh (September or little autumn) and I'd have to get back in school. Funny how I could stand and watch a huge shovel scoop out the very earth and stone I wanted left alone and yet still just like to see the action.

I sort of woke up doing this just in time to see Nehts-eh(t) (Skunk) being chased away from a bulldozer. He had dark skin and light hair. I joined up with him and he said, "I used to play in that swamp. They're filling it all in." The 'dozer was pushing boulders into the swamp which seemed to swallow them up. "It's like quicksand in some place," Skunk says. "Stay here, I'm going to see if I can make it out to that little island."

He sure knew his way around the swamp and quick like a frog, he was on the island. He waved but it didn't look like at me so I turned and saw Jewel coming from the east. Just as I looked back at Skunk, BAM!—BAM!—BAM! A gun went off. Black mud was spattered all over Skunk. "I told you, get the hell out of here, kid!" It was the surveyor helper with the Colt .45 only this time he was doing pick and shovel work. He laughed and shot again. BAM! Skunk went back the way he came.

Jewel said nothing but started off towards the contractor's office. She was now clan mother of the Snipe Clan. I could feel how mad Skunk was and no matter how much I asked him to leave and go back to Garlow Road, he wouldn't. After a while Jewel came back and joined us. I wasn't even sure if we were on the reservation or not because the looks of the place was changing so fast. Jewel was mad too. She said, "I told the boss there about the shooting and he just said, 'Well get the hell out if you don't like it.' " She tried to get Skunk to leave too but Skunk seemed all the more stubborn.

I was wondering what to do when up staggered Sky High, and that's what he was too. Drunk. We told him what had happened and he said, "Well I'd jes go over and drive that big 'dozer into the swamp."

What he said made me look at the 'dozer. It made Skunk look too. Nobody was on it and it sat puffing away by itself. Way down the haul road I could see men hurrying towards the red coffee truck. Skunk was already running towards the 'dozer. He looked like a flea on an elephant when he finally got into the seat. First the 'dozer backed up then it went forward. It went so slow I don't think anyone but Jewel and me and Skunk knew it was moving. Skunk rode it quite a ways because I think he was trying to get the blade up. But it didn't matter. Jewel took off towards Garlow Road. I got into some low elders and hid. Sky High just wandered off towards the coffee wagon. Skunk jumped off the 'dozer and started after Jewel. I gave him a sound like cock pheasants do when they fly up. He came into the elders with me. We watched the 'dozer, together, as it idled out to the edge of the stones. Before it went down into the swamp, it balanced a little bit. I felt like it was time for me to leave and I left. Again, I couldn't get Skunk to go with me. It was his swamp and he was wanting to see the most of it that he could.

I followed Gill Creek back to Garlow Road and found out

that Jewel had told more about being chased out of the contractor's office. She told around that she had warned the contractor that he'd be sorry if he didn't get that man with the gun off the job. I knew that when Skunk's father, Hroo-SNEK'kree (Big Horned Owl), heard about this, he'd be rough. And he was maybe stubborner than Skunk. I was getting hungry but there was a big line to the sandwich and soup kettle. After a while I got in line. Skunk came from the swamp and I let him cut in line. He was a stubborn hero to me. He was still mad. "It never went out of sight," he said. "The exhaust pipe is still sticking out. About a foot of it. If that engine would of just kept going a little longer, I think it would of gone out of sight. And talk about swearing, you should of heard them men swear when they seen what happened. Then they all went down to the office arguing whose fault it was."

That night at a meeting at Double Ugly's the news was that Sky High had been arrested for destroying a bulldozer. The meeting broke up when Heavy Dough came to the door and, through puffs from running, said that there had been some heavy shooting out towards Garlow Road direction. We questioned him as to who all did he think was shooting. "Well," he said, thinking, "maybe it was just one person. About ten or fifteen shots. Damn loud though."

Several meeting members wanted to jump into cars and go see. "Hold it," Very Bear said. "Take your cars home and go on foot crosslots if you gotta go over there. The law might be riding heavy right now."

Heeengs, the oldest woman there, said, "Maybe nobody better go." She was talking Tuscarora. "Your eyes will shine at night if they light you." Nobody went.

The next day we found out what had happened. Much machinery was damaged. Diesel engines had holes through them and all the crane booms near the swamp were laying on the ground bent because the sheaves holding the hog rods were all smashed. It took a heavy rifle and a scope to do this. Skunk's father owned one. He sometimes hunted far north in Canada. Monkey Boy said he was in Johnson Sporting Goods store when Hroo-SNEK'kree(t) picked up some special order bullets. They were .600 Nitros.

"They ain't for Moose," was all he said, according to Monkey Boy.

Now I'm going to ask you to do something. I'm going to ask you to picture a big machine coming at you; maybe a D9 Caterpillar Bulldozer. You are in a fenced-in place; you and that machine. You can't see the operator of that machine but it keeps coming at you. You can move faster than it can but it never seems to tire. You keep wondering if it's going to run out of fuel before you get too tired and have to stop to rest, to get some sleep. After a while you won't know how many hours have gone by. Or days. Or years.

That's the way it seemed to me with this struggle with the Niagara Power Project. I mean, as far as time and events went. Maybe I haven't told of everything happening in the right order. I KNOW that many other things were happening where I wasn't. If so, that's the reason. Time likes to scramble. I don't know how many years went by.

I can remember one more thing happening. It seemed to say that the privates in the war were tired of the generals who hid and called the shots because it was the last harassing thing that I saw the harassers do, and the state trooper involved seemed to not care. Several Tuscaroras had New York State licenses as demolition experts. On this day I happen to see this state trooper sitting next to this brand-new giant yellow bulldozer, guarding it. He was tired, but not tired enough to take off his Smokey-the-Bear type hat that New York State troopers wear. But he was too tired of it all to get excited when a woodchuck rifle bullet somersaulted that hat off of his head. He just sat there, hatless, for a minute or two, before he picked up his hat and walked slowly toward a field telephone to report the incident. When he was no more than fifty yards from the still-clean machine, an unknown number of dynamite sticks blew the machine apart. The trooper looked back at the wreckage but he didn't hurry any extra as he went on towards the telephone. He would just report TWO incidents instead of one. And the harassments sort of died out with that machine.

Goo-ses-hehh-HUHH (November or little winter) came and snowflakes with it. The resistance pulled in its horns to think,

202

worry, and wonder by the fire. It was a time of not much heart but little did the Indians know, the amount of their land they were saving.

In New York City lived a man who was no more than Mr. SPA himself. His name was Robert Moses. He had been in charge of building whatever huge projects the State of New York and the City of New York had thought of. He was getting up there in age but he came on like a firebrand when the Niagara Power Project first began. Nobody knows how far the pressure of millions of dollars can go to take the heart out of a man like Robert Moses. Maybe he didn't know either because maybe he didn't feel like feeling any more of it or maybe he felt so much he couldn't stand it any longer. I'm just pretty sure the Big Idea at Niagara Falls cost quite a bit. If impatience can be added up like money then maybe there was about a squillion dollars worth of it riding on one man. The Big Idea belongs to New York State and not the federal government. But the decisions in court about a small piece of land on the Tuscarora Indian Reservation belonged to the federal judges in federal courts. However old Robert Moses was when the Indians pulled out the first surveyor's stake near Garlow Road, he added enough years before the reservoir was finished that it had nothing to do with his birth certificate anymore. He gave up.

Indians hated his guts and still do. In the long and bitter winter that never really went away when the summertimes came, the reservoir slowly took shape while another chunk of Indian land waited to know if it would be a state park or Indian hunting grounds. Robert Moses waited too and so did the blue teal and the muskrats and the Indians, including those that went to Europe and Asia to fight for the place they were born.

The case was in the last court of appeals. So was the patience of Robert Moses. When the judge gave the decision, it was in favor of the muskrats.

Robert Moses said, "I'm finished. I'll not appeal that."

The news was received on the Tuscarora Indian Reservation without too much jumping and dancing around because Laws, the lawyer, had chalked up a few wins before but they never had lasted. It just seemed like another temporary delay. And it was.

The federal commission, all by itself, appealed, and the case went to the Supreme Court. To no Indian's surprise, the Tuscarora

Indian Reservation lost the decision. Maybe the commission felt obligated to Robert Moses. Maybe they respected him. Maybe they just liked him. Or even maybe the Bribe Medicine never stopped. For whatever reason, the Supreme Court handed Robert Moses the deed for the big bite of land into the Tuscarora Indian Reservation.

As I say, Moses was no longer connected correctly to his birth certificate and the only thing that didn't stink to him anymore were the things he had seen with his eyes. He had seen the best lawyers in the land cross examine some chiefs who spoke so slow that the very slowness was making the lawyers go batty. "You don't understand. The land is not for sale. It is not for me. It's for my children's children and their children's children." And he had seen how hard it was to talk to them. Not because they wouldn't talk to him; they didn't talk with money. They talked with words. And he had seen the reports of contractors going bankrupt because some Indians, mostly women, were doing mischief. But mostly, this part of the earth was almost solid granite and limestone.

So what he did, he made the reservoir a little higher, just short of Garlow Road, which, by the way, is now paved. And he took the deed for the rest of the land and gave it back to the Tuscarora Indian Nation.

Maybe the cross examiners and some of the judges were big-eyed when he did that but the Indians weren't. Some had added a few extra years to their age, too, and some were dead of old age. Probably the ones that care the least are the muskrats and they ain't building no better or no worse houses than they were long before the Big Idea was born.

I was pissed off because the pike couldn't swim up Gill Creek anymore and I still am. But just on the east side of Garlow Road a powerful medicine grows in that same creek. Nobody knows, but maybe all the struggling we did, did not have the power that that medicine has. All during the struggle it grew there in peaceful confidence, just as it does today. Maybe we lost our heads and forgot the power of Mother Earth. Maybe all we had to do was plant some of that oo-nihh'GWO(T)'oit on the opposite side of the road.

The Trailers

DID YOU ever watch the purple grackles coming in from Ooskood-geh (the south) in the springtime? They fly along dragging those long tails with their heads twisting from side to side. Every once in a while they holler, "Khrih!" which, I don't understand all bird talk but later, you notice, they don't say so much.

They are looking for a nesting spot and they seem to be saying, "There's a pretty good spot! But there might be a better one just out of sight," because they always seem to keep on flying. In the springtime.

When the Tuscaroras first saw white people dragging their belongings across the countryside, they must of thought of the purple grackles because that is the name they gave them, Khreehroo-hri(t) (looking-for-a-nest people) or purple-grackle people.

When the work on the Niagara Power Project began twenty-four hour twice around the clock activity, workers began drifting in from all over. Pretty soon uncles and buddies and cousins were coming in like purple grackles from Ohio and Pennsylvania to Florida. Of course, when they got there, they had to have a nest. The city of Niagara Falls, which half of is in Canada, just didn't have the room to hold all these flocks. Indians came in too, to do the steelwork and lots of them got rooms on our reservation. You can imagine what a wicked lacrosse team was formed. In fact, I don't think any Tuscaroras made the team. There were Indians from St. Regis, Caughnawaga, Monawaki, Oshweken — you name it, we had 'em. Two, from somewheres, were living upstairs in our house. And this was only the beginning.

This was only the beginning because when all the space from Niagara Falls to the reservation used up its living places, the white workers came onto the reservation dragging their trailers, looking for a place to put them. The chiefs held council. Maybe two or three councils. Non-Indians are not supposed to live on the reservations and escape property taxes unless they are married to an Indian. Trailers, though, were excused in this time of need as being non-permanent living places. Also, laws are like the wind — who's to say if they are blowing or sucking? And you can't look at laws or winds like you can animals and vegetables. Also, the chiefs knew that the big wheels in charge of getting the power project done had enough pals in Washington or fat enough wallets to bend any laws towards their favor. Anyways, the chiefs said O.K. to the trailers — until the Power Project was over. Father was one of the first to register with the chiefs that he was having a trailer park. Maybe THE first, being as he was a chief too.

If a voice at Dog Street and Walmore had yelled "GOLD!" it couldn't have got more action. Overnight, the reservation had trailers coming out of its woodwork. Maybe at first the desperate trailer owners were ready to rough it. I mean, what is wrong with the childhood dream of camping in the wilds, living like first man and yet have a job nearby too? Well, for one thing, trailer owners have to poo too, and for just the three trailers which was the total of what we called our trailer park at our house, a third of our whole garden plot had to be made into a leach bed. Then of course, the bodies of the trailer owners were no different than ours; almost 100% water, with a need to keep 'em that way, and so our well went dry. By now, the reservation had electricity so THAT had to be octopussed out to the trailers too. Whatever else could be a problem, did, and however grateful the trailer owners were to find spots for their trailers, that vanished. For example, after about three years of this and no way of knowing how long the Power Project would go on, and with the leach bed full, Father found room in other trailer parks for his trailer people and ended his trailer park. I went with Father to the first trailer to tell them about this and the trailer man's wife started bawling. When Father said he had found a place for them, the man said to his wife,

"Shut up honey, it's better than a jab in the ass with a sharp stick," but he moved the trailer out at night so as not to pay up the rent.

If we had problems with just three trailers, think of the problems of those with more trailers; and in numbers, trailers in trailer parks went all the way to a hundred or more. Somewhere along the way, sometime just before we gave up the trailer park ghost, the Tuscarora Nation decided that it ought to be collecting a small tax from each trailer. There may be nothing wrong with this except, Indians almost puke at the sound of the word TAX. That, plus Indians are scarey about demanding others to do something. And, being as, if you want reasons for monkeyed-upness, they're never that simple. For example, if someone asks me why I haven't been around to visit lately, I never say, "Because I don't like you all that much." I say, "I've been so busy." And speaking of liking, the chiefs, like any other leader-type people, are not the picture of angels in everybody's hearts. But what I mean is, supposing I'm greedy. That may be why I didn't visit Tom; because Dick and Harry had a big barn to play in or a basketball hoop on their house. If Tom says, "You never come to MY house," we could get into an argument because I'll fight back to keep Tom from making me feel guilty about my greediness. And NEVER will the word GREEDY or GUILT be used. We'll argue over little things: "You cheat at marbles!" "I do not!" "You do too!" "I do NOT!" So some of the REAL feelings on the reservation are held back until fists fly. Or bullets. Or court fees. So I think it's fair to say that probably the chiefs had trouble collecting this tax fee. Probably some paid while others didn't.

The reservation, as a group of — say — one thousand people is no different than any group of one thousand people. Whatever fears, or loves, or likes, or dislikes, or prejudices, or religious beliefs, or jealousies, or the little flocking togethers of birds-of-a-feather, or whatever it is that MAKES people split into groups — those same things cause splits within the reservation. Maybe Indians are THE most splittable people. Our land has been split. Our tribes have been split. Our culture split. Our beliefs split. Our laws split. Our thoughts and hopes and decisions, then, have a nice long history of forks in the road. Some of the non-Indian roads have brought gladness and some have brought a crushing of hope.

So there's lots of distrust. I used to hide behind a tree when someone came to our house.

My little groups that I was split into was, first, the people
living in our house. I trusted them. And trees. Also dogs and cats
and chickens that lived at our house. Next came cousins my age
and neighbors my age and some wild animals like rabbits. Next
came older friends of my father and mother, and sometimes their
dogs. Close to them came older cousins and neighbors and their
chickens and some of their dogs. (Especially dogs that didn't bark
and wagged their tails a lot.) Next came other relatives and frogs
and any children on the reservation my age who were friendly.
Next came any dogs or cats on the reservation that were friendly.
Also, even before this, I liked birds but they didn't like me or my
slingshot. Next came some Baptists if they were friendly and
friendlier people that were not Baptist; maybe Presbyterian or
Catholic or nothing. Also animals like woodchucks. Next came
Indians that I didn't know very well but that smiled at me. Also
toads and snakes. After that, I was pretty scarey of people and
animals that bit, like raccoons. I hid on black people or white
people that came for medicine. Or strange Indians from other
reservations. Or people with Canadian license plates on their car.
Or anyone in any kind of uniform. And skunks. I hated loud or
mean people from anywhere. Or dogs that bit or cats that
scratched. And airplanes. For them, I ran and hid under my bed.
I was born on the reservation and if all the others born there had
many of these distrusts plus any that I didn't have, then there
might not be too much trust all around, huh? And that just covers
distrust and some prejudices that I didn't even know I was learning. What about if I envied something some other kid had? Oh you
can make a longer list but not me. I might get to disliking myself.

So now here is a reservation with lots of trailer parks on it.
Some were neat and clean with each trailer having its own yard.
Others were crowded and had muddy or rutted driveways and
parking places. Some had weeping leach beds and stunk.

Many Indians didn't have a trailer park. For some, it was
because of the lack of money or land space to start one. Others
didn't think it took any money to start one and let trailers park
anywheres. Some that had land but no money said that they didn't
want trailers; that it was wrong in the first place. Some said it

honestly. Some had both land and money but were against trailers. Or didn't have the time or ambition. Probably a lot of owners were without business sense too and had problems collecting rent. Some, though, just plain saw the whole thing as a cluttering up of the reservation. Others went about their business not caring and not saying anything.

As work on the Niagara Power Project straggled towards an ending, the trailers did not leave the reservation in great numbers. Nobody could say, "On this one particular day, all the work on all of the project will end. On that day, all trailers must leave the reservation." Also, now, some of the white owners had left and had sold their trailers to Tuscaroras who were now calling the trailer their home. The chiefs began trying to sort out some kind of ending of trailer parks to go along with the ending of the Power Project and if they expected that it may not be a happy ending, they were right. Maybe Degonawida and Hiawatha (Hi-Ye(t)-WA-the(t)) had trouble forming the Iroquois Confederacy but I'm sure neither one of them would have said, "O.K.," if, after forming the Iroquois, they had been asked, "Now that you're done with that, how about straightening out the trailer court thing at Tuscarora?" That is, the reservation is really a very peaceful place most of the time. But in every house one can expect to find anywhere from two to eight, maybe ten (according to size of family) rifles and shotguns. These are for hunting. So go ahead and poke a very peaceful hornet's nest and see what happens. See what kind of open season gets declared.

Yes, there are many splits among the Indian people on the reservation — clans, religious beliefs, you name it. But for anybody that isn't an Indian and never lived like an Indian, that person NEVER EVER could understand what the Indians will fight for. I may not be able to tell about it exactly, but I'll try. I'll use myself for an example. I'll use myself and cats because I saw this thing in cats first. It seems that however deep a living thing is shown or given freely of love and kindness and freedom and peace and quiet and food and laughter — just plain good, good, good feeling — THAT whole feeling gets into that living thing's guts. And BOY! does that living thing like it. That is LIFE to that living thing and it wants to dish out that same feeling to everything — living or dead, that is around it. And so PRECIOUS is this feeling to this living thing, that it also develops the same depth of OPPOSITE-NESS to protect the precious "good feeling." Also, if it has had terrific freedom, it will also be terrifically brave; RECKLESSLY brave.

One night, in the middle of the night, I came out of a deep sleep because of this noise, "gaaaags — gaaaaags— gaaaaags." There was a little moon because in the dimness of the window I saw something moving. In my sleepy eyes it looked like somebody's head. In my sleepy ears I thought somebody was ripping the window screens to break into my room. Now here was a living thing disturbing my peacefulness. Instantly, I was ready to kill. What it turned out to be, it turned out to be my young pet cat. It slept in bed with me and my dog. What it had done, it had shit on my bed and was trying to cover it up. That's what the noise was. What gave it away was the smell. Up until that moment, my cat and I were great to each other. Now, though, I punched it against the wall. In its young life, it had had all kinds of freedom, so it was very brave. It attacked me tooth and nail. I went crazy wild. I had had freedom too and was brave too and to have my peace disturbed this badly, I went wild too and threw the cat right through the screening of my second-story window. At first I didn't know that its claws had ripped through my veins and blood was going all over my bed and everything in the dark. So, for a week straight, I stoned that young cat away from the house. In one week, so badly did that cat want the good feeling of life that it had before, that it got skinny and shakey and scarey. I forgave it after a week but being as it was a young cat and not done growing, it was too late. It hissed and ran, hissed and ran. Then a dog chased it and caught it and killed it. I got myself a new kitten.

This time I wasn't going to let that happen again, so I loved it and fed it no matter WHAT it might do on my bed. It was a model T cat (brown with black stripes) just like the other one and in time, it grew up. Except, the new cat had an extra good life. Extra freedom. One day that same dog that killed the other cat came charging after the new cat. What do you think it did? Nothing. At first, it just watched the dog come and then it jumped right on the dog's neck and began tearing its eyes and ears to smithereens. It rode the yelping dog about twenty yards before it fell off and began washing up.

210

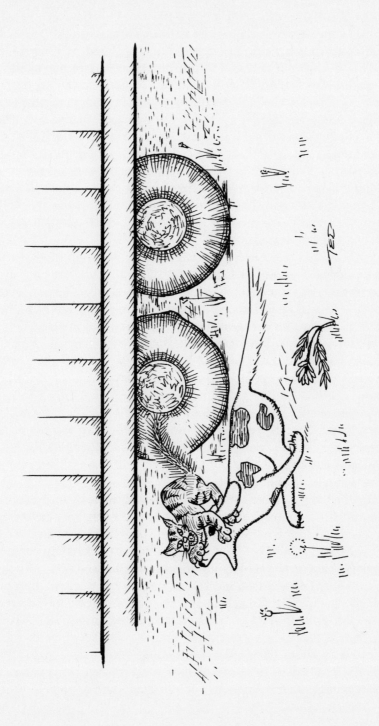

I think every Indian is like that. Because every Indian house that every Indian visits, and everything in that house, gives off that good and kind and precious feeling but don't — and I mean DON'T! — disturb that feeling. If you GO in with that good feeling the house will feel it too, and pretty soon the whole house will want to give you everything it's got and you will want to give everything that you have too. And you won't see any fences nor will you ever put any up. You'll eat cornbread fried in butter in any house and when somebody brings that same feeling to your house, your house will turn itself inside out for them. It can't be helped. That's the way it is. I know. Because when something disturbs my peace, I might as well go looking for a job poking hornets' nests because I'll be perfectly suited for that.

So. What happened with the trailer park thing? Along with however many groups or factions or splits there may be on the reservation, the trailer thing caused one more. Often a split causes all other cracks or differences to, for the time being anyways, heal up or patch up. Then the reservation becomes two main bodies. Well, three. Some didn't care at all. But here is a strange thing. Of the people that did not give one hoot one way or the other, some of these can cause a split. And that's just about what happened here.

The trailer park owners, as a group, put up a fight for whatever rights they felt they had. So on one side, there was the park owners and certain friends and relatives plus the people in the trailers themselves. There had to be people in some of these trailers who had made good, fast, strong friendships with the park owners. This alone might make some park owners go to bat for someone they liked. Also, probably the money that the friends paid for trailer space had become pretty good friends of the park owners too. On the other side of the split were the Indians who complained to the chiefs about the trailers staying on past the work on the project. Also certain ones among THEIR friends and relatives, plus now, the chiefs and THEIR backers-uppers. Maybe even some Tuscaroras now living in trailers. What is tricky, now, is that WITHOUT the people that didn't give a hoot, I don't think there would have even been a thing called "the trailer thing." Not even a real split. That is, a smoother thing would have taken place between the park owners and the chiefs but before that could happen, out of the group of don't-really-carers came the instigators. Young people. Full of fun and mischief. My schoolmates and I were always getting each other into scraps as a form of entertainment. Just as a tree can make a million matches, a match can burn a million trees and it just takes a tiny spark to start a fire. Like a kid saying to a grumpy trailer owner, "NYEAH-NYEAH, NYEAH-NYEAH, you gotta MOO-ove, you gotta MOO-ove." Especially if it's sort of "sung," over and over. That's the little spark, and a grump will always fan it, much to the joy of the singer.

There are numbers of ways of how the "fire" got going but it's easy to see that once hecklers got under the skins of trailer owners, and that gets passed on to the park owner (". . . and what are you going to do about it?") then something could happen. Then the little heckler tells mommy and pretty soon mommy tells the chiefs. However it started, it came to a point where guns came out. On both sides. One park owner's house still has bullet holes in it. The protest and fight against the New York State Power Authority over Indian land was still inside of many people's skin and the protest against the trailers became powerful. A twenty-four-hour encampment of protest was even set up. Bullets are not the most symbolic sight or sound of welcome, especially during the moments when they are measured in feet per second and many trailers did not wait for any court order which can be measured in weeks instead of feet per second. It did come, though — the court order — and the trailers left.

So now the "trailer thing" is just a dot of reservation history because between the splits and cracks and healings — something — maybe right this minute — is monkey farting with that precious gut want of the Indians on the reservation for that terrific good-ness-kindness-no-fence feeling; where the only loud noise is laughter. Flies, though, fall into ointments all the time.

The Tellers

MANY of the older men and women of the reservation would stop whatever they were doing to tell children anything that children wanted to know. I don't mean their OWN children; they couldn't do THAT; I mean any OTHER children, which, there are high numbers of. Parents DID say, "Don't be shy." That made us mad; and BY GOLLY! just to show 'em, we WERE shy then. To people. (Of course we could turn shyness ON or OFF if we felt like it. The reason I say this is, after all, we would talk to strangers or toads or turtles and things, if we felt like it.)

In fact, the way we felt about old folks was: "Isn't it a pity that they don't realize how MUCH us kids know. And it's their own fault if they're scairt to ask questions. Too shy, I bet, or embarrassed. They don't know that while they sit around the after-dinner table talking about the weather, why! WE'RE right out IN the weather and more than that — WE'RE talking secret things like that one of us saw so and so's panties while she was swinging on the school swing the other day and guess WHAT? She wears BLUE panties! — things like that. They just don't ask."

Gradually though, I forgave them. And just to show there was no hard feelings, *I* began asking questions. Men, mostly.

Men like Manylips, Jeeeks, Cap Peters, Juke-a-dom, Old Claudie, LEE'FY-Yett, Digger, Song, Bassable, John Bunker, Simon Cusick, Pete John, Eddie Errand, Georgenash, JEW'gweh — men like that; and one woman, HeeeNGS. They received full forgiveness. And questions. Some were much older than Father.

215

Guess what? Old folks got feelings too. And quite a few ain't scairt to let 'em out. Much as I hated loud noises — well — on the Fourth of July, at Hyde Park, at Gill Creek, in Niagara Falls they have these big fireworks in the sky. They're beautiful. I didn't like the noise — but I couldn't keep my eyes off the sky.

I mean, one time I seen Old Star Silver let out his feelings. He lived all by himself at the northeast corner of the big old wooded swamp at the end of Blacknose Spring Road. That was also the end of one corner of the reservation. I don't know how old he was but he was OLD. He had WHITE HAIR! Age had no effect on his voice though. It was wicked. Loud, I mean. Graveley and raspy too, like George Green and his kids' voices. On nice summer nights, when we, our family, at our house, use to take blankets outside to sleep on the grass, very often we would be disturbed by a swamp full of noise. Even at that distance. It would be Star Silver, telling his troubles to, and preaching to, the Swamp. And YOW-WEEE! Could he EVER warwhoop. And swear.

This time, when I seen him, he must of been off to a early start; middle of day, not night. I was coming out of that trail that leads to that place where bones and flint are. All of a sudden them three, four hundred year old trees in the swamp went wild with echoes. I think my hair stood up. Before Star Silver's warwhoop was done echoing he cut loose with words no man should hear. Nor beast. (I don't think the hru'SNEG'kree(t), the long-horned owls, were scared of him though. Many's the time I heard them at night, sassing him right back.) Oh it was sickening to hear him and not see him, so I snuck up and looked.

His white hair was going everywhich way in the wind; his arms were waving; his neck cords were jumping and pulling; his skin was red red; his eyes were popping; his veins were popping; his mouth was flopping; he was in his underwear and THAT was flapping; his teeth were missing; his body was jerking — and — it was a beautiful sight — like big fireworks at Hyde Park.

I secretly wished I could do that; what I saw. But I said to myself, "Oh, but I could NE-VER! THAT wouldn't be RIGHT! What would people SAY! And besides, hardly anybody's got a voice THAT loud. *I* — I don't like loud noises anyways. Besides — SWEARING! Why, whoever thought that there were THAT many

216

swear words! And talk about AWFUL! He ought to be ASHAMED! But worse yet — DRUNK! — and here he was, Star, not realizing what people might say — just A'LECTURING that big old Swamp to beat the band — and secretly beautiful; like big fireworks. HE would never die of a heart attack or ulcers, Father always said.

I sort of wrecked it, though. Maybe it didn't seem right to see all this for nothing or something, but before I knew what I was doing, I went closer. I had two pennies in my pocket and I gave one of them to Mr. Silver.

"WHAT TH'GAWDAMNFUCKIN'HELL IZZAT FOR?" he bellowed, fixing his eyes to see me better with.

"I want to give it to you," is all I could say.

"HOLY ASS AND BALLS!" he hollered, "ELEAZER'S BOY! — WELL I'LL BE A ROTTEN COCKSUCKER! WHY I REMEMBER WHEN THAT FUCKIN' ELEAZER WAS NOTHING BUT A JESUSTOCHRIST GRASSHOPPER!" Then he smiled. I did too. Now he seemed to turn into a rag doll. He seemed questionable. I mean I felt like questioning him. And I did.

"What was you mad at?" I says.

"Oh hell," he says. "You gotta straighten the world out once in a while."

That ain't a real great thing to say but before evening, I heard more than a penny's worth.

There was another man that used to let out his feelings, Art Johnson. He was probably famouser than Star was because he lived at the middle of the reservation which gave him a bigger hearing audience. I never heard his feelings at his own house but I did at ours. He seemed to like my father even though him and his brother and my father had had a big punching fight over who stole the bottoms of each other's rows while they were picking apples in that old orchard next to Roy Hills.

Sometimes Art came to our house when Father wasn't home and sometimes before he came, what he had drank first was not just plain water. And speaking of water, sometimes he had wet his pants first. At these times, we locked ourselves in on him because we didn't like the smell of pee. But if Father was home, he let him in anyway, but had him sit on the woodpile. How did we know

218

when he was coming? Easy. We could hear his feelings coming up the hill.

"YESSIR! THAT ELEAZER IS A VERY NICE MAN — MAYBE THE BEST! —HE'S A GOOD CHRISTIAN MAN TOO! —NOW THAT'S THE KIND I LIKE! —ELEAZER ALWAYS FEEDS HIS FRIENDS IF THEY'RE POOR!—"

And on and on until Art knocked on the door. Sometimes it would be just me and my sister Weedy and grandmother Geese-a-geese home. Geese-a-geese would be scairt but Weedy and I would just stay behind the locked door and look at each other and hold our hands over our mouths to keep from giggling too loud. Art Johnson would be on the top step now.

"THERE'S NO MAN IN THE WHOLE WORLD LIKE ELEAZER WILLIAMS! OTHERS HAVE TRIED BUT NOBODY MAKES THE GRADE!"

(knock knock) (quiet like)

"— YESSIR —THAT ELEAZER SURE IS WONDERFUL! — LOTS OF PEOPLE THOUGHT THEY WAS GONNA DIE—BUT NO!—ELEAZER KNOWS HIS MEDICINE!—"

(This went on for five or ten minutes.)

(KNOCK! KNOCK! KNOCK!)

"—THAT ELEAZER TURNED OUT TO BE PRETTY GOOD AFTER ALL—"

(shuffle, shuffle)

(BAM! BAM! BAM!)

"—THIS IS THE LAST TIME I'M GONNA SAY IT— ELEAZER IS A GOOD MAN—"

(Silence — then, his trademark!)

"*ART JOHNSON!*—NO SMALL MAN *EITHER!*—BAP- TIZED TOO, JUST LIKE YOU! —— YOU HEAR THAT? —— I KNOW YOU'RE IN THERE! —— ELEAZER! —— YOU GODDAM LAZY SONOVABITCH—"

(Now everything goes the other way.)

"—YOU'RE BOUND FOR DEEPEST HELL FOR SURE!—"

After a while Art would shuffle off the step and start on down the valley. "BY CHRIST I JUST CAN'T BELIEVE THE EVIL IN THAT BLACKHEARTED ELEAZER—HELL IS NO PLACE FOR HIM!—HELL IS TOO GOOD FOR THAT NO GOOD—LOW DOWN—ROTTEN—"

Weedy and I would still be snickering when Geese-a-geese would come down from her room where she had locked herself in. "You mustn't listen to that," she'd say.

As Art Johnson started on up the other side of the valley he would be getting ready for the next house he would come to. "JOHN WESLEY PATTERSON IS A GREAT FARMER AND A GREAT HUNTER—THE BEST BASKETBALL PLAYER THIS RESERVATION EVER SEEN—"

Now some of these old geezers could be fairly cranky anytime, and say so. Crankiness may not be quite the same as Star Silver lambasting the swamp or Art Johnson on his porch telling the reservation how he feels, but it's a steam-letter-offer too. You take Old Jah'sood or Manylips or Old Bassable; they'll tell you quick, if you're stepping on their toes. Old Sy, he was probably the champion of old cranky buggers. He not only told people off or hit them with his walking stick, he smashed objects.

For example, one night Ol' Sy came into the gym to see a basketball game. The first bench he sat on wouldn't keep still because its legs were crooked. Ol' Sy got up and stomped it flat. "THERE!" he said to the collapsed bench, "Try and wobble NOW!"

In his younger days he used to be a snare drummer. "Traps," he called a snare drum. One day he got out his old drum. He was planning heavily on doing a few rat-a-tat-tats like he used to. Well the noise he made was a trifle off the beat. "Oh you don't wanna keep time anymore do you!" he said to the drum, and taking the sticks like two ice picks, he jabbed holes right through the head of it. "Well how's THAT for timing?!!" he shouted at the drum as he kicked it across the floor.

Ol' Sy stood up for his rights right to the very end when a car hit him and ended him. He figured he had just as much right to Dog Street as any car, even if he WAS wearing dark clothes on a black road at midnight.

What I'm getting at is, these old geezers were liable to lambaste anybody or anything, especially if they got up on the wrong side of the bed — and then again, they could talk words just dripping with honey. Like SETHcloss, the jealous old coot, he was like that. He used to sit in the backroom of old blind Olive's store, waiting for some man to get chummy with her so he could yell at her — just as though men couldn't keep from falling all over her. One thing, blind as a bat or not, she could someway tell a one dollar bill from a five or ten. Anyways, one day he said to me, "What are you looking at me for? By rights you don't even belong here. You're nothing but Twa'HREE-niih (Oneida). You're lucky you was even adopted. The Chiefs' Council was good enough to give your clan two chiefs and let 'em sit in council. WAS YOU GRATEFUL? NO YOU WASN'T. Instead you Wolves got the biggest mouth." And all I done was look at him. To top it off, he was doing all the talking and I don't even know what reservation he came from. Then he turned right around and said, "Just the same, it's nice that we all stick together. Not only that — your mother's a good cook, even if she only has one leg. She's always right there when there's lots of people to feed too." This wasn't the usual way to hear things though because THIS guy was trying to tell me things I didn't even want to hear and some things I already knew. But the thing is — others did that too sometimes, like old Cap Peters-Hi-velocity did one time — first one feeling, then the other.

Old Cap lived at the top of Blacknose Spring Road. He wasn't too tall and his face, his head, made me think of a small wrinkled pumpkin with white hair. I say white hair so's you'll know how old he was. I don't think his name was really Cap Peters-Hi-velocity. Indians just like to nickname each other for some reason or other. Sometimes it's because of what they can or can't do. For instance Digger, he digs the graves in the graveyard in case you die. But now, Creeping Paralysis, he got that name because he was scairt to walk on steel beams one windy day. Or like, No-blanket; he forgot his coat one cold day and he shivered and shook 'til quitting time. But now like RCA; he got his name from a record player because his name was Victor. That's how I think old Cap got his name — from the bullet company, Peters Ammunition Company. Each box of bullets was marked 'Peters Hi velocity';

and Cap's name was Peters. Some used to call him Peters Out.

Old Cap wasn't the best at speaking English. He might say, "Dog bit John, John's hand" or "Stop my house when you turn the corner around." I made fun of this just as much as anybody else. What he was doing, he was talking English like Indian. If you say "little dog" in Tuscarora, you'd say "jeese UHH," but it really comes out, "dog, little."

One day I got to talking with old Cap. I wasn't planning on it but his dog-little came running at me as I walked by. It was yapping its head off so I threw my baseball cap at it to scare it. It took my hat and ran back around the house with it and me hot after it. Indians pay close attention to their dog's noises — even small noises — so with all the yapping, Cap knew the whole story. In fact, I almost ran into him as he met me coming around the corner. He was carrying my hat. "HIH," he said. (That's an old Indian word that eastern tribes used for greeting. It's a sharp ringing sound — like an axe hitting a hardwood block. Probably they called to each other from a good distance. It was like saying, "I'm friendly.") Being as I felt a little guilty for making fun of Cap's English, I told him in Tuscarora, "Hello, I hear the Tuscarora." (Wug hehshyehh'hu(t)-skaw'hroo'hri(t).) That DID it! He mostly never said much, but now, in Tuscarora, he was — I was going to say, Hi Velocity. Of course I spoke English back to him. No sense having HIM make fun of ME. I spoke Tuscarora about like he spoke English.

He started right in, complaining, about how the younger generation is letting go of the old ways. Then he blamed the chiefs for not taking care of this problem. Then he blamed white people —soldiers —government — missionaries, for all of it.

"For all of what?" I said, thinking that everything was just fine.

"Oh you know," he said, "people on this reservation acting greedy — the chiefs half scared of one another, acting like politicians — Indians going to white man's court because they don't respect the chiefs — nobody helping each other out anymore — everybody speaking English. Pretty soon Indians will be marrying their own clan. Pretty soon they'll all be alcoholics. Pretty soon they'll all be crazy. I think half the reservation is crazy NOW."

"I didn't know that," I said.

"Well maybe not so much now," he said, slowing down a little. "But in my time, quite a few became crazy. You take old Holland now. We were good friends one time. But he went crazy. I think that's some of your relation too."

"Why was he crazy? What did he do?"

"Well we all know that Indians can't be white people but some try to be. Even the parents are to blame. Maybe they plant white corn but they tell their children, 'Don't live this way — you can do better than this — get a good education — be rich.' Then the children go crazy trying to be two ways; or trying to study too hard; or can't stand it and they turn to alcohol, like Holland did. Why you should have seen him one time, right out in the pouring rain." Old Cap was picking up speed in his talk again. "He had five or six men and women out on the grass drinking that rotten stuff and they were all bare naked. I looked outside and two of them came galloping by on horseback — not a stitch of clothes on! Now you tell me they weren't crazy? And what about Foster? He was worse yet. He had a woman just as crazy as he was. One day, right at Prospect Park above the Falls she took a notion to jump in the river and sacrifice herself like the Maid-of-the-Mist. She got into that icy water and that woke her up and she decided to get back out of there. Did Foster reach out and help her back out? Well he helped her alright — he pushed her right back in again, right in front of all those people (tourists at Niagara Falls). Of course they locked him up for that. But it's all the white man's fault! Don't you see?" I just kept looking at Peters-Hi-velocity. These were exciting happenings that I didn't know about. Maybe I'd get to hear more. He looked at me. "Don't you see that us Indians can't live the white man's way?"

Old Cap was sitting on his step and I was sitting on the grass. All I did was wait for him to keep talking. Instead he bowed his head into his hands. I didn't know what to do. I couldn't figure out why he stopped talking. Quite a while went by and I tried to think of something to say. Before I could, he looked up again. He spoke again and when he did, his voice was low and quiet. "You believe me, don't you?" he asked. I couldn't make out why he changed. Before I could answer, he said, "Well don't. I don't get many visitors anymore. People don't visit like they used to. I'm getting the same way. I don't visit much. Those that I visit with

223

are not like you. Those that I visit with — we always agree. We always talk about the wrongs of the reservation and we always say there's nothing can be done about it and we always agree. We like to blame the white man. We say, 'things are falling apart,' and we always agree. But you, you just look at me. Well I'm going to tell you something — I'm glad you came today. I'm going to tell you something else. I don't WANT to agree that everything is falling apart. Maybe things are NOT right, but I don't HAVE TO BE part of it. YOU don't have to be part of it — nobody HAS TO. It's just easier. And another thing. We haven't lost everything. We still have chiefs. We're NOT all alcoholics. We're NOT crazy. I simply CHOSE to criticize. I expected you to agree. I wanted you to say, 'Yes, it's the white man's fault and we can't do anything about it.' That way, we could sit here and agree and not DO anything."

I said, "Well, I like to hear about the old happenings."

I guess he thought I meant way, way back and he started telling things like how they used to plant corn and beans. He said they even had some medicines that they called "corn medicine." "Indians now don't even remember what it was," he said, "And now that we don't use it, it's scarce. One medicine was Bottlegrass; now, try and find some. They used to boil up this medicine, then soak the corn seeds in it until they sprout. My grandmother says they had corn so healthy there was a halo around the plants, something like we see sometimes around the moon. They put certain fish, certain hardwood ashes in the ground too. They used to have ten, fifteen varieties of corn and beans too. Now we don't even have Indian beans anymore. They used to plant some beans that climb, right next to the corn, and the beans and the corn grew up together. They had special corn for traveling too. They used to pound it up good and dry it by the fire. You just take a handful when you go on a trip; you don't need much because when you swallow just a little, with water, it swells up in your belly." I stayed and listened but these weren't the kind of stories to excite me. The thing was, Cap Peters-Hi-velocity had started out feeling one way, then turned right around and talked like another person.

One day I ran into GAA-neh. He was a big ironworker, maybe half a lifetime old. Now I don't know if there are any man laws or spirit laws that say that getting drunk is a crime or a sin. I don't thing GAA-neh knew either. Just the same, he would separate his drinking times from his going-to-church times; at least, pretty much. Why I say I don't know about spirit law is, one day GAA-neh came and spoke with my father. GAA-neh had been drunk for about a week straight and wasn't done yet. He told my father that he had just been talking to Hru-SNAA-yiihh. "That's odd," my father said, "Hru-SNAA-yiihh (he's skinny) died ten years before you were born, yet you describe him exactly as he was — as he spoke, too."

GAA-neh would go two, three, four years at a crack alcoholizing then he'd stop, go to church, repent, lead prayer groups, yell at people to follow his example, and read the Bible to them. One day during one of his off seasons (ready to go from drinking to preaching) I met him on Susy's Lane on my way back from school. His walk was a little tipsy and he was preaching to himself, or to the road. ". . . and I'm gonna get the Lord's help to walk the straight and narrow — but dammit! This road here won't keep still — oh, chweaant! Elly'a'see-HUHH!" (Hello, Eleazer little.)

I greeted him and then I decided to tease him a little. "Hey," I said. "Is it alright to swear while you're walking the straight and narrow?"

He thought for a minute. "Well," he says, "Horatio seems to think so. Last time I was at the mission prayer meeting he was right there just a 'testifying for dear life.' Took him a good half hour too, telling his wrongs and rights — an' he says '. . . but I don't know about them kids of mine. I'm forever after 'em — telling 'em what's right. I've told 'em and told 'em and TOLD 'em — but the GA-dam sonsa'bitches won't LISTEN!' "

One day I ran into Horatio himself. As we got yakking he says, "Yeaaah, you kids now days got it knocked up. When I was a kid now — that was just after the old medicine folks quit giving a damn — there wasn't nobody scared of the law. Why should they be? Times was tough and if they landed in the clink, why, that was just free eats and bedding. I remember one time Gooh-goo

and his cousin was on the bum. They pitched horse shit out back
for half a day. They thought they was gonna get paid. All the old
man (father) gave them was a meal and they stomped off mad as
hornets. Next thing we heard they had gone to Highland Avenue
(at that time, a run-down section of Niagara Falls) someplace and
chewed some woman's tit right the hell off. And what did they get
for it? — free eats and bedding."

I asked him why the old medicine people quit practicing. He
said, "For one thing the Law came around. My folks never used to
see sheriffs' cars out here. And hell, we think we got some real
nuts out here; well we got news that white people was pointing a
finger at any-damn-body they pleased and yelling 'Witch.' Church-
people too, they was, and once they put the finger on you, you
was DONE. They'd string you up and burn you alive. No damn
wonder the old folks said 'to hell with it!' The chiefs too. Years
ago there was no such a thing as money; so they never WAS paid
and probably never will. Now you take the President of the United
States or even some small-ass politician in Niagara Falls — never
stood in a bread line and never will. Don't WANNA know such
things exist — don't wanna know that there is such a thing as
Indian laws either. What the hell — we're just as bad. We expect a
chief to work eight, ten hours a day someplace, know both laws
plus keep both the reservation and Washington straightened out
too. So I don't blame the old medicine people for just watching
out for themselves. When I was a kid my folks went and got
a'hold of this damn thing we called Monkey Toes. They got it
from Kree'gi(t)-UHH. She come from Six Nations (Canada). Why
christ that thing looked horny. To tell the truth I was scared of
the fuckin' thing. There was these two things looked like monkey
hands with long nails. There was a bone and a silver spoon too.
Whenever somebody was gonna kick the bucket or messing around
with oo-DEEH-seh, '—dadadadadadada—' that bone started rattling
like an alarm clock. I was small too. I remember one night them
monkey paws went off again, '—dadadadadada—.' My old man — I
don't know how he could tell, but as soon as there was a knock on
the door, he said, 'Don't open it. That's Kree'gi(t)-UHH. She came
after the monkey paws. I was always gonna make up a silver
bullet.' He grabbed the shotgun anyway and Ma yanked the door
open. There was nothing but a big black cat standing there. The

226

old man, he let go with that 12 gauge. You ought'a see the fur fly. But the hell — the next morning we looked outside. Here was the neighbor's small black kitten dead; blown to hell. But we seen one set of footprints, woman's shoes, leading off the porch. Now YOU tell me what the Christ was going on! I'm telling you — them days was a BITCH!"

"Yessir," he went on, "I remember one winter we was down to eatin' gruel (flour and water). Soon's I got old enough I got away for a while. Put some years in at Carlisle Indian School too. Then I got hooked up with that sillyass Jim Thorpe. Them were the days. If it wasn't for sports we'd a went looney. That place (Carlisle) was enough to drive anybody fruits. Indians from all over. All trying to get away from tough times on some reservation, yet all homesick. Some was smarter than hell but couldn't speak much English. If we went to earn some spending money off campus on some farm we had to sign a list of things we weren't suppose to do. One was, 'I won't speak any native tongue.' If anybody did some Indian thing, sing or dance, they'd say 'None of that pagan stuff. We don't want no superstitions around here!' Jim Thorpe used to say, 'If you're superstitious — play it out!' He was that way himself, that's why. He always stepped into the football field with his left foot first. One time big Charley Redwater pushed him in, right foot first. There was a helluva fight. They firehosed them to stop it. But what the hell am I telling you all this for? Your old gent was there. And his brother. Now THERE was a case. He went silly in Philly."

Uncle Go-Beddy DID seem odd to me. He was going to teach me to pitch baseball but he never did. Maybe I was just used to him. He seemed businesslike. He had a briefcase and he was gone a lot. "Nobody said nothing to me about that," I said, "What did he do? How silly was he? He was always 'going to' teach me to pitch baseball."

"Why that poor cocksucker was GONE!" Horatio said. "The reason he never taught you to pitch was because he was lucky he could wipe his own ass. I remember one thing. He was baseball-happy. THAT I'll give him. One time he wrote to Connie Mack and told him that he could win the pennant for the Athletics. He said 'I got a new pitch. I call it SNAKE CURVE.' So he got a try-out in Niagara Falls. Connie Mack had a spy watching. All Go-

Beddy done was hold the ball straight up over his head and twirl it around a few times then throw it — straight as a die — at the catcher. With one damn pitch, he struck himself out. Oh, he could pitch scrub league but he was far from a pennant winner. But I mean he done lots of silly things. Spells of it, I think he had. He was always walking the damn streets with that briefcase of his — always going to 'go make a speech someplace.' Maybe I'm just pissed off because I got taken in by him one time myself. I thought to myself, 'Why that lying sack of shit, he ain't never gonna make no speech,' and I told him so too. What did he do? He invited me to hear him speak down at the Dickersonville school-house the next day. Like a jackass I hiked myself down there. Well, he was there alright. He was standing in front of a bunch of school kids recitin' a poem — something about Stonewall Jackson. Sickening! He had on his old Carlisle uniform too. And that's another thing — that old uniform. He used to put that damn thing on and parade up and down Main Street at the Falls. Every once in a while he'd salute somebody — and believe it or not, some was just fucked up enough to salute him right back. Yaaaa — that guy was sure SOMEthin' — always on the go too. Visiting — always on big business. One day one of the kids got nose trouble and peeked in that briefcase of his. Ha! What you think he had in there? Why he was swiping one of our chickens — planning on eatin' that ga'damn skinny cock-a-doodle-doo. Funny," he said, "you could never hate the poor bastard."

"What makes people go goofy?" I asked.

"Who the hell knows," he said. "Old Holland used to say, 'There ain't nobody crazy — it's only what we think.' Maybe some-day he'll make a hell of a good judge, but if you ask me, they shouldn't let people like him run around free. He had this woman Kate locked upstairs with the windows boarded shut. One evening he came puffing over. 'Lend me five dollars,' he says, 'Kate's taken a turn for the worse. I gotta get a doctor. I got money coming; I'll pay you back tonight or tomorrow.' Well, my wife and I, we talked it over. We let him have it but it drained just about all we had. That night we got to thinking. 'By Christ,' I says, 'What the hell we do that for? Why didn't we go see for ourselves.' He only lived little ways. My wife said, 'That's the way I feel. Let's go see. Maybe I can help her.' When we got there, there wasn't a spark of

228

a light to be seen in that house. Well we snuck on in. Me — I was after the MONEY. Pearl — she had just that much devilment in her. Let me tell you somethin'. To this day we wish to hell we never set foot in that place. Kate was dead — dead for a week or better, and STINK! Oh Christ did she stink. We hightailed it for home to get some fresh air. I couldn't even give Pearl a jump that night just thinking about it. The next day, '. . . do(t), do(t). . . ,' Holland's rapping on my door. I let him in. I'm playing Mr. Innocence himself. And for all Holland might be, he had my five bucks in his hand. 'I got baaaad news,' he says, 'We were just a little too late. Katy passed away in my arms — not TEN MINUTES ago.' There was no way in the world I could help it — I HA-HA-HA'ed for a good ten minutes. Of course I snatched that five back first. 'You missed your fuckin' callin',' I told him. 'You shoulda' been a salesman.' But dammit! — I don't blame them old farts; who WAS they to trust? The United States Cavalry? The marshal? Washington? Homesteaders? Bootleggers? Missionaries? Hell no. There wasn't a soul to trust. And I say it'd be one hell of a lot simpler if EVERY white man WAS rotten. Then you'd know where you stood. Take the Masons — you can pick up the paper and see where they're doing good left and right. Damn clannish, maybe, but they still do a lotta' good things — help cripple kids and that. So old Eddy Errand — you remember that poor old one-eyed bastard, never hurt a fly in his life — he wants to get on the bandwagon too. So he joined the Masons. Well, he signed up in Canada where he was born at — I think they call the Masons 'Orangemen' there. Paid his dues for years, then one day he dropped dead. Well Jazz Wilson's kid was a minister, a Mason too, so he did the burial service — beautiful park — fancy shrubs and flowers — high wrought iron fence and gate around it — the works! It was raining and when Eddy's caravan arrived, why hell, nothing but the best — a big new tent over the grave hole. Eddy, mind you, is flat out in a polished walnut casket. So they hoist the casket up with some shiny contraption and he's ready to go under. Jazzes' kid says the last rite and some big wheel Mason dismissed the crowd — you know, like it's bad enough the man's dead — why watch dirty ole' chunks of dirt fall on him too. Everybody ran for their cars. Jazzes' boy shot the shit for a few minutes and when he ran out in the rain, he didn't know which way was which and he ended up at the ass end of the cemetery, at a locked gate. He ran back to the tent for directions. He said later, 'I came dashing through the tent flaps; what I saw embarrassed me so much I ran right back out in the rain again.' The Masons were taking Eddy out of the walnut casket and puttin' him in the ga'dam rough box to be buried in. And that's the kind of shit that makes you wonder who'n all hell to trust — who'n ALL hell IS crazy? Who's an angel and who's a LYING ROTTEN ASS?" Horatio hooked his suspenders with his thumbs and snapped them against his ribs. "Hey," he said, "That reminds me — I haven't et since breakfast. I gotta grub up. Come around oftener," he said, going into the house. I started for home. I could hear him talking to his wife. "Gimme some eggs," he was saying. "Make 'em nice and snotty."

Sometimes I would be talking to one of these old talkers and I'd say, "So and so said that years ago 'such and such' happened. Is that true?"

Like I said to Joo'ga-DOM, "I hear that when this road was getting widened, they found a dead body someplace close to where we're standing right now."

"Yaaas," he said, "It wassa woman." (Some old Indians had this accent. Maybe not Tuscarora.) "Some used to say, Bright Star. Some menfolks call her Pittsburg Sport. Me, I never paid no 'tention to the body. I don't know if she wass Indian or white. What doss it matter? That's the way it wass too, them times. Some wass jus' back from the war. Some of their friends — they never came back. Times wass tuff. So they feel this way, 'I could haf died for nothing.' Mens like that can kill easy — die easy. What do they care about the law? The law nefer show care too — who wass this Bright Star. Those fellas that knew — they say she wass peddling herself — so the law look down on her. Some here knows who did it. What doss it matter? Living things dies sooner or later. I kill a chicken this morning. My gran'pa, he told me; he sess, 'Creation iss what hass the Power. Creation kills peoples efery day, some way. That iss all right; nobody iss to blame. Who are we, then, to put ourselfs in higher judgment than thiss Creation?' I belief him. When the tuff times wass ofer people feel different. Them that ran after that Pittsburg Sport, they wass scattered among the church pews on Sunday too. Maybe they could pray the best. What doss it matter?"

Some of the men that HAD been to wars wouldn't talk about much else than the terrible things they saw. Others wouldn't want to remember it; wouldn't say anything about war. Hama'hama'- Lincoln was an officer in the Navy; a tough thin wiry old bugger. He told me he saw this old Indian sitting by the water; sitting by the Gulf of Mexico, watching a big flock of birds. He says, "I talked to this old man. I asked him what he was doing. He said he was listening to the birds. 'What do they say?' I asked him. He says, 'They gonna fly a long ways — tonight.' There were thousands of them, all twittering away. The old man says, 'Listen! Some of them are sad. Some are sick. Some are old. They know they can't fly that far. They're going south someplace; all water all the way. Them that can't make it — they wait 'til tomorrow.' I believed that old fella. But just the same, I took a walk down by the docks the next morning. There was that old Indian again. Less than two hundred birds were left. They were pretty quiet. The old man was talking to them. He said, 'You won't be happy if you die here alone. Go ahead. It's better to go. . . .' Dang if all them birds didn't take off all at once and head for South America 'til they were out of sight. That old fella walked away from me, but he said once more, 'Some won't make it.' It was sad." That was Hama'hama'- Lincoln's war story. That's all he ever told me. What fooled me — he was tough, but he told me a not tough story.

Not long afterwards, Hama'hama'Lincoln died. Saw'wa- NEEESE told me about it. As much as Indians seemed to be going to work in factories and not visiting each other much; not working the land; they still kept closer track of each other than it looked like. Sometimes they called Hama'hama'Lincoln, 'Abe.' Saw'wa- NEEESE said, "Abe got to drinking pretty heavy towards the last. When his pension check came, he was off to Sanborn, to Marlboro Inn. One day I was battin' the breeze with WAAS-oit, keeping him from overworking on his garden. We saw the mailman stop at Abe's mailbox. Waas said, 'Watch Abe come out. Today his pension comes.' Abe never came out. We decided to walk over — see, may- be he's sick. Soon as we came in his yard I knew something was wrong. By gosh, that little dog of his sent chills right up my spine. He had that dog on a chain and it was half crazy, barking scare-bark. That poor little thing would RUN, hit the end of the chain and turn somersaults, then dash back and do it again. There was no answer at the door. After while Waas says, 'We better go in.' We found Abe inside. He was sittin' on the shit pot, balanced; head forward, ass down. He was deader than a doornail — yessir — he was deader than a doornail. We went out and turned that little dog loose. Son-of-a-gun DID he EVER run — right down the road going east. He must have seen oot-NAA'wog" (ghost).

Some people, though, lived by themselves and seemed to keep to themselves. Like old Star Silver. You would think that living that far from anybody else that he wouldn't know what was happening to others, wouldn't know what was going on on the reservation. Here's what Star Silver said. "One everning I heard something. It came from the southeast; from that woods behind where WEE'rheh lives. It sounded like a damned old water pump — hand pump when it gets rusty. 'What in HELLS' zat?' I says to myself. So I took a hike over. When I got closer I thought maybe it was a shittin' small screech owl, not growed up yet because that noise kept moving. When I got there I knew different. I remembered that noise. They used to call it 'Close-Person Warning.' I went and told WEE'rheh but that lazy bitch never done nothing about it. Her mother died the next day."

Old Star Silver though, he was full of subjects. He was saying ". . . It's funny how some folks pay attention to things, maybe something valuable. But them same darn people's kids won't pick up one stinkin' bit of it. But they WILL pick up SOME thing. Something is always passed on down the line. Now you take NO-blanket. His grandfather and his father never watched out for their own health. Same thing now with NO-blanket. One time he got sinus trouble. Never bothered with Indian medicine — just let it go. After while his fuckin' forehead turned BLACK. Why the silly ass damn near died from it. He was laying on his back in Ransomville Hospital for over three weeks. Them doctors stuck his ass FULL of holes. Pen-a-silly'en or something like that. When he come out they told him, 'You ain't got to worry about clap for three years.' "

Then once he was saying, ". . . I remember how your grandfather Dehhh'WEEESE used to holler at YOUR father, 'WA'CHOO DO THAT FOR! DON'T TALK BACK!' "

"Hey," I said, "That's what my father says to me NOW. I wonder who started that, Adam and Eve?"

"Maybe Adam Hru(t)-gweese," he said laughing. (Adam Turtle. He was some past relation of mine).

"By Christ," he went on, "We can make fun of them old bastards but I'll tell you something. Don't underestimate them old heads. Some couldn't even talk English. Not long ago they had a big fire up north. The whole woods was going up in smoke. Lots'a Indian homes in danger. Well they could stop it if they could pump the water from the creek to the top the hill. That was their only chance. Well them forest rangers, they only brought in a bunch of small pumps — none of them strong enough. They was ready to pull out when old Houng'gwanee and his boys came up the creek in birch barks. Couldn't talk a word of English. He just lined them canoes up, so far apart, up the hill. Then he pumped water into the first one, another pump to the second one, and so on right up the hill and they hosed that damn fire to death. No. Them horny old timers didn't just piss time away in a pinch. What about Haa'hree BEE'sehh? He had no business roofing with his boys at his age. But what happened when they hired that white kid and his foot went through that hole? A bucket of boiling asphalt in each hand too. Before that kid's hands hit bottom in them buckets old Haa'hree had him flying flat out across that roof like a skinned rabbit, peeled his shirts and sweaters and gloves right up over his head. You seen them old Snappin Turtles — before you can blink, they can pick off them Na-HRE(T)' HRE(T) (sunfish). All that kid lost was some skin off his wrists. Now that's the stuff a fella's kids could use — IF it gets handed down. I don't suppose it all will though," Old Star said, looking into the big swamp. "I'll be six foot under one of these days myself, but I wouldn't mind hanging around long enough to see what this reservation comes to. I s'pose kids will be going on to college. Maybe one day they'll be drag assing back with a buttful of degrees and a license to dig up old Indian skulls or somethin'. Already I seen one of the youngfolks out here carryin' one of them electric treasure finders."

"Did he get anything?" I asked, kind of excited.

"Yeah," Old Star said. "Exercise."

Quite a few Indians HAD already gone to college. One was

my aunt; my father's sister; she was a nurse. Sir William said maybe she was a witch too. One winter after we moved to Dog Street he was walking along the hill back of the old house. He said he seen somebody's footprints in the snow. Barefoot. He said, "I thought to myself, 'who would do a thing like that — go barefoot in the snow.' I followed them tracks but I kept watching way ahead — I thought maybe it was ooh-DUT-cheahh (Indian boogeyman or spirit warner of sexy misbehavior). I followed them tracks to the middle of that cherry orchard then, poof! they just ended. They were clear, quite fresh, and there was no drifting. I took them tracks backwards and I ended up back at that old house." He meant where I used to live, where I was born. Only my Aunt Min lived there anymore but she was suppose to be in New York City, nursing people.

She never got married and she used to send me books, and they were always for people way, way past my age. One time I asked what she learned in school. She said, "Oh, different languages. I studied chemistry and nutrition and I learned to stay away from food stores. You might as well eat paper." (I used to chew paper once in a while. Pretend it was gum. Then I used to spit out the juice — pretend it was chewing tobacco.)

"First of all," she said, "all the fruits and vegetables and grain comes from some big money crazy farmer that has to buy fertilizer just to make anything grow anymore. More than half the vitamins and minerals and trace elements that our body needs from this earth to fight disease haven't even been discovered yet. I took some rotten-smelling black earth right out of the swamp one time and put it under a strong microscope. That dirt was just CRAWLING with life. Then I mixed it with two kinds of regular fertilizer and left it overnight. The next day that earth was DEAD. Well you remember," she said, "when your pigs got sick. They could hardly walk. They had rickets because they didn't get any sunshine in that old log shed and all they ate was middling from Allen Milling Company. I told your father to let them out; let them loose. You remember what they did. Hogs are smarter than us scientists. They went out and ate pure dirt. In one week we couldn't catch them. Oh sure, fertilizer will make plants grow, but they're not healthy. They get diseases so the chemical companies can jump for joy. Thousands of dollars are spent on discoveries for

234

cures for plant diseases. Then bugs and worms — they come flocking to any weak plants."

"How can a plant be too healthy for a bug or a worm?" I asked her.

"Maybe it's not necessary to know WHY," she said, "I don't know why, but did you ever see a bug or a worm on a May apple (wild mandrake)?" I had to admit I hadn't. Then she said, "What about elderberries and blackcaps and wild strawberries — oo-wa(t) berries and herbs? Why don't they get diseases and die? But it only matters that you and I know that mother earth knows more chemistry than people ever will. I learned, in one of the best colleges in the world, that elements can not be changed, only compounded. (That's what I was — confounded — at her words, but I let her go on.) But plants do it all the time. But the food stores — what else do they sell — meat — and what did these animals eat? Grain from big farms. Food grown in that dead soil. And what do people eat? Meat AND produce? Yes, but food that's even worse. Big food stores handle lots of food. They are only in business to make money. They can't afford to let thousands of pounds of food spoil on them so the chemical companies get busy again and offer 'new' and 'better' chemical preservatives. And the more this happens the more we hear about cancers and heart and bone diseases. So the chemical companies get busy and make chemicals and drugs for plants and animals and people. Everybody gets rich because nobody's healthy. Years ago Indians ate rotten meat, and corn rotted in decomposing swamp mud. I mean they let it rot on purpose. I probably couldn't eat it now, just as I can't eat limburger cheese, but who knows? Maybe they had something. They never had cancer. What it boils down to — what it just seems to me is — what good is it that is in the teachings of the universities of the world? They are not teaching people how to NOT HAVE disease. The chemicals — the drugs that kill the germs of disease also kill germs in us that we need for health. We need the health of May apples, not of blighted wheat. I've been feeling something lately. I've been feeling like I need to get out of the city. I pay a lot for food that's supposedly grown without chemical fertilizers. I like the vegetables your father grows. I feel that I need to live out here and grow my own too. I feel that your father knows what he's doing when he puts plant matter, manure, hickory ashes —

things of this earth — back into the soil. I feel it best to leave the city."

When Aunt Min went back to New York, she took me with her to see the big city. Let me tell you something. If you haven't been there, don't go there. It ain't like a big woods at night where the bugs and the trees and the wind talk to you. If you talk to anybody in New York City, they just stare at you. Also, in the woods you can go anywhere, day or night. In the big city, every door is locked at night. Even Min changed as soon as we left for the train to go. She put up her long black hair into a bun at the back of her head and never let it out again. She was someplace between sixty and seventy years old but she had never got married. On the reservation she spoke to any man, but in the city, I never saw her speak to any man; not even one. She was getting to be a little hard of hearing but when we got to New York, she went stone deaf — "deef," some of the old Indians used to say. We took one little bus ride but all other times we were worse than moles, traveling underground and popping up here and there. On that bus ride, just because she was deef now, she embarrassed me. Maybe she thought I couldn't hear either. She'd cup her hand over one side of her mouth to aim the sound of her voice right at me, even though we were sitting side by side in the bus. "THERE'S GRANT'S TOMB," she'd shout, or some such thing. Besides, I couldn't care less if Grants was going out of business or not. I could SURE understand why she "felt it best to leave the city." Besides, it's VERY noisy in a city; but you can't hear anything. I wanted to go home before I went deef too. One trick I learned and maybe you ought to try it too. My Aunt Min thought of it. She put me on a train to go home even though that was the thing I was scared the most of. But she gave me some cards with writing on them. "Where is the toilet?" "Where is the drinking water?" "Which train to Niagara Falls?" (from Buffalo or You'THROOh-rehhh). Things like that. Well I figured I could talk better than cards. I was wrong. People paid no attention to me. As soon as I showed the cards, though, somebody said, "Oh dear, he's a mute," and I never had to speak another word all the way home. I just laughed when I told my folks about that and they said, "Shame on you." You can do that too. You can just laugh if somebody says, "Shame on you," if you use cards.

236

Once in a great while, Mother would buy a dozen oranges. One day she did that. I was sucking on one of them when I looked at my hands. They were all bright orange color. Somebody had painted the oranges to make them look healthy. I threw the orange down and ran to the little stream of water that ran out of our drinking water spring and washed my hands. I though of what my aunt had told me about bought foods. "Maybe that orange means bad luck," I thought.

I was glad that my Aunt Min had told me such a rare thing. Maybe she WAS a witch. The next day we got the news. A thing even rarer had happened to Min. On the very last day of her work —on the underground trains that she was riding, to retire from New York City forever —a man stabbed her to death. A state trooper came with a black and white car to tell us about it. He said the man that did it was in jail. He also said that this man's bloodstream was full of drugs. I ran to the woods to tell the news but when I got there, the woods already knew. Not a breath of air spoke and all the leaves were looking downward.

Way out on the southeast end of the reservation, a relative of mine lived. She was very kind to me but I didn't see her very often. People said she was a strong witch but I only thought of her kindness. I thought she was the smartest woman in the world. Her name was Heee'engs.

I could ask her ANY question. She told me before she died that I was too young to learn power yet but that my father could show me that when it was time. One day I met her and Saw'hri'- Mah hr'I in the woods gathering medicine. I didn't have nothing better to do so I went with them. They were looking for Hroo DAA yuk. (Don't know English name.) We come to a place where Heee'engs said, "It grows right here." I couldn't see a single plant anywheres but I could smell it. Heee'engs pulled out a small rag bag of medicine. She put some on the ground and said "Neow'- WIHH" (thank you). Where she put the medicine I saw one plant. I happened to turn around behind me. Hroo DAA yuk was suddenly all over the place. The women didn't take very much of it.

One day soon after Aunt Min died I made it my special business to go and talk with Heee'engs. I had been thinking about

the health of wild fruits and berries and nuts. Could a person live
on just this? What about Indians long time ago? What did they eat
in winter? If anybody could tell me, Heee'engs could. She seemed
to know everything. She seemed to know way ahead of time, what
was going to happen — especially the weather — I bet she knew a
thousand signs. She said that snow fleas told her which wax to use
on snowsnakes. (A winter sport where Indian men threw a spear-
like wooden shaft, called a snowsnake, down a log track, for distance.) She listened to screech owls and watched the movements
of animals. If a cow or horse shook its body she knew how soon
rain would come. If someone killed any game in autumn she
looked at the fur of its feet to see how cold winter would be. She
was able to get seagulls to come around and tell her about rain,
and boy! can they EVER squawk. While I was with her gathering
medicine that time I asked her why she kept looking at trees. She
said, "There used to be a little power called 'Cyclone-Warning.' I
haven't seen it for long time. It looks like a porcupine quill with a
hair tail. If you see it stuck in a tree with the tail waving, that
means 'Cyclone' is coming."

I myself knew quite a few signs. Everybody did. A sundog
means warm weather. Lots of cornhusks means cold winter. Of
course clouds and robins tell easy signs of weather. Also, when
you can hear noises clearly, like chopping in the woods, for a long
distance; that means rain or snow too. But Heee'engs; she noticed
everything. If somebody skinned an animal she checked on how
much fat it had. She opened its stomach to see what it ate. She
watched the direction of shooting stars or if a new moon was
laying down or standing up. She said to me, "Don't point at a
storm — bad luck. Don't point at a rainbow — bad luck." Once she
said, "If you see chickens roosting in the daytime, tell your
mother to bring in the clothes off the line, it's going to rain."
I don't know how she could tell weather from the Northern
Lights because it didn't just mean "rain" or "dry weather" or
"cold." I like the name, Northern Lights in Tuscarora. It says,

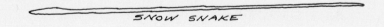

SNOW SNAKE

"the-sky-is-performing," and it gives the feeling that the sky is a solid thing that I could touch.

I guess I could go on and on about the things Heee'engs paid attention to. These were all simple things to her. It was like hearing a car coming down the road and without looking, you could say, "A car is coming" and it WOULD be. Even if she was in a house she paid attention. If the fire made a little bunch of explosions, rain was coming. She said that years ago there used to be a great big black and white woodpecker that was the best weather prophet but it died out. She told me too, that if I ever was fishing for sturgeon and one jumped out of the water, not to kill it — to go home because it was telling me that rain was coming. Oh I tell you, she knew thousands and thousands of things but she wouldn't tell me yet, how to CHANGE weather. Song, though, told me what he saw her do. He met her gathering medicine too and they got to talking medicine until a storm came up. Song said she was carrying a walking stick. "She wasn't done talking yet so all she did was jab that stick in the ground and point it at the coming rain. The storm swung off to the side but I had to keep gabbing because it was raining hard on the next woods over." I guess it's enough to tell you that Heee'engs knew her stuff alright!

So I made this special trip to talk to Heee'engs about Indian food. She wasn't too tall of a person and she was very skinny. Her eyes were kind of sunk in but they were very black and shiny. So was her hair although I think she was very old. I got there early but she was up already smoking her pipe and paying close attention, with them black eyes, to what the smoke was doing. I don't think she ever blinked her eyes — unless she did it exactly at the same time that I blinked mine. Maybe she even slept that way.

Before I could ask her anything she said, "I knew you were coming. Are you hungry? You have food on your mind." When I told her what I came for and when I asked her what did the old Indians eat, she rolled her eyes up and flopped her head on her shoulder and let her tongue land out as much as to say, "I'm dead tired already just thinking of answering that."

She spoke a half a dozen Indian languages but when she began answering she spoke mostly Tuscarora to me. "I think it would be best if I began telling you some of the things that they DIDN'T eat," she said. "Salt was one thing. That was mainly medicine — for sore guts. Different ones wouldn't eat certain things and they had their own good reasons; like bad luck to eat animals that have holes in a cemetery. Or maybe they wouldn't eat animals or birds of their own clan. Maybe some wouldn't eat snakes because they didn't like the idea or it was bad luck to THEM. Maybe some wouldn't eat owls because owls brought them good news. But there was one thing NObody ate. Loons. Loons are to protect Indians. They have good power. Never kill or eat a loon."

While Heee'engs was talking, she had put down her pipe. She had about fifteen different medicine leaves that she used for tobacco. I thought her pipe had gone out but she stopped talking and looked at her pipe. A little stream of smoke had come out of it. Heee'engs went to her door and looked out towards Chew Road. She seemed to be waiting for something. I looked out the window but I saw nothing. In a minute or so though, a woman came into view walking on the road. It was WEE'hrehh. "I'M BUSY TO-DAY!" Heee'engs called out to her. I could hear WEE'hrehh say something about that she just wanted to tell Heee'engs that she got all her tomato canning done. Heee'engs nodded to her and waved her off "good-bye" and sat down again. "I wish people would stop coming to me with their problems," she said. "It's high time they paddled their own canoes. WEE'hrehh had some-body stealing her tomatoes so she comes running to me. I put guards on her tomato patch — blacksnakes in the daytime and night hawks at night." As she said ". . . night hawks at night," she flipped out a little medicine bag that hung around her neck. I take it she meant that she never left her house to do these things. "I won't eat night hawk," she said. "That's got good power too. If you find their nest, you better not be bothering the little ones. The older ones can dive on you and 'boom' in your ear. You can go deaf." Maybe my Aunt Min had done that.

Heee'engs made us some Wa CHEE huh hruhhk tea (penny-royal). "Years ago," she said, "the Indians ate medicine because everything was medicine, or else they MADE it medicine. What they planted mainly was corn, beans, squash. But first they made medicine. Then they put the seeds in the medicine while the sun traveled one fist length. Then they put the wet seeds in a jar to crack open a little bit. They used to plant at full moon, about the time when the Juneberry blossoms (shad). These three things, corn, beans, squash, are called the Three Sisters. Never did they put the seeds in the earth without telling the Creator first what they are going to do; and they ask the Creator's help for them to grow."

Heee'engs smiled as she spoke. She put a chunk of wood on to keep the water hot and lit her pipe again with a long sliver. I pictured it in my mind that it would be hard for her to raise her voice against anybody or anything. "Somebody else is coming," she said as she sat down, "but let them. I feel good now." Pretty soon I heard heavy footsteps by the door. I thought it was a man but it was HrooSAAnoo-oit (crab, big). She owned the house that Heee'engs was renting. Maybe that's why she just walked right in.

"Good morning, Heee'engs," she said with music in her voice. "Isn't it a beau-ti-ful day. How are you?"

A big voice came out of Heee'engs that I didn't think was in her. "NOW YOU KNOW GA'DAMN WELL THAT YOU DON'T GIVE A GOOD GA'DAMN HOW I AM!" she said in English. Me and HrooSAAnoo-oit were startled but Heee'engs just pointed the stem of her pipe at the open door.

Now it was HrooSAAnoo-oit's turn. "You ugly bitch!" she said.

"Get out of here with that lying sweet talk," Heee'engs said. "It's enough to make a maggot puke."

In less than a minute I had seen two people change feelings. Before HrooSAAnoo-oit was all the way out the doorway on her way out, Heee'engs was smiling and talking again as though nothing had happened.

"That's another thing Indians used to eat," she said. "Crabs, (crawfish) just the tails; fry them or roast them or boil them or put them in soup or cornbread. The same with just about everything else. They cooked in different ways. They smoked a lot of meat too. Eels, fish, clams, oysters, mussels; some ate snake meat, but not me. Snake has power too. But to tell you ALL the things they ate. . . ," Heee'engs just shook her head, ". . . well, to start with, I can name you fifteen different kinds of corn. All you see now is Ga'neh ha GEH'hrod (Tuscarora white corn) and

Ga'NOO(t)-gee(t) (calico corn). All was medicine too, especially the silk of calico corn. Remember, they gave medicine to the seeds first."

"What was that medicine?" I asked. I figured our corn could'a used some.

"U'Sa'ga'ada' and gusdis'ni," she said. (Onondaga which I don't understand.) She went on, "There was more kinds of corn than that too, and about forty different kinds of beans. I can name twenty-five or thirty. Then there was all kinds of squash, pump-kins, gourds, cucumbers, and melons. Some melons they used to cook. Everybody used to work together too, like a quilting bee or chopping bee that we have yet. They all talk to Ra'wiNEEyu(t) (Creator) too first. That's the strongest power. They do this each time, before they clear the trees, or plant, or hoe, or harvest; also they have ceremonies to give thanks or bring rain in between. Two more important things was always in the fields too — Indian tobacco and sunflowers."

"Yeah, but what about wintertime?" I said. "That sounds like lots of food, but what about wintertime?"

"Oh they were worse than squirrels," she said. "They dug food pits all over with poles and bark and sod on top; but let me just tell you about the food — we're just getting started. Before I go any farther though, let's see what we have already. Start with corn. They had different varieties for breads, different varieties for soups, some for traveling (ground, baked white corn) (na'you ta'HA-QUOT'tu(t) or 'what you walk-long-ways-with-type'), some for puddings, some for dumplings, and that's just to start with. Now you take cornbread. Some was plain, some with beans of many choices, some with many choices of wild fruits and berries, some with different choices of nuts, and any of these different kinds of breads of different kinds of corn could be sweetened with maple syrup or not. Corn was only one kind of flour too. They made flour of seeds and roots, acorns, chestnuts, beans, lots of things. They could mix these flours and add any kind of medicines for ceremonies or power or flavorings. I guess you can see what kind of question you ask when you ask about the food of long ago. One time I had bean bread with crab tails and frog legs in it."

This began to sound to me like the learnings of medicines.

No wonder there was no written language. There wasn't TIME to write; or if anyone did, they'd STILL be writing. Still—food seemed easier to remember; maybe not the recipes but just all the things that I had ever eaten; like black ants, they taste like wild grapes. While I was thinking, Heee'engs had got up and was walking around but she was still talking. "... flint corn and popcorn too," she was saying. When I noticed what she was doing, getting something for us to eat, I told her that I had just eaten—a lot too, because I tried to eat enough for all day. She just kept right on frying cornbread in butter. "Just pre-tennnnnnd you're hungry," she said. Maybe she witched me, I don't know, but I ate everything up plus two pieces of elderberry pie with butternuts in the berries.

I asked her how she could remember all that. She said, "If you know medicine, you can see pictures." She got her pipe and picked out a couple medicine leaves and stoked them up. She leaned back in a big chair and rested her feet up on the kitchen table, just kind of kicking things out of the way for room. She gazed up towards where the wall and the ceiling came together. "Get ready," she said, "I'll tell you what I see. It's quicker this way."

You better get ready too. I'll try to remember everything but she let go with quite a list. "You know most of the plants," she said, "They never ate plants with white leaves—that's power medicine, but they ate white fungus—many kinds; all except amanita, which they had medicine to equalize that poison. They even ate them stinkhorns. Some fungus is great medicine. But plants now (I'll translate to English as best I can) nettle, wood betony, watercress, wild garlic, dandelion, burdock, yellowdock, leeks, sensitive fern (deer, what-they-lie-on), mustard, milkweed, pigweed, purslane, peppermint, sorrel, smartweed, spotted-leaves— some they ate the roots of—jack-in-the-pulpit (boil first, or it'll burn your tongue off), lilies, cattails, skunk cabbage (cook first or it'll burn you), arrowhead (water plant), arrow arum (water plant), cucumber root, Solomon's-seal, hog plum (in North Carolina only), pokeweed, toothwort, wild potato vine (morning glory variety, cook first, bitter), cow parsnip, groundnut (wild beans), pepper root, wild potato (wild sunflower variety), groundnut (dwarf ginseng variety), wild potato (long-red-deep eyes), wild potato (horn shape-purple), spring beauty. . . ." It WAS as bad as the medicines. I wanted to stop Heee'engs but she went right on reciting from pictures ". . . stalks of early shoots of ferns, grapevine, sumac, wild raspberry. . . ." Oh I knew I shouldn't have asked. I was beginning to see pictures too and I could hardly listen.

"Hey," I yelled, "I can't keep up." But Heee'engs was in a trance and couldn't hear worse than me. "Ooooooo," I said to myself gritting my teeth. I rapped myself (lightly, of course) on the skull like Geese-a-geese used to do and cupped my hands behind my ears for best hearing. Heee'engs was rattling on.

". . . red and black currants, red and black cherries, ground cherries (dogberry), May apples, wild plums, chokecherries, wild grapes, mulberries, squaw berries (some say, partridgeberry), wintergreen berries, tree berry (Vibernum) nannyberry, Juneberry, cranberry, blueberries (high and low), gooseberries, strawberries (three kinds), elderberries, purple flowering raspberries, blackberries (black caps and yellow caps), thimbleberries (ground and bush. . . ." I couldn't stand it any longer. I was going deaf again; and blind. I jumped up in front of Heee'engs and waved my arms. This time she stopped.

"Let's rest, let's rest!" I said to her, "My hearing is going backwards."

"That's because you listen too hard," she said. "I'm dry anyway." She got up and made goldenrod tea. "There's many different kinds of goldenrod," she said, "but the one that looks like little elm trees are good medicine. On a hot day you can put your hand under the flowers and it feels cold."

After I drank the tea I felt like I could hear good again. "What did they drink?" I asked.

Heee'engs acted scared. She looked behind her and behind me. Then she sat still as though she was listening for something. She got up and, glancing around as she came towards me, she cupped her hand over her mouth a little and whispered in my ear. "Water," she said.

After we got done laughing she explained to me that Indians were always joking and acting like that. "In them days though," she said, "I would have had to put on a better act than that. Everybody was wide awake to everything—just like a Dare."

244

(White crane that nobody could get close to because it could see
and hear with powerful eyes and ears.)

She went and got a pillow for me and told me to lay back
and listen easy; then she went on talking. "I won't talk from
pictures anymore and I'll tell you some of the things they drank.
They had many many kinds of soup without salt so they didn't
have to drink often. I don't have to tell you how many medicine
plants there are that you can make tea from — hemlock, black
birch, spicewood, wintergreen, yarrow, witch hazel, red raspberry,
sumac berries, horsemint, sassafrass — things like that were common teas. They made drinks like a coffee from corn, sunflowers,
roasted chestnuts — oh they had plenty of drinks — sap of wild
grape, maples, buttonwood, ash, walnut, and wild cherry. Ash not
much because it flows so slow. Wild cherry is bitter so they added
water and maple sugar. Some used to just break a small limb off
and catch the sap that way. Some used to just chop a flat gash in a
tree and drive a wet piece of wet wood into it so that it hangs
down a little. The sap will follow the wet wood and drip off.
Indians didn't drink much because they ate lots of the greens I
told you about, raw. The shoots of many plants are juicy, just
like the roots and bulbs of water plants and lilies. They ate green
corn raw too and made many dishes of it. We don't do that anymore. The recipes for soups and puddings of corn, beans, squash,
pumpkins, cooked melons, bulbs, nuts, and fruits are endless.
They used to eat mashed beans like we eat mashed potatoes. Or
mashed squash or pumpkin. They used to make nut meat gravy.
Nuts and seeds are full of oil. They used to mash them and boil
them for oil — especially sunflower seeds. That is strong medicine,
that oil. We can go on and on because they knew how to dry
food too, and that tastes different. Different kinds of fish planted
under corn makes a different taste to corn too. When they dry
some things just before it's ripe, that taste different too. Every
meat of every bird or animal or turtle or water things — fish, frogs,
clams, eels, crabs, oysters, mussels — they all taste different. The
meat taste different dried out. Different meats from different
parts of the body taste different. Beaver tail is highly prized.
Turtle has half a dozen different flavors. Meat wrapped in basswood leaves to bake taste different. Lots of meat was smoked.
Different wood makes different smoke taste. And don't forget, the

woods was full of flavoring plants. If you had a big pot of wood-pecker soup, maybe the next meal your mother would add laurel (bay leaves), or dried mushrooms, or some wood charcoal, or seeds of. . . ."

" 'WOODPECKER soup?! CHARcoal?' " I yelled.

"Sure. Charcoal is good flavoring. It floats too. All you do is pick it out, then eat. Bird meat is good too. The women used to make bird traps, especially around the braided corn when it was drying outside yet. It's just a hole in a piece of bark with a bass-wood skin loop on the inside. Birds poke their heads in the hole and get caught. Squirrels too. I told you," she said, "The only thing I know that Indians didn't eat for sure was loons. They didn't waste much." While she was talking, a wasp flew in through the door and went into a hole in a little house made of dry mud on a lath where plaster was missing. She got up and got a broom and 'buks'ed the wood near the mud house. The wasp came out and she whacked it against the wall with the broom. It fell on the floor and she stamped on it. Then she poked and banged the edge of the wasphouse until it fell. It broke on the floor. She reached down and picked up a baby wasp. It was all white. She popped it into her mouth. I could hear her chew it. That was enough for me. "Indian candy," she said.

I didn't really care but I said, "What does it taste like?"

"Waspy," she said, grinning. "The way your mouth is hang-ing, it looks like you can taste it too."

"I can," I said.

"What does it taste like?"

"It tastes like I better be going home."

Quite often, if I heard something interesting, I'd see who else knew about such things. Maybe after hearing a good ghost story, I'd go on a ghost-questioning spree. I was pretty sure not many could add to anything Heee'engs had told me but I asked anyways. Song was the guy I cornered. He was the best of any-body to listen to because as he spoke Indian, his voice flowed up and down, nice and slow, like a song. He said, "Oh sure — young wasps are good. Seventeen-year locusts too. They used to call it health food. My grandmother used to make soup and we could eat anytime. One evening I saw her hang a lantern on the apple tree by the house. When it got a little darker she went out with a wet rag and whipped it around next to the lantern. She put that rag right in the soup and cooked it. When I asked her why, she said, 'Gnats make good flavor.' She showed me other things too. I used to chew young wheat. You know how it makes that white gum. One day grandmother told me to mix it with slippery elm. I did. After that, the gum wasn't so much like rubber. We used to chew dead pine pitch and beeswax too; and basswood buds. I hear the best is that spongy tissue from female deer tits but I never tried that."

Being as Song spent more time in the woods than in the kitchen, his talk WAS different — more of animals or things of the woods. "Indians used to try to be like animals or birds — whatever they wished for — maybe eat deer meat to make them run like a deer. Or drink turtle blood to live a long life. They used to eat mice but only the one that has a short tail. I don't know why. We don't believe the way they used to — maybe just a FEW things. I saw Onondagas using deer tallow in their snowsnake wax for speed one time. But things have changed over the years. Corn used to grow tall. Indians used to give the kids a piece of cornstalk to suck on so they would grow tall too."

"What makes things change like that?"

"Use," he said. "When I used to handle big logs in the woods my arms were big and strong. Now they're small and flabby. But Indians used to know that it goes farther than that. If you don't tell your corn to grow tall, it won't. If you don't use Indian medicine, it will go away. We used to have wild rice — wild oats, but we got lazy and didn't use them anymore. They disappeared. We don't use elm bark for dishes or pails or rattles anymore. We don't make any more barkhouse. The elms are disappearing too. There used to be a bunch of flying squirrels living around my house. They were the best weather prophets. They used to stick their little heads out of them holes and holler, 'rain coming, rain coming.' Gradually I began to pick up a newspaper and look at the weather there instead. In one year them flying squirrels all disappeared. They knew that I wasn't using their weather reports anymore so they went away. Now I find out that the weather news in the paper tells lies sometimes. I remember when I went to school, if we talked about animals knowing the weather, our teacher would say that these things were just old superstitions. 'But of course,' the teacher said, 'Indians used to be a backward people.' "

"Backward from what?" I asked.

"Backward from what the teacher believed. Well, you stop and think about it, Indians DID do lots of things that were opposite from white people's ways, but I can't say one way is 'backwards' from the other, just opposite."

"What did Indians do opposite?"

"Now you take the old hunters. They never carried pots and pans along when they went on a big hunt. They didn't have to eat at a certain time either. If they killed a deer they didn't put the meat inside of a kettle then heat the outside of the kettle. They just take the guts out and lay the deer on its back, put water in the cavity and maybe the heart or liver or some other small game and maybe some wild potatoes. Then they heated stones and put the hot rocks in the water and cooked that way. Why carry pots and pans?"

"What else was opposite?"

"Well, the old Indians used to use medicine BEFORE they got sick. Now people wait until they get sick, THEN they use medicine."

"How did they know BEFORE they got sick, that they were gonna get sick?"

"Indians paid close attention to all signs, to all dreams, and they USED this knowledge. Nowdays people, even people in the government, can't even see war or hard times coming, let alone earthquakes or cyclones. Even just the thought that Indians were 'backwards' is opposite of how the Indians could think of the white people."

"Well I, for one, would like to know when I was going to be sick BEFORE I get sick, and I don't even know the signs to USE before they disappear. Maybe that all disappeared already."

"Maybe," Song said, "But I have a feeling that some day people will feel like you do, and begin to watch for signs again. Whoever does, will begin to see these signs again. I'm sure they will USE them too, because by that time, I think they will need them."

248

Now you have to understand that I didn't just spend every minute of my time going from person to person asking questions. In fact, sometimes it was quite a while before I got the chance. I went to school and picked fights and played sports too, just like you did. Also, some old Indians didn't seem to know any more than I did, or else they just didn't feel like talking sometimes, the same as we are on certain days. So quite a bit of time slipped by on me.

It was sometimes disappointing to hear Indians say, "I don't know." After my father died, I was disappointed with myself because there were quite a few things I didn't know the Indian names of because I had never asked. Even my mother had forgotten the names of some of the trees in the woods. Of course her time had been spent in the kitchen, not the woods. I was getting older and the old Indian men were dying off. I had an uncle named HAA-hree. He had grey eyes and light hair. He had played professional basketball in his younger days and when he walked, straight-backed with his butt sticking out, it always seemed as though he was expecting somebody to dash up from his blind sides and take a ball away from him. He used to hum or whistle a lot and it seemed like he went through life like he drove a car. My mother and I went to Buffalo with him in his car one day. My father used to drive about ten miles per hour under the speed limits but HAA-hree drove about ten OVER. Not only that, he was all over the road, in and out and around other cars, passing wherever there was a few inches clearance for his car. Right up Main Street in Buffalo like that, whistling or humming away. All of a sudden he might take a notion to swerve down some crummy street. "Short-cut," he'd say in Tuscarora. Even if we got lost, he'd wiggle his way back out of it, and to him it was still "short-cut." I began to notice that all this time, whenever he spoke, he never used English. When we got back home I got an idea. I ran through the woods breaking off limbs.

I ran up to Uncle HAA-hree and said, "Can you tell me the Indian names of these trees?"

"What's the matter with you?" he said in Tuscarora. Then, he started naming "jigHE(T)du(t) (hard maple), HU(T)'throo(t) (thornapple), Jooh g'wa g'we(t)NEH'neeh (black walnut), WUH'ck (white ash), ooHOOOS stu(t) (basswood), th'wa hew WAH(T) (apple), ga soo(t)GWAATH'thehh (butternut), youhh d'yehh hruhh GEE'WA gihh (bitter hickory), ja wa h'yuss SUHH hrihh (elder), naw hihhh WO(T) (prickly ash), naw HRAWWgwee(t) (sumac), HOOGKS (slippery elm), gaHROD gwahh (elm), youSNAA yihhh (blue beech), HROO(T) daw(f) (hickory)." Those were all the branches I had given him. I thought I could fool him. I had brought along a short piece of bittersweet vine. (The orange berry kind, not nightshade.) I had broken it off low so it would be straight, not curly yet. This was like a final test. I poked it out at him. "Na guthwa HREE(T)ehh," he said, taking it out of my hand and throwing it up on top of the roof of our house. "It brings good luck to you when you do that," he said. "It's good medicine for broken bones too, but don't use too much — it's pretty strong."

"Well," I thought to myself, "somebody's still alive that I can tap for information." But guess what? HE died too before I got to ask him another thing.

In one of my talks with an old Indian named Georgenash, he had said, "Whatever you're near, however you spend your time, whoever you spend your time with, however these things are — that's the way you'll become." That's what was happening to me. I lived on Dog Street now. I didn't go into the woods as much anymore. Most of the grownups worked at factories now. Not as many Indians were planting much food anymore. I was going to school and getting good report cards. That's the way I was becoming — the way I spent my time. Everything in the books I read was becoming the place of information and "the tellers" that I used to question were going into coffins and lowered into holes in the graveyard and covered up.

One day somebody said, "Romeo Green is back."

By this time I was in a place where I gave some kind of answer like, "I didn't even know that there was ever such a color."

When I found out that he was an old Tuscarora, I began asking around to find out how come I never heard of him. Well, it seems that some years before my time some Indian parents were told in a nice way that their children would do better in a boarding school. So little Romeo took off for higher learning. I don't know what schools Romeo went to, maybe Haskell Indian School or Carlisle plus Georgetown University. Somewhere along the way he

got interested in music. So he learned a few notes at a place called Juilliard. In fact he learned enough notes to become a member of some symphony orchestra, and there he lived ever after, until now.

One day I was dog-trotting along past Scoop's house and I heard some music. I knew Scoop had electricity now but no radio, only a few bulbs that he hated to turn on for too long a time. Also the music seemed quite jazzy. It seemed to be coming from the back of the house so I walked around the house and came to see my first look at Romeo Green.

He was quite a big man and his face looked something like the painting of Tecumseh except with a white man's haircut and new overalls. The music was coming from a record on a phonograph with wires coming out of Scoop's window. Romeo was sitting in a lawn chair with a big book which, later, I saw that it was poetry. I could see the cardboard thing that the record had come out of. It had a picture of a man with a saxophone on it; also the name, Stan Getz.

Right away Romeo began to talk and at first he got the jump on me. That is, HE was asking questions instead of me. I found out too, then, that grownups find it easier to talk about some things with children than with people their own age.

Mostly, he asked me who, of the older folks, was dead on the reservation. Somewhere along the line of our talk he suddenly grabbed the big book of poetry and threw it into the middle of the big honeysuckle bush. "Some of the greatest poets," he said, "are buried right here on this reservation. But the sad thing is, nobody knew that, not even the poets themselves. You remember Bee-land? He was one of them."

I began to picture Bee-land again. At first I pictured him mumbling the English language on Christmas night as he gave instructions about The Feast. But then I remembered always trying to sit close to him in church so I could hear him speak to the Creator. He always spoke Tuscarora then. He would also always be chewing something — maybe slippery elm. This caused a ball of muscle on the side of his head to jump in and out as he talked and chewed. And now, as Romeo spoke of poetry, I could see this ball of muscle again, like a hammer in his head, pounding silver into words and dropping them out of his mouth.

252

". . . We — we are the blood-looking clay of this Earth.
You — You of the Power that creates us —
Lay the eggs of Your thoughts within us
As the mud wasp fills a little house of clay
Let this be the medicine of our ways
That You may reap the health of our spirits.

Breathe into our heads
The seeds of kindness that will sprout within the clay
    of our thinking,
To sprout upwards — as the vines of wild grapes
For You to taste the echo of the love-sap.

Fill the earthen vessels where within our voices dwell
— With Your cleansing sweat of rainfall
So that when we speak our tongue
The strong odor of truth will fill your lungs.

Braid us all together like the drying ears of corn
But tight — but tight
We need the imprint of forgiveness for each other,
Plain upon our earthen husks.

Smooth our wounds with Your Hand so tender
Smooth the clay becoming ripe — so that
You can see into the mirror-water-skin
Of Your created creation. . . ."

And on and on Bee-land would go, in direct contact with the
Creator. I felt a little guilty sitting near Bee-land so I could horn in
on his words. But now that I let you in on it too, I don't feel quite
so guilty.

Romeo spoke to me something like my Aunt Min did. That
is, some of his long words went over my head. He spoke of
wondering why he had taken so long to realize why he wasn't
happy with the symphony orchestra. He said, "I finally came to
realize that a lot of politics and falseness was going on all around
me. I was passed up several times for becoming the master conductor of the orchestra. When I wrote some pieces I was told that

parts of them were too dissonant for public approval. It was as though only certain things could be done, could be talked about. I didn't feel a need to become the conductor but I would have liked the chance to say so. One day I woke up. I was doing the same thing as everyone else around me. I was buying magazines like *Psychology Today, Intellectual Digest, Scientific American* — and I was going to cocktail parties and trying to sound MOST intelligent, the same as everyone else there was doing. We were solving all the world problems in talk only; never DOING, just talking. I was at one of these parties when I woke up. I remember that night. I just got sick of it all. I was just going to leave when someone across the group of men said, 'Chief! What would one of your old medicine men say if you asked him why, when evil and good are polarities, do they appear in the same syndrome as genius and insanity — just a hair's breadth apart?' Maybe it was good that this man asked this question. Maybe it was THEN that I woke up. I said, 'A medicine person would see no need on this earth for the answer to that question. But maybe to be polite he would say that since all things are in orbit, there is no such thing as a straight line. There is no such thing as polarity, except in the frail choice of man. If you take the line between your polarities and curve it into a circle, you would have your own answer.' Then I left my last cocktail party. And here I am with new overalls on, and that's my vegetable garden you see over there."

By the time I left Romeo, he was talking in the Tuscarora language. It had come back to him. I took a shortcut through the trees to get home but I couldn't seem to hurry. I was thinking of Bee-land and his poetry again. No more would I be hearing Bee-land speak. He was back into the earth. "The Tellers" were all dead or dying. I didn't feel very good. I wasn't even walking anymore. Right next to me was a young pine tree. It was one of the 4-H trees that I had planted. It was almost as tall as I was now. I put my hand on its sappy little trunk.

"OoKHREHH'weh," I said to the little pine, "who's going to be 'The Tellers' now, now that 'The Tellers' are dead?"

At first the little tree didn't answer, but I waited. After a while it said, "You and I will be 'The Tellers.' Someday children will say, 'What did the Old Folks say?' and they will be asking about US — about what YOU and *I* are talking about right now."

254

THE RESERVATION

was composed in 11-point IBM Selectric Century Medium, leaded two points,
by Metricomp Studios; with display type
in Century Schoolbook by Dix Typesetting Co., Inc;
printed offset on VB 55-pound Antique Cream, Smyth-sewn and
bound in Holliston Crown Linen over boards by
Vail-Ballou Press, Inc;
and published by

SYRACUSE UNIVERSITY PRESS
Syracuse, New York 13210